# 'TIS THE SEASON TO DIE

When I went back inside to get the Poodles, the phone was ringing. It was Aunt Peg and as always, she got right to the point. "Have you looked at the morning paper yet?"

"No, I haven't had time. Why?"

"Your Henry the bus driver is on page one."

Wedging the phone between ear and shoulder, I quickly unwrapped the *Stamford Advocate*. I zeroed in on a small picture of Henry just below the fold. *Local Man Dies Under Suspicious Circumstances* the caption read.

"Suspicious circumstances?" I said out loud. "What suspicious circumstances?"

"Read the story," said Peg. "It's obviously right in front of you."

"I don't have time. Give me the highlights."

Peg began reading from the paper. "Mr. Pruitt collapsed in his yard Monday evening and was taken by ambulance to St. Joseph's Hospital where doctors were unable to revive him. He was pronounced dead later that night. An initial autopsy indicated that the likely cause of death was cardiovascular disease; however sources at this newspaper have learned that Mr. Pruitt's remains are being held by the medical examiner pending further investigation."

"Further investigation? That doesn't sound good."

"Of course it doesn't sound good," Peg said crisply. "It's not supposed to. Read between the lines, Melanie. The newspaper is telling us that your friend Henry didn't die of natural causes. It looks to me as though he was murdered . . ."

Books by Laurien Berenson

A PEDIGREE TO DIE FOR

UNDERDOG

DOG EAT DOG

HAIR OF THE DOG

WATCHDOG

HUSH PUPPY

UNLEASHED

ONCE BITTEN

HOT DOG

BEST IN SHOW

JINGLE BELL BARK

RAINING CATS AND DOGS

CHOW DOWN

HOUNDED TO DEATH

DOGGIE DAY CARE MURDER

GONE WITH THE WOOF

DEATH OF A DOG WHISPERER

THE BARK BEFORE CHRISTMAS

Published by Kensington Publishing Corporation

# Jingle Bell Bark

## A Melanie Travis Mystery

## Laurien Berenson

**KENSINGTON BOOKS**
http://www.kensingtonbooks.com

KENSINGTON BOOKS are published by

Kensington Publishing Corp.
119 West 40th Street
New York, NY 10018

All Kensington titles, imprints, and distributed lines are available at
special quantity discounts for bulk purchases for sales promotion,
premiums, fund-raising, educational, or institutional use. Special
book excerpts or customized printings can also be created to fit
specific needs. For details, write or phone the office of the Kensington Special Sales Manager: Kensington Publishing Corp., 119 West
40th Street, New York, NY 10018. Attn. Special Sales Department.
Phone: 1-800-221-2647.

Kensington and the K logo Reg. U.S. Pat. & TM Off.

ISBN-13: 978-1-4967-0003-2
ISBN-10: 1-4967-0003-1
First Kensington Hardcover Edition: September 2004
First Kensington Mass Market Edition: October 2005

eISBN-13: 978-1-4967-0004-9
eISBN-10: 1-4967-0004-X
Kensington Electronic Edition: October 2015

10 9 8 7

Printed in the United States of America

# 1

Most people start the new year on January first.
Not me, I'm a school teacher; I start out fresh in the fall. I've always found something rejuvenating about the tang of crisp autumn air, and the sound of feet shuffling through dry, fallen leaves. The coming of that new season never fails to lift my spirits and renew my enthusiasm for the year ahead.

In keeping with this renewal I've taken to making resolutions at the start of each new school year. Now that I'm a few years into my thirties, I find the demands I choose to place upon myself have simplified. That whole eat-right, exercise-more, and lose-weight thing? Not happening around here. I mean, really, aside from super models and sitcom stars, who has the time? Some days I consider myself lucky if my shoes match.

Each other, that is. Not my outfit.

So this year when September rolled around, I made a different pledge, one more in keeping with the way my life was going now. I wanted a dull moment, I decided. Just one would do. An hour, or even half of one where nothing was required of me and there was nowhere I had to be. I wanted to kick back, put my feet up, and experience a little boredom.

The idea sounded so simple. I knew other people had managed it. Why couldn't I seem to do the same?

Perhaps the fact that I was a single mother had something

to do with that. Davey is the light of my life and the other half of my heart. He's also a typical eight-year-old boy: loud, boisterous, often dirty, and always entertaining. And if he wasn't enough to keep me busy, our two housemates, Standard Poodles Faith and Eve, were always ready to fill in the blanks.

The two big Poodles are mother and daughter and they share a number of traits. Both dogs are thoughtful and mischievous. They're also smarter than many people I know, which isn't necessarily a good thing when you consider that I work in education.

The other person who's been known to occasionally lead me down the path of most resistance is my Aunt Peg, also known as Margaret Turnbull of Cedar Crest Kennels, breeder of Standard Poodles par excellence, newly appointed AKC judge, and a woman who has all the finesse of a Bullmastiff with a broken toe when it comes to going after what she wants.

Aunt Peg often tries to run my life and occasionally succeeds. Recently, however, the majority of her domineering tactics had been directed toward my sister-in-law, Bertie, who was expecting her first child with my brother, Frank, in December. Never a mother herself, Aunt Peg was nevertheless a font of unsolicited advice. I knew it was selfish on my part, but still it was a relief to see Aunt Peg focus her attention on another relative for a change.

Which is a long, roundabout way of saying that of late my life had been running rather smoothly; nearly the entire fall semester had passed uneventfully. With Thanksgiving just behind us, both my students and I were looking forward to the holiday season and Christmas break.

And since he wasn't finding third grade to be too demanding, the biggest thing on Davey's agenda was the production of a Christmas play at the Long Ridge Arts Center. Davey and his best friend, Joey Brickman, had been cast as two of the three Wise Men. Not starring roles exactly, but ones that came with the incentives that they could carry props, give away presents, and didn't have to dress up as a camel.

Davey had practiced his two lines so often I could say

them in my sleep, and probably did. If so, Sam Driver, my fiancé, didn't seem to mind. This was our second try at being engaged, the first attempt having come to an ignominious end eighteen months earlier when Sam had abruptly left town for parts unknown. This time, we were hoping for a better result.

This time I thought I might actually have things under control. Unfortunately, it's just that kind of overconfidence that comes back and bites you in the butt every single time. Trust me, I know these things.

There's a belief among today's parents of school-age children that any moment left unscheduled is a moment wasted. Gone are the days when kids played outside until dark, and games were designed to be fun, rather than promote learning and educational advancement. Now it seems as though any child who hasn't completed math and reading readiness courses by kindergarten is already off the fast track.

For Davey's sake, I tried not to get too caught up in the frenetic race-for-success mentality that was so pervasive in Fairfield County. But then I was left with the concern that my laissez-faire attitude might be responsible for allowing my child to fall behind his peers. Besides, since most of his friends were engaged in one activity after another, if Davey wanted to have any social life at all, he had to get involved.

Which brought us to the Christmas play at the arts center. With soccer season over and basketball yet to begin, the choices for December narrowed themselves down to Cotillion and the Christmas play. Faced with a choice between white gloves and a Wise Man's robes, Davey opted to try out his fledgling acting skills.

Auditions were held over Thanksgiving break. That was really just a fancy way of saying that notices had been posted at a number of likely locations around town, then the organizers had waited to see how many children might show up. In past years, I'd been told, attendance had been so light that Ms. Morehouse, the play's director, had been forced to dole out speaking parts to several of the smaller parents. I'd worn clogs with platform heels to the audition, just in case.

This time around, however, Cotillion must not have exerted its customary draw. At the appointed time, the auditorium at the arts center was filled with a battalion of kids, all seemingly high on Christmas cheer. In the chaos that ensued, Davey and Joey had been lucky to land their minor speaking roles. Parents of children who came later found themselves being sent home with directions on how to make a sheep costume. By my count, Ms. Morehouse would be lucky if the flock-to-be didn't overwhelm the small stage.

When school started up again after the break, the addition of play practice to the schedule necessitated a change in Davey's routine. Weekdays I worked as a special needs tutor at Howard Academy, a private school in Greenwich, Connecticut. Davey, who went to public school near our house in Stamford, rode the bus. His bus driver, Henry, was a kindly man, cherished by the mothers on the route, who felt safe in trusting him with their children. Lately he'd taken to carrying a box of milkbones for the Poodles.

Monday morning, as I got Davey ready for school, I kept one eye on the clock. Henry was notoriously punctual, and since I needed to speak with him about the schedule change, I wanted to be waiting outside when he arrived.

Davey had shown up in the kitchen minutes before, dragging a backpack that was at least twice as heavy as any book bag I ever remembered taking to school. Even six months earlier, he'd seemed like a little boy. Now I was struck suddenly by how much he had grown up.

It wasn't just physical development, though that was part of it. His jeans, bought a size too big, had until recently pooled around his ankles. Now they fit, which probably meant that in six weeks they'd be too small. In the months since summer, his blond hair had darkened again. The sandy brown shade gave him a more serious look. Big brown eyes, so like his father's, gazed right past me and fastened on the bowl, spoon, and box of Cheerios I'd left sitting on the table. He crossed the room with the same quick, graceful strides that served him well on the soccer field and slid into a chair.

"All set for school?" I asked.

Standing at the counter, I was putting baby carrots in a baggie to add to his lunch. I'd never been entirely sure whether Davey actually ate them or whether they were slipped surreptitiously into the cage of the class rabbit. Either way, he seemed to appreciate their addition.

"Mmmm." He poured a bowl of cereal, sloshed on some milk, and dove in.

"You have all your homework?"

His shoulders rose and fell in a weary sigh.

"What?" I said mildly.

"You ask me that every day."

"Some days you say no," I pointed out, heading toward the back door. A whine from the step outside had alerted me to the fact that Faith and Eve were ready to come in.

Having an enclosed backyard where I knew the Poodles would be safe, even when I wasn't watching, was a luxury. One I would have been hard pressed to afford if Aunt Peg hadn't taken matters into her own hands and arranged to have the four-foot cedar fence erected one day while Davey and I were at school. My aunt had her standards for responsible dog ownership, and heaven help the family that fell below them.

As usual, Faith came running inside first, while Eve hung back and followed more slowly. Since the two Poodles were nearly the same size, I hadn't yet decided whether the younger dog's deference was due to her age or her slightly more cautious temperament. Once inside, however, Eve dashed past her mother and bounded to Davey's side.

Her tail, shaved at the base and adorned by a large black pom-pon on the end, wagged back and forth. Judging by her greeting, you'd have thought it had been weeks rather than mere minutes since they'd seen each other last. I watched as Davey slipped her a handful of dry Cheerios.

"Be careful of her hair," I said, sounding like the nagging mother I try hard not to be.

I couldn't help it. In this instance it was reflex. And self-defense.

Faith, who was retired from the show ring, wore her dense black coat in a very becoming short blanket of curls. Eve, in the midst of pursuing her championship, was in a continental trim. Like Faith, her face and feet were shaved. In addition, her hindquarter and legs had also been clipped down to the skin, save for a rosette of hair over each hip and bracelets around her ankles.

The hair on the front of her body, known as her mane coat, was thick and profuse. It had been growing since she was a baby, and despite frequent trimming and shaping, was more than a foot long in some places. If Davey spilled his milk in there, I would have to devote the next hour to painstakingly getting it out.

Ask me how I know.

"I'm not going to spill my milk," Davey said.

I opened my mouth to speak.

"Or my orange juice," my son finished for me. He knows me entirely too well.

Chewing her cereal, Eve moved away from the table and went to check out the water bowl. I slipped Faith a biscuit to make sure they were even in the treat department. The older Poodle carried it under the table and lay down to examine her prize. She has always been a finicky eater. Sometimes I think she enjoys having biscuits more than actually eating them. Eve, on the other hand, would clean out the cupboards if she could figure out how to use a can opener.

"You remember you'll be getting off the bus at the arts center this afternoon instead of coming home, right?" I said.

We'd rehearsed his route the night before, but I still needed the reassurance of running through it again. Over the years I'd found that my job as a mother consisted of endless repetition. Not only that, but it was guaranteed that the one thing I didn't mention ten times was the one my child would forget—and then make me feel guilty for not reminding him.

"Got it." Davey finished his cereal and started on his juice. I whisked up the empty bowl and rinsed it in the sink.

"And Joey will be doing the same thing. So the two of you should stay together."

"We've been to the center a thousand times," Davey said. "I'm not going to get lost."

"Yes, but this is the first time you'll be going on your own, straight from school."

"We'll be fine. Once you give Henry the note he'll make sure we get off in the right place."

He would, I thought, and felt immediately better. Henry had been driving the bus for longer than Davey had been in school. In all those years I doubted if he'd ever misplaced a single child.

Davey and I were on the front steps when the school bus turned the corner onto our road. Winter mornings, it took twice as long to get a child out the door. Davey's parka was zipped, his knit cap pulled down firmly over his ears, and there was a mitten on each hand. Though we had yet to see snow, the temperature was hovering just above the freezing mark. Our breath blew out in little puffs as we walked out to the curb and waited.

Seconds later, the bus lumbered to a stop in front of us. The door whooshed open. Warm air billowed out. Davey scrambled past me and up the steps. He was probably afraid I would try to kiss him good-bye in front of his friends.

"Cold enough for you?" Henry asked. This time of year, it was his standard greeting.

His lined face creased in an easy grin; I'd never seen Henry in a bad mood. I guessed his age to be about sixty, but he'd taken good care of himself. His jaw was freshly shaven, his eyes clear. A down parka hung over the back of his seat; a bulky green sweater kept him warm. He wore knit gloves with the fingers cut off and, as always, a baseball cap covered his thinning hair. Seeing that I wanted to talk, Henry shifted into park and reached for the mug of coffee in a holder by his knee.

"I'll say." Since I was only planning on being outside for a minute, I hadn't bothered to fasten my own coat. Now I was grateful for the heated air escaping through the doorway. I extended my hand inside with a folded note. "For the next few weeks, Davey's going to be getting off three days a week at the arts center."

Henry nodded. "Decided against Cotillion, did you? Good choice."

There wasn't much going on in the neighborhood that escaped the driver's notice. "Davey thought so, too," I said.

Henry added my permission slip to a pile of others in his tray. "Half the kids on this route went out for the Christmas play this year. You got yourself a sheep?"

"Wise Man."

"Behold a star in the east," Henry intoned.

My brow lifted.

"First line, right?"

It was.

"Things don't change much from year to year. You watch out for Rebecca, now. She runs a tight ship. Time she gets through with you, you may wish you'd signed up for white gloves and waltzing." Henry's eyes twinkled as he delivered the warning.

I didn't think twice about teasing him right back. "So she's Rebecca to you? The rest of us call her Ms. Morehouse."

"Yeah, well." Henry shifted into gear and reached for the lever to pull the door shut. "You know what they say, age has its privileges."

The door slid shut; the brakes released. The bus groaned and rolled away. Davey had a window seat. I waved as he went by. Engrossed in talking to his friends, he didn't respond.

As I turned back to the house, I saw two black noses pressed against the front window. Four paws beat against the cold glass eagerly as the Poodles danced on their hind legs waiting for me to come and get them.

I went inside to start the week.

# 2

Once I reached Howard Academy, the day flew by. For one thing, half my tutoring sessions were canceled. Think about it: the day after Thanksgiving break, in a private school in Greenwich? Between the kids who were still schussing down the slopes and the ones who were still sunning in the Caribbean, the place was nearly empty. Even some of the teachers hadn't bothered to show up. That's life in the fast lane for you.

I worked with a few students, took Faith and Eve for several walks around the academy's spacious grounds, ate my sandwich of turkey leftovers for lunch, planned the next day's lessons in case anyone showed up, and decided to call it a day. Leaving early, I had plenty of time to drop Faith and Eve off at home before heading over to the arts center. Most afternoons I'd simply pick Davey up after play practice ended. That day, I decided to stop in early, sit in the back of the auditorium, and watch how things went.

The Long Ridge Arts Center was located in backcountry Stamford on a narrow, twisting road barely more than a single lane wide. Despite its out-of-the-way location, the families in the area flocked to the center, drawn by the diversity of its offerings. There were classes in ballet and jazz, yoga and theater, photography and cartooning. And if enough requests came in for a program that wasn't offered, chances were the center would hire a teacher and find a way to put a class together.

Privately funded and largely supported by grateful parents, the arts center was a huge asset to the community. In earlier years, Davey had attended after-school classes in speech and drawing. This was the first time he'd elected to take part in the Christmas play.

By the time I arrived, a fleet of yellow school buses was already lined up outside the building, disgorging hordes of eager students. Inside, the lobby was bustling. On other occasions, I'd stopped to admire the students' artwork adorning the walls, but now I went directly through into the auditorium.

Nearly forty children were milling around in the front of the room. It took me a minute to spot Davey. He was up on the stage, standing off to one side with Joey Brickman and several other friends. Satisfied that they'd arrived safely, I pulled off my wool coat and scarf and slipped into a seat in the back row.

Only a minute passed before Rebecca Morehouse strode out from the wings. She clapped her hands loudly. "People! People! Let's get organized now."

Amazingly, the chatter stopped. Three dozen children stopped running, dancing, and playing, and turned to see what she wanted. I stared, awestruck. Bringing even half that many kids under control quickly was no easy task. This was like watching magic in action. Either that or witchcraft.

Silence accomplished, Ms. Morehouse strode across the stage with the regal bearing of someone who was accustomed to performing. She was an older woman, probably not a whole lot younger than Aunt Peg. But whereas Peg's hair had gone gray years before, Ms. Morehouse's hair was tinted a becoming shade of blond. Her crisp wool suit looked as though it bore a designer label and it accentuated a figure that was not only battling the effects of time, but clearly winning. Cool gray eyes peered out from a flawlessly made-up face.

For my part, at least I could say that my hair had been brushed that morning and the corduroy pants I was wearing were mostly clean.

"What did I miss?" Alice Brickman came hurrying into the auditorium and slid into the empty seat next to me.

Alice has been one of my best friends for years, ever since we met in a play group when Davey and Joey were only a few months old. There's something about the shared bafflement of first-time motherhood that bonds women in a hurry. Alice and her family lived right down the street from us, and in the intervening years, Joey had gained a younger sister named Carly, who had recently started first grade.

"Nothing yet," I said, as Alice shrugged out of her faux sheepskin coat. "They're just getting started."

Up on the stage, Ms. Morehouse was taking attendance. Holding out a clipboard, she read off each name from her list, searched among the faces until she'd located the child, and then marked them all present.

"Excellent," she said when she was done. "As you all know, play practice will take place every Monday, Wednesday, and Friday from now until Christmas. You will be expected to attend every practice and every performance. Unexcused absences will not be tolerated. Nor will tardiness. This production will be run in a professional manner and it is assumed that you will behave accordingly."

"Good Lord," Alice muttered under her breath. "Who hired the marines? This is a Christmas play, not basic training."

I had to agree. "Do you think she realizes she's dealing with elementary school children?"

Pausing in what she was doing, the director turned to send a frosty glare out into the mostly empty audience. There was no way she could have heard us from that distance. Nevertheless, Alice and I both shut our mouths and sank down in our seats.

"Busted," Alice whispered behind the hand she'd lifted to cover her lips. I would have laughed if I'd dared. This was like being back in second grade.

"Come on," I said instead, gathering up my things. "Let's go outside."

Out in the lobby, there was an alcove where refreshments had been set out on a table. It was quiet enough there that we could talk. Alice and I poured ourselves a couple of cups of coffee from the urn, and added a dollar each to the donation jar.

"I'm not sure we should leave them alone in there," she said. "Any minute now, that woman is bound to discover she's got a stage full of kids and not professional actors. What if she blows a gasket?"

I set my coffee down on the counter, waiting for it to cool. "Judging by appearances, I don't think Ms. Morehouse has a gasket. Or anything else that might be likely to blow."

"Sure, be cavalier. Just because your child isn't the trouble-magnet Joey is."

Every child was a magnet for trouble, I thought. Though Alice's son did seem to have more than his share of bad luck. "He is when he's with Joey," I said truthfully.

"Thanks." Alice snorted. "That's a big help. Come on, let me show you something. It's a miracle the way this scheduling worked out."

She led the way down one of the long hallways that branched off from the lobby. A dance studio was at the end, and several mothers were clustered around a one-way viewing window that looked like a mirror to the class full of young ballerinas inside.

"Carly?" I guessed, finding an empty space and having a look.

Alice nodded. "Joe and I took the kids to see *The Nutcracker* last Christmas in New York. Joey was bored stiff, but Carly fell in love. I thought it was probably just a phase, but a year later here she is, still going strong. Miss Diane says she shows a lot of promise, not that I care so much about that. I just want her to have fun."

Carly certainly seemed to be doing that. In a sea of little girls in black leotards, Alice's daughter was the one with the big smile on her face. Like her mother, Carly had strawberry blond curls and pale, freckled skin. Her eyes were alight with enjoyment as her fingers gripped the barre, standing with her back straight and her toes pointed slightly outward.

"I see what you mean about miraculous scheduling," I said. "I don't know how you manage two kids. I have enough trouble keeping everything straight with one."

"For starters, I don't have a job," Alice pointed out.

"Or Aunt Peg." Somedays Peg was more trouble than a whole houseful of children. "Then again," I added to be fair, "I don't have a husband."

"You've got Sam. It's practically the same thing." Her gaze drifted downward to the diamond engagement ring on my left hand. As of yet, there wasn't a wedding band to accompany it. "In fact, it would be the same thing if you'd ever get your act together."

There was that.

I changed the subject. "And I have the Poodles. Dogs are a big responsibility too."

"I'm glad you brought that up." Alice stepped away from the window. "Let's go back to the lobby and sit down for a few minutes. There's something I've been meaning to ask you about."

Thanks to my association with Aunt Peg and the fact that I'm involved in the dog show world, I've become the resident "dog lady" of the neighborhood. People have questions, and they seem to think that I'll have the answers. A call might come at ten o'clock at night. "Spike's running a temperature of 101. Does he have to go to the vet right now or can it wait until tomorrow?" One like that was easy to answer, since the normal temperature range for a dog was different from that of a human and Spike wasn't actually running a fever. The Brickmans didn't have a dog, however, so I was curious to hear what Alice wanted. We topped off our coffee cups and settled in a pair of chairs in the sun by the front window.

"This is a secret," she began in a hushed tone. "You have to promise not to say a word."

"Okay. Who is it a secret from?" I was really hoping she wouldn't say Joe, her husband. In my experience, secrets like that tend to mean big trouble.

"The kids," Alice cast a furtive glance around. "All the kids. Davey too. I want it to be a surprise."

Ahh, a good secret. I liked those. "You're getting Joey and Carly a puppy."

Alice nodded happily. "For Christmas. You know how much Joey loves Faith and Eve. He's been bugging Joe and me about this forever and we decided it's time. He's old enough to handle a pet. We think the responsibility will be good for him."

"Stop right there," I said. "I think getting a puppy is a great idea. But whatever you do, don't make the mistake of thinking that Joey will actually be the one taking care of him. It's like having a baby. You know how husbands always say they'll pitch in and help out, when what they really mean is they'll do ten percent of the non-gross stuff at times when it's convenient for them?"

"Yes," Alice agreed readily. We'd *all* been there.

"Well, getting a puppy is exactly the same thing. Everyone means well, especially in the beginning. But essentially the responsibility for taking care of the dog is going to end up with you. It always turns out that way."

"I can handle that. We always had dogs when I was little. I've kind of missed not having one around."

Right answer, I thought. "What kind of dog are you looking for?"

"Not a Poodle," Alice said quickly, like she wanted to get that out of the way. I think she was afraid of hurting my feelings. "Your dogs are great, but all that hair would be just too much for me. Sometimes I wonder how you cope."

Sometimes I did too. The thing about Poodles was that once you'd lived with one and you'd enjoyed their wonderful temperament, you couldn't imagine wanting any other breed. So doing all that grooming began to seem like a fair trade-off. But looking at it from the outside, I could see how people might think that Poodle owners were nuts.

Which was fine with most Poodle owners. From our point of view, not everyone had the ability to appreciate what a joy it was to own such a truly superb breed of dog. Their loss, really.

"What then," I asked. "A Lab?" Blacks, yellows, chocolates; they were the quintessential Fairfield County dog. Sometimes it seemed like no family was complete without one.

"No, but you're close. Joe wants a Golden Retriever. That's what he had when he was little, a big old dog named Goldie. That's fine with me. I've heard they're supposed to be really good with kids. And that's what's important."

"They are," I agreed. "Though you're still going to be in trouble when it comes to hair. Goldens shed like crazy."

Alice shrugged. "That's what vacuums are for."

Not at my house, I thought.

"I'll talk to Aunt Peg," I said. "She knows everybody. I'm sure she'll be able to put you in touch with a couple of good breeders."

"Thanks for the offer, but you don't have to bother. That's the great part. I already have a puppy all picked out."

"You do?" That was fast.

"Yeah, that's actually how this whole idea got started. Over the weekend Ms. Morehouse had a box of Christmas puppies in her car. You and Davey must have left right after the audition was over, but I was a few minutes late getting here. Ms. Morehouse took a bunch of the kids outside and showed them this cute batch of puppies she had."

"Wait a minute," I said. "Hold the phone. Go back." Usually I'm pretty quick on the uptake, but I was having a hard time wrapping my mind around the facts of this story. "The puppies were *in her car?*"

"That's right." Alice didn't seem nearly as bothered by this fact as I was. "She had them outside in the parking lot."

"Weren't they cold?"

"I have no idea. I didn't think about that. I mean, they have hair, right?"

Now I was frowning. "Just how old were these puppies?"

"I don't know. Five weeks? Maybe six. Joey said she told them the litter was timed especially so that they would be ready for Christmas."

That was *not* good news. A reputable dog breeder would never plan a litter around Christmas. The holiday season was stressful and hectic, and just about the worst possible time for introducing a new and very vulnerable member to the family.

"Christmas puppies," I muttered, shaking my head. "In a box in her car. Did Ms. Morehouse tell Joey why they were there?"

"Well, yes." Alice was beginning to look troubled by my response. "So the kids could see them and play with them, and then tell their parents about them. She said that's the way she sells all her puppies."

"*All* her puppies? How many litters does she have?"

"I didn't think to ask," said Alice. "Does it matter?"

Of course it mattered. Because if Alice wanted to add a puppy to her family, she should want that puppy to come from the best possible source. A breeder who didn't have new litters for every holiday, one who had put time and effort into ensuring that her breeding stock was healthy both genetically and physically. She should want to know that the puppies had been socialized and brought up right, that they'd been wormed and had their shots.

It was one thing to feel sorry for a litter of puppies found in a box and to adopt one out of sympathy. It was quite another to consider paying good money to a lady who was selling puppies out of one.

"I assume she's charging money for these puppies?" I asked.

"Of course," said Alice. "They're very cute. And they're

purebred Golden Retrievers, just what Joe wants. They're seven hundred dollars apiece."

"That's a lot of money."

"Good puppies should cost a lot of money; that's what Ms. Morehouse said."

She was right. The problem was, I hadn't heard anything so far to indicate that these actually were good puppies.

"Besides," Alice continued, "these puppies cost a little more because they're a special litter, born just in time for Christmas. She said they were selling really fast. If I want to be sure of getting one, I have to put a deposit down today." She reached down and patted her purse. "I've brought the money with me. A hundred dollars, with the rest due on Christmas Eve when I pick the puppy up. Ms. Morehouse said she'd throw in a bright red collar with a bow for free. Isn't that nice of her?"

For seven hundred dollars, I would be wanting my puppy to come with a lot more than a red collar and a bow, I thought. Like a health guarantee.

"What about genetic testing?" I said. "Did you ask about that?"

"Well . . . no," Alice admitted. "I don't even know what it is."

"All breeds of dogs have heritable diseases. I'm not really up on Golden Retrievers, but I know you need to look out for hip dysplasia and probably PRA, which is a progressive eye disease. I'd imagine there are other things that need to be tested for, too."

"Oh, that stuff." Alice looked relieved. "I don't have to worry about any of that. Ms. Morehouse said it's only the really inbred dogs, like the ones that go to the dog shows, that have those kinds of problems. Her dogs are just fine."

"That is not true," I said firmly. "In most cases, the breeders who show their dogs are the only ones who *are* testing for genetic problems and trying to eradicate them. Just because Ms. Morehouse hasn't done the testing to find out if she has problems, doesn't mean they're not there."

"But she would know, wouldn't she? I mean, she said the puppies' parents were healthy."

"Did she show them to you?"

"No, but it's not as if she had a chance to. I only saw the puppies briefly last week when I picked Joey up, and then I spoke with her last night on the phone. But I'm sure she has nothing to hide."

That made one of us, I thought.

"Suppose a guy pulled up outside, opened his trunk, and said he was selling CD players," I said. "Would you buy one?"

"Probably not."

"Why not?"

"Because the fact that he was selling electronic equipment out of the back of his car would make me suspicious." Alice paused, then added, "But this is entirely different."

"How?"

"For one thing, everyone knows who Ms. Morehouse is. She's been producing the Christmas play for years. And for another, you could go to any mall and buy a CD player, so why would you take a chance on doing it here? At least I know enough to know that you're not supposed to buy a puppy from a pet store. You're supposed to find a good breeder and I did."

I was tempted to refute that last statement, but the look on Alice's face stopped me.

"Please don't ruin this for me," she said softly. "Or for Joey and Carly. These puppies are really cute and everything will turn out just fine. You'll see."

Ah heck, I thought. It was Christmas, the time of year when miracles were supposed to happen. Maybe she was right.

# 3

"You did *what*?" Aunt Peg asked. Her tone was deceptively mild. I knew that tone well. It meant that the wrath of the infuriated dog person was about to descend upon me.

It was Monday evening, after dinner. Aunt Peg had shown up with a list of plans pertaining to the upcoming holidays that she wanted to discuss. She'd also brought a box of oatmeal raisin cookies that looked good enough to be homemade. Since I knew perfectly well that Peg only cooked for her Poodles, I was betting she'd discovered a new bakery on the route between her house in Greenwich and ours in Stamford.

I helped myself to a cookie before answering. I also decided to try approaching the topic we'd just been discussing in a more roundabout manner. "You know Alice Brickman," I said.

"Of course I know Alice. She's Joey's mother. Lovely woman." Aunt Peg's brow dipped. "I dare say she doesn't know very much about dogs."

"What makes you think that?"

"Last summer when you brought her to the Danbury dog show, the way she walked around the grooming tent, going right up to all sorts of strange dogs and cooing in their faces. I was rather afraid she was going to get her nose bitten."

With good reason, I thought. "I'm afraid Alice thinks anything smaller than she is should be addressed in baby talk."

Aunt Peg rolled her eyes. Faith and Eve have much the same reaction when Alice speaks to them, but being polite, well-brought-up Poodles, they don't show their disdain quite so visibly.

"So now she wants to buy her children a puppy," Aunt Peg said. "Good for her. Every child should have a dog."

Words to live by around here. I nodded.

Aunt Peg was waiting expectantly. Waiting for me to explain how such an apparently good idea had morphed into quite the opposite. "She came to you for advice," she prompted. "And of course you would have had plenty to offer."

"I would have," I said in my own defense, "except that by the time I found out about Alice's plans, she'd already found the puppy she wanted. By the way, we have to keep our voices down." I glanced toward the doorway. Davey was doing his homework upstairs. "This whole thing is supposed to be a secret. The puppy is going to be a surprise for Christmas."

Aunt Peg's mood was not improved by the addition of this unhappy news. "Please tell me you explained to her that bringing home a new puppy on Christmas day is the worst sort of idea. All that noise and confusion, relatives coming and going, and nobody having the time to devote the proper attention to acclimating the poor thing to its new home; *that* is simply out of the question."

"I did try—"

"And I can't imagine why you didn't let her know that I'd be happy to put her in touch with some reputable breeders."

"I tried that, too—"

"And yet somehow," Peg said frostily, bringing us back to where the conversation had started, "you ended up telling her that it was perfectly all right for her to obtain a pet that will be a beloved member of her family for the next dozen years from the backyard equivalent of a puppy mill?"

"Something like that," I admitted.

"I give up," said Peg.

But of course she didn't. Things were never that easy when Aunt Peg was around. In all likelihood she was just taking a deep breath and preparing her next argument. Either that or she was contemplating getting up and marching down to the Brickmans' house to tell Alice that the way she had chosen to conduct her life was simply *not done*.

Little did Alice know that the fact that the temperature was in the low thirties and snow was falling lightly outside was probably going to save her from a stern talking-to. I got up, walked over to the back door, and turned on the outside lights, just in case Aunt Peg had forgotten about the weather conditions. In the yellow glow of the bulb, snow eddied up and down with the wind. Peg frowned at the sight and stayed put.

"You'll have to do something," she said finally.

I'd known that all along.

"I figured I'd start by trying to find out more about Rebecca Morehouse. Do you know her?"

"The name doesn't sound familiar. Should I?"

"You know everybody in dogs."

"My dear girl, someone who peddles puppies from a box in the back of their car is not 'in dogs' by any stretch of the imagination. What kind of puppy is this that we're talking about?"

"Golden Retriever."

"Good choice for the inexperienced dog owner," Peg said. At least she approved of something. "Purebred?"

"Maybe, maybe not. I haven't seen them. Alice said they were very cute."

"Of course they're cute. *All* puppies are cute. Pet shops thrive on just that very thing. The problem is that not all puppies are healthy or well raised. What else do we know about this woman?"

"She works in the theater department at the Long Ridge Arts Center. She's the director of the Christmas pageant. She's been in charge of it for years."

"Ah yes." Aunt Peg smiled happily. "I understand my nephew is to have a key role as a Wise Man. He had me running his lines with him over the phone yesterday."

"That couldn't have taken very long," I said. "He only has two."

"Don't complain, it could be worse. I'm told this year's flock of sheep may well spill off the stage."

"Not if Ms. Morehouse has anything to say about it." Faith, who had been snoozing beside the couch, got up and put her head in my lap. I ran my hands around the sides of her head and scratched beneath her ears. A Poodle "in hair" can only be patted in very specific places. Even though Faith had been out of show coat for more than a year, I still couldn't bring myself to rub the top of her head. "She keeps those kids under pretty tight control. You should have heard her reading them the rules earlier."

"Funny," Peg mused.

"What is?"

"That her standards should be so high when it comes to her work and so low when applied to producing puppies. I think this Rebecca Morehouse may be a bit of a conundrum."

And Lord knew, we needed more of those.

"When is Davey's next play practice?"

"Wednesday after school. I thought I'd introduce myself to Ms. Morehouse afterward. Maybe ask her a bit about her puppies. If Alice is determined to buy one, the least I can do is try and get some more information for her."

"You don't suppose the poor things will be sitting outside in a box again?" Aunt Peg sounded justifiably outraged.

"I doubt it. Alice said she had to turn in her deposit today because most of the litter was already spoken for."

"People should know better . . ." Aunt Peg muttered darkly.

Isn't that the truth?

\* \* \*

"I need a new note for play practice," Davey said the next day after school.

He was sitting at the kitchen table doing his homework while I stood nearby, working my way through Eve's long mane coat with a pin brush and a Greyhound comb. Usually I do most of the major grooming in the basement, but it was December, the basement was cold, and Eve and I had both decided we would be more comfortable in the kitchen. Fortunately, her grooming table is portable.

"Why?" I looked up. Notes had been known to go astray, but Davey couldn't have lost that one. I had handed it to Henry myself.

"There's a substitute bus driver and she doesn't know where anyone is supposed to go."

My hands kept working as I considered that. "Maybe Henry will be back tomorrow."

"I don't think so. She said we all needed to bring new permission slips from our parents so she could get everyone's routes sorted out."

Which is why, at eight-fifteen Wednesday morning, I was once again standing outside on the icy sidewalk, waiting for Davey's bus to appear. If nothing else, motherhood teaches you the virtue of patience—whether you want to learn it or not.

The bus was a couple of minutes late. Davey used the extra time to make snowballs from the dusting that had covered the grass overnight and throw them at the front door. His aim was pretty good but, predictably, by the time the bus arrived he'd gotten as much snow on himself as he had on the house.

Probably hoping I wouldn't notice that he was clutching one last snowball, Davey dashed past me and scooted up the steps. Even though it was clear I'd been waiting, the door immediately began to whoosh shut behind him. I made it to the curb just in time to rap on the side of the bus as it began to move away. Groaning reluctantly, the vehicle slowed, then stopped.

"What?"

The new bus driver opened the door a crack and glared in my direction. She looked barely old enough to possess a driver's license, much less to have graduated from high school.

"I'm Davey Travis's mother."

Gum popped between her teeth. "Yeah, I guessed that."

"I have a permission slip for this afternoon and Friday."

The girl shrugged and extended a hand. "The kid could have given it to me."

Maybe, if his mittens hadn't been soaking wet. I pulled myself up straight and used my best teacher's voice. "What is your name?"

"Annie Gault. What's it to you?"

At that point, it was beginning to look as though I might need that information for my letter of complaint. I'd heard other mothers grumble about drivers who were rude or unsafe, but fortunately I'd never experienced the problem myself. Having Henry in charge of the route the entire time Davey had been riding the bus had spoiled me.

"Do you know when Henry will be back?" I asked.

"I don't even know who Henry is. All I know is I got a call yesterday telling me that this was my new route from now until I heard differently."

She yanked the door shut. The bus moved slowly away from the curb, then gathered speed as it traveled down the block. By the time it turned the corner at the end, it looked like it was going too fast for the icy conditions.

Frowning, I watched until the bus was out of sight and wondered what had happened to Henry. Maybe I ought to call the bus company and find out. No way was I going to leave Davey's well-being in Annie Gault's care any longer than I had to.

When I walked back into the house, the phone was ringing. It was Alice; her voice was quivering with indignation. "Did you meet *that girl?* Ms. Pierced Eyebrow?"

Now that she mentioned it, there *had* been a silver hoop

sticking out of the side of Annie's face. I'd always wondered how people managed to avoid getting those caught on stuff. "Annie Gault," I said.

"At least you got a name. I didn't even get that much. She just snatched the note out of my hand and took off."

"Consider yourself lucky." My eyes strayed to the clock on the counter. If I didn't leave in the next five minutes, I would be late. And Russell Hanover II, the school's headmaster, took a very dim view of tardiness. "She slammed the door in my face. I had to bang on the bus to get her to open it again."

"Kids these days." Alice sighed. "Why do you think nobody teaches them manners anymore?"

"Probably because it's too much trouble. What do you suppose happened to Henry?"

"That's what I was calling to ask you. I hope he didn't get reassigned. Maybe we could mount a campaign in the neighborhood to get him back."

"I was thinking of calling the bus company," I said. "Maybe during my lunch break today."

"Oh, that's right, you've got to go," said Alice. "I don't want to make you late. Let me know what you find out. If he's sick or something, maybe we can go visit him."

I'd been packing up my papers and looking for Faith and Eve's leashes, but that brought me up short. "Visit him?"

"Sure. He lives right around here somewhere. Maybe a mile away. We talked about it once when the city of Stamford was considering changing some zoning over on Old Long Ridge Road. I've never been to his house, but I bet it wouldn't be hard to find. He's probably right in the phone book."

Paying Henry a visit hadn't occurred to me, but now that Alice brought it up, it wasn't a bad idea. Henry wasn't a young man; I wondered if he had anyone looking out for him. Besides, I needed to talk to Alice about her prospective puppy anyway. This might be a good way to kill two birds with one stone.

"Sounds good to me," I said. "I'll get back to you later."

* * *

By midweek, most of the kids had managed to find their way home from Thanksgiving break. But with only two and a half weeks until Christmas vacation, spirits were still running high. In my job as special needs tutor, I don't teach actual classes; instead I work in private sessions with those students whose schoolwork is deemed to be falling below par.

Howard Academy houses a primary and a middle school, teaching children from kindergarten through eighth grade. The school has an impeccable record of placing its graduates at the finest secondary institutions in the country. From there it is anticipated that the students will go on to Ivy League colleges and prestigious jobs, while remembering the academy that had given them their start with frequent and generous donations.

I might have been more skeptical about that process except for the fact that it seemed to work so well. Bitsy Hanover, the headmaster's wife, orchestrated numerous fund-raisers throughout the school year to which alumni responded with alacrity and enthusiasm. As I'd been reminded by Mr. Hanover on more than one occasion, maintaining the school's reputation for academic excellence was an important component in this success. Thus every student was expected to perform at the highest possible standard.

That was where I came in. And if occasionally, due to those circumstances, my work day was a little more pressured than I might have wished, that downside was more than offset by the fact that I loved the kids I got to work with. My job also offered a wonderful perk in that nobody minded if I took the Poodles to school with me, which was why Faith and Eve spent most days snoozing on their big cedar beds in the corner of my classroom.

At lunchtime, before heading to the large refectory where students and teachers dined together, I pulled out my cell phone and placed a call to the bus company that serviced all of North Stamford.

"Hi," I said when a woman picked up. "My name is Melanie Travis. My son, Davey, rides one of your buses to Hunting Ridge Elementary School. The driver is a man named Henry."

"Yes, Henry Pruitt." Her voice sounded unexpectedly wary.

"I noticed that he's been out for a day or two and I was wondering if you could tell me where he was."

"Are you a relative of his?"

"No, just an acquaintance."

"I'm sorry. It's against company policy for us to give out any information about our employees."

Geez, I thought. They were a local bus company, not the Pentagon. "Could you tell me when you expect him back?"

"I'm afraid I can't answer that question either." Her tone was clipped. "Please be assured that all your bussing needs will continue to be met in a timely and professional manner."

Right, I thought. Like that was going to make me feel better. I wondered if she was reading to me from the company brochure.

"One last thing," I said, beginning to feel somewhat wary myself. "Is Henry still employed by your company?"

"As I told you a moment ago, I'm not at liberty—"

Frowning, I hit the button and cut off the connection. Earlier I'd been mildly concerned about Annie Gault's driving skills. Now I was genuinely worried about Henry.

Alice's phone number was on speed dial. As I hurried down the hall to the lunchroom, I left a message at her house telling her to find out Henry's address and meet me after school.

None of this felt good to me.

# 4

When the Poodles and I arrived home that afternoon, Alice was sitting on our front step. I pulled the station wagon into the short driveway, stopped in front of the garage, and hopped out. "Aren't you freezing?" I asked. "I hope you haven't been here long."

"Only five minutes or so." She stood up and brushed off the seat of her pants. "Here in the sun it's actually quite pleasant."

"Why didn't you just get my spare key out of the garage? You know where I keep it."

Door now open, we were both waiting while Faith and Eve sniffed every available spot in the front yard before deciding where they wanted to pee. They'd already been walked several times during the day so it wasn't as though they were desperate. No, this was a territorial thing. Heaven forbid that their own yard should carry the scent of another dog.

"Too much bother," said Alice. "Besides, you have no idea how rare something like this is for me. To simply sit quietly, with no children needing me right this second, no husband calling from work to tell me he's bringing a client home for dinner, no housework that has to be done. . . ."

Nodding, I led the way into the perpetually disheveled interior of my small house. "Better the pristine outdoors than the messy indoors."

"Something like that." Alice smiled and I did too. We'd known each other far too long to take offense at hearing the truth.

Faith and Eve came flying up the steps together; I shut the door behind them. Alice and I pulled off coats, scarves, and gloves, and piled them on the coatrack.

"How long does it take to get dogs trained like that?" she asked.

At the moment, the Poodles were heading toward the kitchen where they were hoping I would give them a biscuit from the pantry. I assumed that wasn't what she meant. "You mean housebroken?"

"Exactly. We had a dog when I was little, but I don't remember anything about the training process. I guess my parents must have been in charge of that. All I know is that every so often Rufus would make a mistake in the house and my mother would scream and scrub and act like the sanitary police were going to be descending upon us at any moment."

Nice image. I'd never had a pet when I was little, so everything that had happened first with Faith, and then again with Eve, was entirely new to me. "These guys were really quick to housebreak. But Poodles are different. At least that's what Aunt Peg tells me."

Alice walked over to the refrigerator and helped herself to a diet soda. "Do you think your aunt might be willing to sit down with me and give me a few pointers on how to deal with a new puppy?"

"I'm sure she'd be delighted to."

"Even though I'm not getting one from her?"

"I can't see why that would make any difference." Since both Poodles were sitting expectantly outside the pantry door, I got out the peanut butter biscuits and passed a couple around. "Aunt Peg is all in favor of responsible dog ownership. And while she adores Poodles herself, she can certainly understand that not everyone feels they have to have one. That's why there are approximately one hundred and forty-nine other breeds to choose from. Not to mention your basic, garden-variety mutts. Aunt Peg just wants to be sure that people who have dogs do right by them."

Alice pondered that. "She's going to be upset about where this puppy came from, isn't she?"

"Yup." No point in denying it. Since Alice had grabbed a chair and settled in, I poured myself a drink too.

"Look at it this way," she said. "You don't approve of Ms. Morehouse's methods. But if people buy her puppies, they'll be leaving her place and going to better homes. That's got to be a good thing, right?"

"Not necessarily. Because the fact the people are willing to pay Ms. Morehouse a decent sum of money for puppies she hasn't put all that much thought and effort into producing only encourages her to keep on breeding. Not only that, but she doesn't seem to care whether or not her puppies are going to good homes. Did she interview you when you talked to her about buying one?"

"Umm," Alice thought back. "Not exactly."

"Did she ask any questions at all?"

"She took down my name, address, and phone number."

"Which has nothing to do with whether or not you would be a good dog owner. Did she ask if you had a fenced yard?"

"No."

"If you'd ever owned a dog before?"

"No."

"If you had any children and what their ages were?"

"Well, she knew about Joey, obviously. He's in the play." Alice was beginning to sound defensive.

"But not about Carly. For all Ms. Morehouse knew, you might have had half a dozen children under the age of six."

"No, I couldn't have," Alice said firmly. "Trust me, my marriage wouldn't have survived it."

"You can see what I'm getting at, though."

"Yeah, I guess so."

I was leaning back against the counter. Faith ambled over, carrying a thick chew toy made of braided rope in her mouth. She pushed one end into my hand, checking if I wanted to play tug-of-war. I snatched the toy from between her teeth and waved it in front of her nose. Delighted, the Poodle jumped up and grabbed the toy back.

"Ms. Morehouse told me that housebreaking was going to be a snap," Alice said, watching the game. "Is she wrong about that too?"

"Maybe not," I allowed. "As long as you're dedicated. And consistent. And you don't mind taking your new puppy outside for a walk every couple hours."

"Every couple hours?" She stood up, rinsed her soda can in the sink, and tossed it in the recycling bin. "I thought dogs only had to go out three or four times a day."

"Adult dogs, maybe. But puppies? No way. They can't hold it that long."

"I guess this is going to be more involved than I thought. I have a lot to learn, don't I?"

"Don't worry," I said. "Aunt Peg makes a great teacher."

Alice had met my aunt a number of times. She knew what she was letting herself in for. "I'll just bet," she muttered.


As Alice had predicted, Henry Pruitt lived in the same North Stamford neighborhood where he'd been driving a school bus for the past half dozen years. His house was on a block very similar to the one Alice and I lived on: a post–World War II development of small homes on quarter-acre lots meant to welcome returning veterans with affordably priced housing. Half a century later, Henry's street looked to be a mix of young, yuppie families and older residents who'd been in place for years.

Numbers above the mail slots on most front doors made Henry's house easy to find. It was a light gray cape with white trim. The porch was neatly swept and the roof looked new. Even in winter, the yard was well tended.

I pulled the Volvo in beside the curb and coasted to a stop. Together, Alice and I peered out at the house. All at once, neither one of us was in a hurry to get out of the car.

"Well, now I feel sort of stupid," she said. "I mean, everything looks fine. What are we going to say when we knock on the door and Henry answers and asks what we want?"

"That we were worried about him and wanted to make sure he was okay?"

"He's going to wonder why we thought he might not be. The poor man's probably taking his first vacation in a decade. He'll think we're a couple of stalkers, coming to his house just because he's missed two days of work."

"Maybe he'll think we're a pair of kind, caring individuals." I tried to sound hopeful; Alice did have a point.

"Stalkers," she said again as a curtain shifted in one of the front windows.

I heard the unmistakable sound of barking coming from within the house. Big dogs, unless I missed my guess. And more than one.

"Come on." I reached for the door handle. "We've been announced. Now we have to go in."

As we navigated the front walk, the barking grew louder and more frantic. Climbing the steps to the porch, I heard a distinct thump as one of the dogs threw itself against the inside of the door. I knew many people kept big dogs as watchdogs, but now that these had done their job and revealed our presence, I wondered why Henry hadn't called them off. The noise inside the small house must have been deafening.

Alice hung back near the steps, but I crossed the porch and reached for the doorbell. I pressed hard and heard it ring within.

Toenails clacked against a front window as one of the dogs pushed the curtain aside and pressed his nose to the glass. A broad golden head with soft brown eyes stared out at us. The dog began to whine under his breath.

"Look," Alice said, staring. "It's a Golden Retriever."

"Two."

A second head joined the first. Judging by the way their bodies were wriggling, the dogs' tails had begun to wag. The watchdogs were happy to see us.

"Ring it again," said Alice, and I did. We waited another minute but there was still no response. The dogs continued to watch us through the window, their warm, moist breath fogging the cool glass.

"I guess Henry isn't home," I said finally. I wasn't quite sure whether to be concerned or relieved.

"Probably just as well," Alice agreed quickly. She was already heading for the steps. "Let's go."

I glanced over at the dogs again. Something seemed off somehow, though I wasn't sure exactly what. "Maybe we should leave a note. You know, saying we stopped by and asking Henry to call and tell us everything is okay."

"I'm sure everything must be fine." Alice reached back and grabbed my arm. "Henry's probably just out somewhere running errands. Maybe he was low on dog food."

"Maybe . . ." I agreed reluctantly. As I followed her down the stairs, I could still hear the dogs. Now the two of them were whimpering unhappily.

"Yoo-hoo! Ladies, wait!"

I'd been so tuned in to the dogs' distress that it took me a moment to realize someone was calling us. Thankfully, Alice was quicker. Already halfway down the walk, she stopped and then turned, treading carefully across the frozen grass to the neighbor's yard.

The woman who'd hailed us was standing in her doorway. The door itself was mostly shut, presumably to block out the cold. The woman's head and one arm poked through the slender opening. I hurried to catch up.

"Are you the daughters?" she asked as we approached.

Alice and I looked at one another. "What daughters?"

"Henry's girls. Come to see about—" The woman stopped and stared hard, seeming annoyed all at once to find us standing in her yard even though she'd been the one to call us there. "Who are you?" she asked abruptly.

"Friends of Henry's," I said quickly before Alice could answer. "Come to check on him."

Her eyes narrowed. "I haven't seen you around here before."

"Henry drives our children on the school bus," Alice said. "We've known him for years."

The woman's features softened. She sighed and pushed her door open. "I guess you'd better come inside then."

"Is everything all right?" I asked.

I didn't get an answer. Instead the woman waved a hand irritably in our direction. "Hurry up, you're letting all the warm air out."

Alice and I did as we were told. Together we scurried through the opening and shut the door behind us. Compared to the brisk temperature outside, the air inside the house was stiflingly warm. I reached up and unwound my scarf, then unbuttoned my coat. Inside for only a moment, I was already hot.

"I'm Betty Bowen," the woman said. "Henry and I have been neighbors here for more than twenty years. John and I moved into this house as newlyweds all that time ago. Don't think we ever expected to be here this long.

"Lots of people, they feel the need to trade up when they start a family, but we never did. Good thing too, since John didn't live past his forty-fifth birthday, and Johnny and I ended up with a house that was mostly paid off so's we didn't end up on the street."

"Johnny?" I asked, even though I knew I probably shouldn't.

Betty Bowen reminded me of my next-door neighbor, Edna Silano. Edna was an older woman, living alone, who didn't have that many people to talk to. Get her started and she would tell you her entire life story, beginning with her trip to America from the old country.

"My boy. That's his picture there." Betty gestured toward the mantelpiece. The wooden ledge was covered with framed photographs. At a glance, they seemed to chronicle the highlights of her son's life. The most recent picture was a high school graduation shot. Alice walked over for a closer look. If they'd have been dog pictures, I might have done the same. Since they weren't, I stayed where I was.

"So you must know Henry pretty well," I said, trying to steer the conversation back on topic.

"It's a terrible, terrible thing." Betty sighed loudly.

"What is?" I asked. Alice looked up.

"What happened to poor dear Henry."

For a single beat, my heart stood still. I knew I should ask, but I couldn't bring myself to do it.

Alice managed for me. "What are you talking about?"

"I'm sorry to have to be the one to tell you," Betty said. "But Henry's gone to his rest. That poor man died the night before last."

# 5

"Oh no," I said softly.

Alice looked similarly stricken. "Henry's dead?" she repeated.

Betty simply nodded.

"What happened?" I asked. "We just saw him on Monday. It must have been very sudden."

"It was," Betty confirmed. "And unexpected, too. He just keeled right over. I guess it was his heart that went. He was outside with those big dogs of his when it happened. Johnny came right in and called nine-one-one but there wasn't a thing anybody could do."

"I'm so sorry to hear that." There was a chair beside me. I sank into it gratefully. I hadn't known Henry well, but he had seemed like a genuinely good person. "So you thought we were his daughters?"

"That's right. Come to see about the arrangements. I've been expecting them for two days now."

"Do they live around here?" asked Alice.

"Not even close. One's in California and the other's in Alaska, if you can believe that. Both all grown up and out on their own. They don't spend much time around here. Henry's been in that house a good ten years, and I can't say that I recall ever meeting either one of them. I assume the authorities have notified them. And they damn well better show up soon because something sure as heck needs to be done about Pepper and Remington."

"Are they the dogs?" I asked. "The two Golden Retrievers we just saw?"

"That's them. Henry loved those two like nobody's business. Now they're just sitting over there in that house waiting to see what's going to happen to them next."

I stared at her, horrified. "You mean nobody's taking care of them?"

"I wouldn't say that exactly. I've looked in on them a couple of times. You know, filling the water bowl and putting out some food. I'm not much of a dog person myself, and those two are living proof why. They're making a god-awful mess of that house."

"Of course they're making a mess," I sputtered. "If they've been cooped up alone in there for two days, what choice do they have? You mean nobody has walked them or let them outside at all?"

"Johnny thought about doing something like that, but I told him to leave well enough alone. Those are big, rambunctious animals. What if he let them out and they ran away? Then it would be our fault that they were missing. When Henry's daughters show up, they'll have to make their own arrangements."

All well and good, assuming that they arrived quickly. But already two days had passed without any sign of Henry's relatives. Who knew how long it might be before someone appeared? Pepper and Remington couldn't stay cooped up in that house all by themselves. If Henry had cared about those dogs, he would have been outraged by the very idea. I knew I was.

I stood up and looked at Betty. "Do you have a key to the house?"

"Oh no," Alice said from behind me.

Determinedly, I ignored her. "I assume you must, since you've been going in and out."

Betty nodded. "After Johnny and I got Henry into the ambulance and on his way to the hospital, we went over there and made sure everything was locked up tight. Of course, at the time we hoped he'd be coming back. It wasn't until later that we realized he wouldn't. Henry kept his keys on a hook by the door. I've got the whole key ring here."

"I know what you're thinking," said Alice. "And it's a crazy idea."

"Those dogs are all but abandoned. What choice do we have?"

"Not we. *You.* If I ever showed up at home with one of those giant dogs, Joe would kill me."

I stared at her, perplexed. "Haven't we been talking about the fact that you're planning to get your kids a puppy? Well, this is what cute little puppies look like when they grow up. Or hadn't you thought that far ahead?"

"Of course I've thought about it. But I figured we'd ease into this dog-ownership thing gradually. That's why we're starting with a puppy."

Her logic made no sense at all, not that I had time to debate the point. Puppies, though smaller, were much more work than adult dogs. I supposed Alice would be finding that out soon enough. But if she didn't think she could handle one of Henry's dogs, what made her think she could handle one of her own?

"Then I'll take them both," I said.

These were, perhaps, not the sanest words ever to pass through my lips.

"You will?" Betty asked, sounding surprised. "What are you going to do with them?"

"For the time being, I'll give them a place to stay where they'll at least be well cared for. Then we'll see what happens when Henry's relatives show up. Maybe his daughters will want them."

"I can't imagine why," said Betty. "Like I said, they don't come and visit much. They've probably never even seen those two."

"I guess I'll have to find homes for them, then."

Brave words considering I had no idea how hard it would be to do something like that. All I knew for sure was that I couldn't walk away and leave Remington and Pepper to an uncertain and possibly neglectful fate.

"That seems like a fine idea to me." Betty sounded delighted to abdicate responsibility. "Leave me your phone number, and if anyone shows up and wants to know where those dogs have gone off to, I'll have them call you."

I wrote down my information while Betty went and got the key to Henry's back door. She pressed it gratefully into my hand. "It might need some cleaning up over there, if you know what I mean."

I could well imagine. Beside me, Alice snorted indelicately. I guessed that meant we both could.

"I can't believe you're doing this," she said as we left Betty's house and went trooping back to Henry's house.

"I have to do this," I said. "I couldn't live with myself if I didn't."

"What on earth are you going to do with two huge Golden Retrievers? You can't be thinking of taking them home. You've never even met these dogs. What if they're vicious?"

"Most Goldens have wonderful temperaments." We stepped up onto the stoop and I fit the key into the lock. "Besides, why would Henry have vicious dogs?"

Pepper and Remington were barking again. Seeing us from inside, they'd followed us though the house as we'd gone around. Now both dogs were in the kitchen, yelping and throwing themselves enthusiastically against the back door. I hoped I was going to be able to get it open and slip inside without one or the other making an escape.

"Where will they stay while you're at school?" Alice asked, peering unhappily over my shoulder at the boisterous pair.

"Good question," I admitted.

"Not to mention the fact that it's almost Christmas. You can't tell me you don't have a million other things to do."

She was right again.

"This is utter madness," said Alice. Since my responses thus far had been less than satisfactory, she poked me hard in the ribs. "Who would take on the care of two big, strange dogs on the spur of the moment at this time of year, just because they needed a home?"

I paused and straightened. My expression brightened. Put like that, I suddenly knew the answer.

"Aunt Peg," I said.


As Betty Bowen had warned us, Remington and Pepper had indeed made a mess. While I found two strong leather leashes and snapped them to the Goldens' collars so I could take the dogs outside for a much needed walk, Alice set about cleaning up.

I told her to wait until I came back in; I insisted I'd do the job myself. But Alice waved away my objections and stooped down to open the cabinet beneath the sink, checking for cleaning supplies.

"I'm a mother," she grumbled. "It's not like I haven't seen worse."

Remington and Pepper were so excited by the prospect of a walk that they dragged me out the door and down the steps. Under normal circumstances, the pair was probably leash trained. Now they were barely controllable.

Not that I could blame them. Semi-free for the first time in days, they had plenty of excess energy. They raced and played, barking with glee. Tethered to them by the length of two six-foot leashes, I just did my best to keep up.

It was at least fifteen minutes before the dogs' high spirits showed the slightest sign of flagging. By that time I was thoroughly whipped. Nothing like a couple quick laps around the block to hammer home the point that my life was a little light on aerobic exercise. Like eating more fiber and learning to appreciate opera, it was one of those things I was planning to get to when my schedule cleared.

Steering the pair back inside, I immediately noticed a dif-

ference. The house smelled a whole lot better than it had
when we'd left. Alice, wearing bright yellow rubber gloves
that covered her arms all the way up to the elbows, was looking quite pleased with herself.

"Lysol, and lots of it," she said. "As soon as I drag these
bags outside to the garbage, you'll never even know there
was a problem in here."

While she did that, I looked in the cupboard where I
found a big bag of Iams kibble. Two dog bowls were sitting
empty on the floor; I rinsed them out and added them to the
pile. Alice helped me carry everything outside. While I was
loading up the car, she returned Henry's key to Betty Bowen.

"Betty said to convey her thanks," Alice said as she slid in
the passenger side. Pepper and Remington, placed in the
storage area in the back, had clambered forward into the
back seat and were now hanging their heads into the open
space between Alice and me. Any minute now, we were going
to find them in the front with us. "I think she was pretty relieved to get rid of them."

"I can imagine." I reached back and tried to shoo the two
dogs away. Tongues lolling, grinning like a pair of doofuses,
they refused to take the hint.

Alice cast them a glance. "I'm glad you didn't listen to
me. They do look a lot happier."

"They must have been lonely locked up inside that
house," I said. "Not to mention, I'm sure they were wondering what happened to Henry."

Alice and I both fell silent. I'd been so busy dealing with
the two big Goldens that I hadn't had time to stop and absorb
the news of Henry's death. Now the loss hit me all over
again.

"He was a nice man." Alice sighed. "I guess the least we
can do is make sure that his dogs are okay."

"Amen to that," I said.

\*    \*    \*

I dropped Alice off at home so she could get her car and go pick up the kids—hers and mine both—at the arts center. Then I got on the Merritt Parkway, thankfully against rush hour traffic, and drove to Greenwich where Aunt Peg lived. Briefly, I considered calling and warning her that I was on my way, but I didn't entertain the notion long. Much as I expected my aunt to be sympathetic to the Goldens' plight, given time to think she would no doubt come up with an alternative plan of action that would have me driving all over the state. Much better to simply show up unannounced and plead their case on the spot.

Aunt Peg lived in backcountry Greenwich in a farmhouse on five acres of land, most of it fenced to contain her Standard Poodles. Currently she had six living in the house with her. Five of those were retired show champions. The other, Eve's littermate, Zeke, though still in hair, was nearing that status himself.

As always, the herd of Poodles announced my arrival the moment I turned in the driveway. The doorbell was superfluous at Aunt Peg's house; I didn't even bother to knock. I simply climbed the wide front steps and waited on the porch for her to come to the door. It didn't take long.

"Didn't I just see you day before yesterday?" Aunt Peg asked by way of a greeting. "Where's my nephew? Have you come for dinner?"

This last was strictly a rhetorical question. Guests who hope to be fed at Aunt Peg's house are well advised to bring the meal with them.

Before I could answer, my aunt's well-honed dog radar had already zeroed in on my car where Pepper and Remington were waiting. Even though it was cool out, I'd left the windows open a crack. Now both Goldens had their noses wedged into the small opening. Streams of drool ran down the glass. Obviously they weren't too concerned about making a good first impression.

"Who on earth are they?" Aunt Peg asked. Quickly, she

stepped out onto the wide porch and shut the door behind her. Her Poodles, left behind in the front hall, knew immediately that something was up. They raced around to the front window to have a look.

"Remington and Pepper," I said brightly.

"Do we know them?"

"We do now. Your kennel is still empty, right?"

Aunt Peg was no dummy. She could see where this was heading.

My aunt's involvement with Standard Poodles had begun decades earlier, during her marriage to my Uncle Max. For much of the latter half of the twentieth century, their Cedar Crest Kennel had been a force in the breed. Their Standard Poodle champions had been contenders at shows all up and down the East Coast. Upon Max's death four years earlier, however, Aunt Peg had begun to scale back.

Her dedication to the Poodle breed remained undiminished but these days she was breeding only rarely, and doing more judging than showing. The small kennel building behind her house, once home to generations of Cedar Crest champions, was no longer in use. Peg's Poodles had shrunk to such a manageable number that she was able to enjoy their company as house dogs.

"Of course it's empty. You know that perfectly well. But that doesn't mean I'm looking to take in boarders."

"How about a pair of orphans?"

Aunt Peg tried to look stern and failed utterly. She's always been a sucker for a dog with a sad story. Moving past me, she was already heading down the steps toward the driveway.

"I suppose we'd better have a look," she said.

# 6

Aunt Peg is a pragmatist where other people's dogs are concerned. She understands that not everyone trains their dogs to the level of behavior she takes for granted in her own Poodles. When she opened the car door, she immediately reached in and took hold of one Golden's collar, while using her body to block the exit until I could grab the other. Nobody was going to escape and run away on Aunt Peg's watch.

A gate on the other side of the driveway led to a fenced three-acre field with the kennel building at the far end. We led the Golden Retrievers through the gate and turned them loose. At once, Pepper and Remington dashed away, racing joyously in huge, looping circles.

"They've been cooped up inside a house all by themselves for the last two days," I said. "Their owner died Monday night and nobody made any provision for their care."

Aunt Peg had come outside without a coat on. Now, watching the two dogs play, she was smiling and shivering at the same time. "I want to hear everything," she said. "But first I need to get the heat and water turned on in the kennel. It will take a few minutes to warm up."

While Aunt Peg strode across the field and attended to that, I went back to the car and got the dog food and bowls I'd brought with me from Henry's house. By the time I reached the kennel, the furnace was already humming and warm air was beginning to stream out through the vents. Peg was pulling blankets out of a cupboard and building a plush bed in one of the big runs. I left the supplies in the outer room, where my aunt had once done all her grooming, and then went to check on the two dogs.

Pepper and Remington had finally stopped running. Now they were standing side by side in the middle of the big field, uncertain what to do next. When I called them by name, both heads snapped up. Moving together, they started toward the kennel.

Aunt Peg joined me in the doorway. "Good boys," she said encouragingly. "That's the way. Come on." Her voice held just the right inflection, with a tone that dogs seemed to trust instinctively. The Golden Retrievers covered the remaining distance and came trotting happily into the building. I closed the door behind them.

"First things first," said Peg. She'd already set out a big bowl of fresh water; now she was considering the kibble I'd delivered. "How bad was it where they were? Did they at least have access to food and water?"

"A neighbor did that much for them." I explained Betty Bowen's involvement. "Mostly I think they were just really lonely."

"And confused too, I'll bet." Peg reached down and stroked Remington's long back. The Golden leaned into the caress, rubbing his body against her legs like a cat. "Who was their owner? And how did you happen to find them?"

While Aunt Peg started soaking some kibble, I related what I knew about Henry Pruitt. Regrettably, it wasn't much.

"So their owner is dead," she mused when I was done. "And the two daughters who presumably will inherit the estate may or may not want them."

"Probably not," I said. "At least not if Betty Bowen is correct. At any rate, they have yet to put in an appearance. If the daughters were aware of the dogs' existence, don't you think they would have made *some* attempt to check on them?"

"One can only hope," Peg said, though her expression indicated that humans had let her down on that score before.

"I'm expecting that we'll have to find homes for them. I was hoping they could stay here in the meantime."

"Of course they'll stay here," Aunt Peg said firmly. In her mind, that part of the problem had already been settled. "It's what comes after that that needs to be figured out."

"Do you know any Golden Retriever people who could put us in touch with their local rescue group?"

"These two don't need to go to rescue. That would be a last resort. First we need to find out where they came from. If they were bred by reputable people, chances are both their breeders will take them back."

Like many of her peers who bred for the dog show world, Aunt Peg's puppies were sold with a contract guaranteeing that she would take a dog back at any point in its life if it was unable to remain with its current owner. Considering how much time and thought had gone into planning and executing each breeding, not to mention finding exactly the right homes for those puppies she didn't keep, Peg felt it was only prudent to keep a judicious eye on her offspring's welfare even after they'd left the nest.

Even in the best of homes, circumstances could change unexpectedly. Death, divorce, loss of a job could all create situations where dog ownership was no longer possible. Aunt Peg wanted it clearly understood that any Poodle who bore the Cedar Crest name would always have a home with her.

"You're right," I said. "I should have thought of that. But what makes you think there would be two breeders? I just assumed these guys were brothers."

"They're not."

"How do you know?" I hated it when Aunt Peg was so certain of something that wasn't at all clear to me.

"For Pete's sake, Melanie. Look at them."

I *was* looking at them. In fact, I was staring. All I saw was two very similar male Golden Retrievers. Remington was slightly larger; his coat was also a lighter color. Other than that, they looked remarkably alike to me.

Aunt Peg drummed her fingers on the countertop, waiting for me to get a clue. It wasn't happening.

Finally she gave up. "I can't believe you don't see it! Those two barely have a single trait in common. Pepper has quality written all over him; it's obvious he came from a good line. I wouldn't be at all surprised to hear that he has littermates who have finished their championships. Remington, on the other hand, is probably a pet store puppy. Lucky for him he seems to have a good temperament because he certainly isn't going to get by in this world on his good looks."

There was no point in asking how she could do that: look at a pair of dogs she'd never seen before and make what were probably accurate predictions about their parentage. By now I'd been involved with Standard Poodles long enough that I could tell a good one from a bad one. I couldn't sort out an entire class with Aunt Peg's effortless ease, but I could definitely cull the wheat from the chaff. Other breeds, however, were still a mystery to me.

Not to Aunt Peg. Her eye for a good dog was honed to such a degree that even those she'd just met could immediately be slotted into their proper categories. I didn't doubt for a minute that she was correct in her assessment. And assuming that Pepper *had* come from a quality line, I wondered if that meant he'd been bred by someone she knew.

Clearly my aunt's thoughts had traveled in the same direction as mine. "The easiest way to track down their breeders is to get a look at their papers. Henry obviously took good care of these two. Let's hope their registration slips were important enough to him that he kept them somewhere safe. What kind of man was Henry? Orderly, organized?"

"I'm afraid I don't know," I admitted. "He was just a very nice man who drove Davey's bus."

Peg harrumphed under her breath. She liked her relatives to be better informed. Her Poodles' AKC registration slips were kept in an accordion folder. A separate file was maintained for each dog; all pertinent health, breeding, and show records were easily accessible and up-to-date. It had to be asking too much to think that Henry might have done the same.

Aunt Peg poked at the kibble with a spoon. Deciding it had soaked long enough, she divided it into two stainless steel bowls and offered it to the dogs. We watched as both dug in eagerly. Having lived with a finicky eater for three years, it did my heart good to see them gobble down the un-adorned kibble. Still, I was betting it wouldn't take Aunt Peg more than a day to have these two eating homemade stew like the rest of her crew.

"What are you doing tomorrow?" she asked.

"Teaching school," I said. "It's Thursday." When it suited her purposes, Aunt Peg was apt to conveniently forget that I worked for a living.

"After that."

"I have a feeling I'm chasing down Remington and Pepper's papers."

"Quite so. Give me directions, tell me what time, and I'll meet you at Henry's house. The job will probably go faster with two people searching than with one."

It sounded like a plan to me.

Alice's husband, Joe, was working late at his law firm in Greenwich. By the time I got back to the Brickmans' house, Alice had the boys doing their homework and she'd ordered in enough pizza for all five of us.

"You're a lifesaver," I said gratefully.

Alice waved away my thanks. "It's just part of the job. How'd your aunt feel about coping with two unexpected vis-itors?"

"One thing you have to say for Peg, she's never at a loss for what to do next. Pepper and Remington are living in her kennel and she and I are going back to Henry's tomorrow afternoon to see if we can find their AKC papers."

"Is that necessary to find them new homes?"

"No, but if we can figure out who their breeders were, we can probably just send them back where they came from. That'll be the easiest solution all the way around."

Alice and I both stopped talking and watched as Carly, still clad in her leotard and ballet slippers, twirled in one kitchen door and out the other. I'd grown up a tomboy and was now raising a son. Little ballerinas were a foreign concept to me. I had no idea whether Alice's daughter had talent or not, but she certainly was cute.

"Tell Davey to get off the bus tomorrow with Joey," Alice said after a moment. "He can stay here until you're ready to come get him."

"Thanks. That would be great."

"I know." She grinned as the doorbell rang, signaling the arrival of dinner. "Great's my middle name."

It wasn't until the next morning, as I put Davey on the bus that Annie Gault was driving, that I realized I hadn't told him about Henry's death. Henry had been a part of my son's life, albeit a small one, for a number of years. I supposed I was going to have to come up with a way to break the news to him.

When I went back in to get the Poodles, the phone was ringing, just as it had been the day before. This time it was Aunt Peg.

As always, she got right to the point. "Have you looked at the morning paper yet?"

"No, I haven't had time." In fact, I'd just brought it in from the driveway. The newspaper was still encased in its protective plastic wrap. "Why?"

"Your Henry the bus driver is on page one."

Wedging the phone between ear and shoulder, I quickly unwrapped the *Stamford Advocate*. Rising gas prices and unrest in the Middle East had the banner headlines. I zeroed in on a small picture of Henry just below the fold. *Local Man Dies Under Suspicious Circumstances* the caption read.

"Suspicious circumstances?" I said out loud. "What suspicious circumstances?"

"Read the story," said Peg. "It's obviously right in front of you."

"I don't have time. Give me the highlights."

"Well, for starters, Henry Pruitt wasn't just a bus driver."

"Oh?" I walked across the kitchen to the back door and called the Poodles inside. Both girls knew the routine; they were standing on the step waiting for me.

"In his younger days, he was apparently quite a successful businessman." Aunt Peg paused, then found her place and began to read. *"Mr. Pruitt retired in 1997 as vice-president and COO of Sterling Management Group, a commodities brokerage firm in Greenwich."*

"That's interesting. What do you suppose he was doing driving a school bus?"

"Wait, there's another quote. It's from someone at Davey's school named Michelle Raddison."

"I know her." Before starting work at Howard Academy, I'd been employed at Hunting Ridge Elementary myself. "She used to run the main office. Now she's the vice-principal. What does Michelle have to say?"

"Here it is. *Henry told all of us that retirement didn't suit him. He liked feeling useful, and with his own children having grown up and moved away, he loved being around the kids. He always said there was no shame in doing any sort of job as long as you did it well."*

Unexpectedly, I felt a lump gather in the back of my throat. "I wish I'd taken the time to get to know him better."

"Keep listening," Peg said. "There's more. *Mr. Pruitt collapsed in his yard Monday evening and was taken by ambulance to St. Joseph's Hospital where doctors were unable to revive him. He was pronounced dead later that night. An initial autopsy indicated that the likely cause of death was cardio-*

*vascular disease, however sources at this newspaper have learned that Mr. Pruitt's remains are being held by the medical examiner pending further investigation."*

"Further investigation? That doesn't sound good."

"Of course it doesn't sound good," Peg said crisply. "It's not supposed to. Read between the lines, Melanie. The newspaper is telling us that your friend, Henry, didn't die of natural causes. It looks to me as though he was murdered."

# 7

Well, that was just the kind of cheerful thought I needed to start the day.

Henry had seemed like such a nice, unassuming man. I couldn't imagine why anyone would have wanted to do him harm. Then again, I'd been content to think of him merely as Davey's bus driver. I'd had no inkling that earlier in life he'd been quite successful in a whole different arena. Obviously, there was plenty I hadn't known about Henry Pruitt.

Thanks to Aunt Peg, however, and her plans for Henry's dogs, I was destined to find out more.

She and I met in front of Henry's house that afternoon. Having come straight from school, I had Faith and Eve with me in the station wagon. Peg, already waiting on the sidewalk when I arrived, greeted the Poodles through the window before turning to me.

"I assume this is the right house," she said. "He doesn't have a fenced yard."

I cracked all four windows and locked the Poodles in. "Not all dog owners do."

She knew that. And I knew that. We'd both been all over this territory before. Which never stopped Aunt Peg from making her point anyway.

I joined her on the sidewalk and stared at Henry's small, tidy cape. Since that morning, I'd been wondering whether the police would have come back and cordoned it off. I'd half expected to find a strand of yellow tape fastened across the door to block our access. Nothing of the sort had happened, however; the small house looked just as it had the night before.

"How did you get inside?" Aunt Peg asked. "Surely the house must be locked."

"Betty Bowen, the next-door neighbor, has a key." I started in that direction. "She was here yesterday. Let's hope she's home today. I probably should have thought to call ahead and check."

"A fine time this is to be remembering that. I hope you haven't brought me all the way over here for nothing."

I considered mentioning that it was she, not I, who had initiated this visit. But somehow, the small satisfaction I might derive from being briefly right seemed hardly worth the lecture on the responsibilities of dog ownership that was sure to follow. Instead I held my tongue, stepped up onto the Bowen porch, and rang the doorbell.

After a minute, I heard the sound of footsteps come pounding toward the door. Surely Betty wouldn't have such a heavy tread, I thought briefly. Then the door was flung open by a slender young man with spiked hair, a studded belt, and a pair of headphones, from which music squawked audibly, curled around his neck.

"Hey," he said.

"You must be Johnny," I said, though he looked quite a bit different from the clean-cut boy I'd seen in the high school graduation photo the day before. Only his dark, somber eyes were the same.

"That's right."

"Is your mother here?"

"Nah, she's out shopping. She'll be back later." He started to close the door.

Aunt Peg reached out and placed her palm firmly against the wooden panel, forestalling that idea. "Perhaps you can help us."

Johnny looked dubious. "With what?"

"We need a key to Henry Pruitt's house," I said. "Yesterday your mother lent me the one you brought back after Henry was taken away."

"So you're the two ladies who took off with the old guy's dogs."

He was only half right, but I didn't bother to correct him. "We didn't take off with them," I said instead. "We took Remington and Pepper somewhere where they could be properly cared for until homes could be found for them."

"Whatever." Johnny shrugged.

"Whatever indeed." Peg nodded toward the headset where music was still playing. "Is that Eminem?"

"Yeah. How'd you know that?"

"Why on earth does everybody think good music is only for the young? I don't see any reason why I can't enjoy it too. Now listen, we need to get something out of Henry's house. And in order to do that we have to borrow your key. Run along and get it for us, would you?"

Musical affinity notwithstanding, Johnny still didn't look convinced. "How do I know you have permission to be in there? It's not like you were friends of his or anything. I've never even seen you around here before."

"Very good," said Aunt Peg. "Your powers of observation merit a gold star. As does your willingness to look out for your neighbor even after he's gone. However, yesterday your mother chose to entrust Melanie and myself with the care of Henry's dogs. In order to do that job, we need to get some more information. If you like, you can come over to the house with us to make sure that we don't abscond with anything of value."

"That's all you want?" Johnny asked. "Information?"

Peg and I both nodded.

"And you won't mess up the place or anything?"

As if it hadn't been a mess yesterday before Alice and I had cleaned up.

"No, we just need to find some papers."

"Well . . . I guess that'll be all right."

Johnny's acquiescence was probably at least partly due to the stubborn expression on Aunt Peg's face. I'd seen that look before, and it didn't bode well. No doubt Johnny was wondering how much more of his time she was planning to take up. Had he asked, I could have told him that this conversation was most assuredly going to continue until Aunt Peg found herself holding a key in her hand.

"Hang on a minute," he said. "I'll go get it."

"What an accommodating young man," Peg said as we waited on the step.

"It wasn't exactly as though you gave him any choice."

"Quite so. On the whole, I find that's the best way to handle most people."

As someone who'd been frequently handled by Aunt Peg myself, I could vouch for that.

Johnny returned a minute later, key ring in hand. He'd fit the earphones back into his ears and was now moving to a beat we couldn't hear. He handed over the keys without comment. Peg and I waved our thanks.

As Alice and I had done the previous day, Aunt Peg and I let ourselves in the back door. She stopped just inside and sniffed delicately. Peg didn't comment but I knew she could imagine the condition the house had been in the day before.

"It seems odd," I said, pausing to decide where to look first.

"What does?" Peg, who's never hesitated in her life, was already striding through the kitchen into the living room.

Dutifully, I trotted along behind. "That just anybody can come walking in here. Short of Henry's daughters arriving and securing this place, you'd think the police would do it. Especially if they think there was something suspicious about Henry's death. What if we were the murderers, coming back to destroy all the clues?"

Aunt Peg flicked a glance in my direction. "You've been watching too much television."

"No, I mean it."

"That's what worries me. We're not destroying clues, Melanie. We're not even looking for clues. We're looking for official AKC documents."

She said the words with reverence. Like we were on a mission from On High. Like that excused the fact that she and I might be trampling through a potential crime scene.

"Okay," I said. If the police weren't concerned, far be it from me to make a fuss. "If you were important papers, where would you be?"

"In my office." Aunt Peg looked around the small living room. "If I had one, that is. I don't even see a desk down here. Let's try upstairs."

Once again, I was left to follow in her wake. It felt kind of creepy, wandering around in the house of a man whom I hadn't known well and who had died under suspicious circumstances. Aunt Peg, however, seemed to feel no such qualms. She went marching up the stairs as though she had every right to go looking through Henry's things. What can I say? The thought of dogs in peril has an empowering effect on her.

By the time I reached the second floor landing, Peg had already located a desk and small file cabinet in a spare bedroom. "Now we're getting somewhere," she said, kneeling in front of the squat cabinet and opening the top drawer. "Let's hope that Remington and Pepper were important enough to Henry that he held on to their registration certificates. In a pinch, even a pedigree would do. I imagine I could probably hunt down a breeder if I knew what lines they came from."

I leaned in and looked over her shoulder. Peg thumbed quickly through the files. Those in the top drawer seemed to be related to Henry's business dealings, past and present. She slid that drawer shut and tried the next. Right up front she found what she was looking for. A folder with the Golden Retrievers' names on it contained a pair of business-size envelopes bearing the return address of the American Kennel Club in North Carolina.

"Bingo." Peg rocked back on her heels and opened the

first one. The certificate had been issued to Longacres Hot Pepper, owner Henry Pruitt. Pepper's sire and dam were both champions, and both of those dogs bore the Longacres prefix as well. The breeder's name was Cindy Marshall.

"Anyone you know?" I asked.

Aunt Peg nodded thoughtfully. "Cindy's been around the dog show scene for at least a decade. I don't believe we've actually met, but I certainly recognize the name. I imagine she'd know mine as well. She lives in northern New Jersey, maybe Gladstone or Basking Ridge. I believe she's a member of the Somerset Hills Kennel Club."

"In other words, she's the type of breeder who would probably take Pepper back and find him a good home if Henry's daughters don't want him."

"I'd be shocked if she wouldn't," Aunt Peg said firmly. "Let's see what we can find out about Remington."

The second Golden Retriever had been registered under the name of Henry's Pal Remington.

"Cute," Peg muttered. It didn't sound like a compliment.

I scanned the short certificate. Remington's sire was a dog named Golden Boy the Great. His dam was listed as Daisy Dipsy Doodle. I chuckled under my breath. At least presumably they'd been purebred. Then my eye traveled down the page to the name of Remington's breeder and my smile died.

"Well, that's interesting," I said.

"Rebecca Morehouse," Aunt Peg read. "I just heard that name recently. From you, wasn't it?"

"Yes, she's the woman who's directing Davey's play at the arts center. The one my neighbor's planning to buy her Christmas puppy from. Small world."

"Small neighborhood, anyway. I wonder how Mr. Pruitt came to buy one of his dogs from a reputable breeder and the other from a local puppy mill. I guess we'll never know the answer to that."

"Unless Rebecca wants to tell us." I walked over to the desk whose surface contained a blotter, a pen set, and a laptop computer. Idly, I began pulling drawers open and looking inside. "I was going to talk to her anyway about Alice's puppy. When I do, I'll ask about Henry and see if she's willing to take Remington. With luck, you'll have your kennel empty again by the end of the week."

"There's no hurry on that score." Aunt Peg braced a hand against the file cabinet and pushed herself slowly to her feet. "Melanie, what are you doing in that poor man's private desk?"

I looked up. "Exactly the same thing you were doing a minute ago in his private filing cabinet. Snooping around."

"At least I had a good excuse."

"So do I. I'm trying to find his address book. It's all well and good for us to decide that Pepper and Remington need to be placed in good homes, but until Henry's relatives show up and say for sure that they don't want them, we don't really have the right to do anything. If we can find his daughters' names and phone numbers, we could give them a call and ask what their plans are."

"Good idea." Peg came to join me. She started opening drawers on the other side. "Wait a minute, here's something."

"What?"

"Photographs." She picked up a sleeve from a local developer and dumped out a thick stack of double prints. "Maybe they'll tell us something."

"Like what?" I leaned over and had a look. "What Henry's daughters look like? How will that help?"

"I don't know. You're the one who wanted to snoop around. You think of something."

Something that would justify our pawing through even more of Henry's private things? I didn't think so.

But since the pictures had already been spilled out onto the desk, I had a look at them. Henry must have been the photographer; he didn't appear in any of the shots. Most were pictures of his house and the surrounding neighborhood. Included, too, were photographs of the Bowens' house, a local park, and the junior and senior high schools.

"How very banal," said Aunt Peg.

"Maybe he was trying out a new camera. Or maybe he was thinking of moving and wanted to have a record of where he used to live?"

"If I do say so myself, that's about the silliest idea you've ever come up with." She gathered up the photographs, slipped them back into the envelope, and placed them back where they'd been. "Nor do I see an address book. Maybe that neighbor woman knows how Henry's daughters can be reached." Aunt Peg pushed the desk drawer firmly shut. "Let's go see if she's back, shall we?"

We checked to make sure we'd left everything as we'd found it, then locked the back door behind us. "You know," Aunt Peg said as we started back across the yard. "It occurs to me that maybe we should have worn gloves. Now I suppose we've left our fingerprints all over everything."

Alice and I had done the same the day before.

"Too late now," I said. "On the other hand, if the police want to know what we were doing in Henry's house, we have a perfectly logical explanation."

"If they're dog lovers," Peg muttered.

Betty Bowen hadn't returned home during the time we'd been inside Henry's house. And Johnny had probably been watching us out the window; he opened the front door before we were even halfway up the walk. I couldn't help but wonder why he didn't have something better to do in the middle of the afternoon. I guessed his age at a year or two on either side of twenty. Why wasn't he in college or at work?

"Find what you wanted?" Johnny asked with a smirk. He threaded his index finger through the key ring I held out to him and twirled it out of my hand. "That Henry, he was pretty busy for an old guy. He had stuff going on all the time."

"Did you know him well?" I asked.

The young man shrugged. It seemed to be a habitual expression of his feelings toward the world. "We've been living next door to each other forever, so I guess we've crossed paths. I used to mow his lawn when I was little."

"Not any more?" asked Peg.

"After he retired he started doing it himself. Kind of put me out of a job. Like I said, Henry was always up to something over there."

"You wouldn't happen to know how we could get in touch with his daughters, would you?"

"Nah. All I know is that they live far away. My mom might know, though. Do you want me to have her call you?"

"That would be great. Thanks."

I dug a piece of paper out of my pocket. Johnny found a pen and I wrote down my number. I'd barely finished before he snatched the slip of paper and shut the door in our faces. Johnny might have been accommodating but his manners could use a little help.

# 8

Aunt Peg headed home after that, and I drove Faith and Eve back to the Brickmans' where I had planned to pick up Davey; except that as it turned out, he wasn't there. "The kids were playing outside and saw Sam's car drive up," Alice explained. "Apparently, that seemed like a good enough reason for everyone to go and congregate at your house. I called ten minutes ago and got Joey and Carly home, but Davey and Sam are there waiting for you."

That was a nice surprise. Sam had been out in Illinois visiting his family over the Thanksgiving break. I hadn't expected him to return until the weekend.

Though Sam and I had been engaged since spring, we hadn't exactly worked out any details about the wedding yet. The last time we'd started making plans in that direction all hell had broken loose, and Sam and I had ended up spending more than half a year apart. Call me superstitious, but with everything between us now going so well, I hated to do anything that might alter that fortuitous state of affairs.

Davey yanked open the front door as I was getting out of the car. "It's about time you got home. Look who's here!"

Sam walked up behind my son and placed his hands on Davey's shoulders. Davey had been growing like mad lately but he had a long way to go before he'd approach Sam's six foot two. As usual, Sam's shaggy blond hair was in need of a haircut and his clothes were casual. In other words, he looked great. But then, he always did to me.

"I wasn't expecting you," I said, opening the back door so that Faith and Eve could hop out.

"I know," said Sam. "I came back a couple days early."

The Poodles didn't waste any time sniffing around the front yard. They dashed right up the steps and greeted their visitor. By the time Sam was finished saying hello to them, I'd also managed to get myself into the house.

"How come?" I asked. "Is everything okay?"

"Everything's fine." Sam slipped his warm hands beneath my jacket, his palms sliding around my waist, and pulled me to him. "I just missed you guys. Next year you'll have to come out to Illinois with me."

"And meet your family?" I gulped.

Sam chuckled under his breath. "I've met yours."

He had a point. Between Aunt Peg, my ex-husband, and my charmingly irresponsible brother, who'd recently married and turned his life around, not to mention another aunt and uncle who'd left the convent and priesthood respectively, my family was a bit of a challenge. Sam had not only met all my relatives, he'd been kind and patient and treated them all like normal people. Which sometimes I was only half convinced they were.

"We'd love to go to Illinois with you," I said, then sighed. Sam's lips were nibbling suggestively on my earlobe, but with Davey watching the proceedings, a proper greeting was going to have to wait.

"Hey, sport." Sam looked at Davey over my shoulder. "How'd you like to take Faith and Eve and put them out in the backyard?"

"No." Instead Davey sat down cross-legged on the floor. Chin in hand, elbow braced on one knee, his position was implacable.

"No?" He was usually very cooperative; I disentangled myself from Sam's embrace and turned to see what was wrong. "What's that about?"

"Sam and I are doing something together. So finish up here and then you can put the dogs out while we go back to work."

"Finish up here?" I laughed in spite of myself.

"You know, kissing and junk. Get it over with, because Sam and I have stuff to do."

Trust me, romance is tough with an eight-year-old in the house.

"Okay, we're done," I said.

"Until later," Sam said under his breath.

I peeled off my coat and tossed it on the coatrack. "What are you two working on?"

"Dinner," Davey announced. "Sam's teaching me how to cook."

"Really?" I headed down the hallway toward the kitchen. I was pretty sure I'd been planning to serve frozen beef stew. "What are we having?"

"Lamb chops, rice pilaf and broccoli with some yellow sauce that's tricky to make."

"Hollandaise," Sam said. He opened the back door and the two Poodles scooted past him.

"Sounds great." I decided I was perfectly willing to be treated like a guest in my own house. "I'll let you boys go to it."

While they cooked, Sam and I filled each other in on what had been going on in our respective lives. In my case, much was left unsaid. It wasn't until dinner had been eaten and the dishes washed, and Davey had gone upstairs to work on his homework, that I was able to tell Sam about Henry Pruitt's unexpected death, and the two Golden Retrievers that were now making themselves at home in Aunt Peg's kennel.

To my surprise, it turned out that Sam knew one of the participants in the story. Like Aunt Peg, he'd been involved in the dog show world for a long time. And though he'd only moved to the East Coast three years earlier, he had a wealth of friends with connections to all aspects of the dog community.

"I met Cindy Marshall last year in New York at a workshop for aspiring judges," he said. "I'd be happy to give her a call if you like."

"I'd love it. I feel slightly guilty about having saddled Aunt Peg with this unexpected responsibility, especially right before Christmas. The sooner I can figure out what to do with Pepper and Remington, the better."

"Only slightly guilty?"

"Well," I said in my own defense, "it's not as if Aunt Peg hasn't gotten me involved in all sorts of situations that were none of my business."

"That," said Sam, "is the understatement of the year."

He called information, got Cindy Marshall's phone number, then sat down at the table and dialed. Hovering behind him, I eavesdropped shamelessly. After the first few minutes of small talk, Sam passed the phone to me.

"Here," he said. "You'll be able to explain things a whole lot better than I will."

"Of course I remember Henry Pruitt," Cindy told me once we'd introduced ourselves. "He was the nicest man, always sending Christmas cards with pictures of Pepper on them. I love selling puppies to people who want to keep in touch, and of course it was tremendously gratifying to know that Pepper had such a good home. I'm so sorry to hear the news about his death. Was he a friend of yours?"

"He was my son's school bus driver. Sad to say, I didn't know him terribly well. Quite by accident I've ended up with his two dogs, since there wasn't anyone else to take them." I told her about Henry's daughters, who had yet to put in an appearance, and that Pepper and Remington were currently living with my Aunt Peg.

"If Peg Turnbull has them, I'm sure they're in good hands," Cindy said. "But of course I'd be happy to take Pepper back. He's only four years old. I get plenty of calls from families with young children who would rather have an older dog, or from people who don't want to deal with the hassle of raising a puppy. I'm sure I can place him in another good situation."

"That would be great," I said. "Aunt Peg said you probably wouldn't mind—"

"Mind?" Cindy's voice rose an octave. "It's not a matter of minding or not minding. I bred that dog. I brought him into the world. His welfare is my responsibility. Just because I sold him to someone else doesn't mean I've relinquished the need to do my duty by him . . ."

I sat through the lecture with a smile on my face. I couldn't wait to hook Cindy Marshall up with Aunt Peg. The two of them were going to get along famously.

I finished up by giving Cindy Aunt Peg's phone number. She promised to get in touch right away.

"That was easy," I said to Sam when I'd hung up.

"Did you expect any differently?"

"You know perfectly well, not everyone can take back a full-grown dog on a moment's notice."

"Not everyone should be breeding dogs," Sam replied.

"You sound like Aunt Peg."

"Normally, that wouldn't be a bad thing." Sam reached around and pulled me into his lap. His hand settled on my thigh and began to work its way upward. "But right now I'd just as soon not remind you of your older relatives. How close are we to Davey's bedtime?"

"Soon," I said, my breath catching on a gasp. "Very soon."

"Good thing," Sam murmured.


The next afternoon found me once again at the Long Ridge Arts Center waiting for play practice to end. Since I wanted to speak to Ms. Morehouse anyway, I'd told Alice I'd pick up all the kids. This close to Christmas, she didn't need to hear the offer twice. I think Alice was on the way to the mall before I'd even hung up the phone.

As I'd done before, I slipped into a back-row seat to watch the rehearsal. The story being enacted was the familiar biblical one. I watched as Mary and Joseph were refused a room at the inn. The boy who was playing Joseph patted "Mary's" arm tenderly. As she turned away, the pillow that was belted to her waist to simulate pregnancy came loose and fell to the floor. The cast dissolved into giggles.

"Yeah, right. If only it were that easy."

I spun around in my seat. My sister-in-law, Bertie, almost nine months pregnant and counting down the days impatiently, was standing in the back of the room.

"Hey," I whispered. "What are you doing here?"

"Peg told me where to find you. I was over at her house visiting, but she was making me crazy, you know? So I decided to come and check out the play."

"Hang on." I grabbed my coat, slipped out of my seat, and led the way out of the auditorium. Out in the lobby we could talk without fear of incurring Ms. Morehouse's wrath. "Let's grab some coffee," I said.

Bertie shook her head. "At this point in my life, caffeine is just a fond memory, along with things like wearing a belt and actually being able to see my own feet."

"I think you look great."

When I'd been pregnant with Davey, I'd been puffy and bloated. Less than a week from her due date, the tall redhead was still stunning, if a bit unwieldy. She maneuvered herself gingerly into a low chair.

"Good Lord," she said, sinking back into the cushions, "you may need a crane to get me out of here."

"Don't worry, we'll find something. Maybe that pulley they're using on stage to make the big gold star rise over the manger."

"That'll do." Bertie heaved a sigh. "And to think, I was so sure I'd sail right through this whole thing. Gain no more than twenty pounds. Eat all sorts of healthy food and exercise faithfully every day. Heck, I figured I'd be showing dogs right up until the baby popped out."

Bertie was a busy professional handler whose services were becoming increasingly sought after. A year earlier, she'd married my younger brother, Frank, who was manager and co-owner of a coffee house in North Stamford. They'd settled together in Wilton, where Bertie had room to house a kennel full of clients' dogs, and until recently she'd continued to ply her trade at shows all over New England. In the last month, however, she'd sent the majority of her string home to their owners for a break until spring.

"I could have told you that nobody who's seven or eight months pregnant wants to be running around a dog show ring," I said, taking a seat across from her.

"You *did* tell me. I just didn't believe you. I figured women have babies every day, so how hard could it be? Of course, it never occurred to me that I was going to hang on to mine for a year and a half."

"Nine months," I said. "You're not even overdue yet."

"How is that possible?" Bertie grumbled. "I feel as though I've been pregnant for half my life. Enough already."

I bit back a grin. Clearly, hormones were playing havoc with my sister-in-law's normally sunny disposition. "So you went to visit Aunt Peg."

"I needed to get out of the house. I needed to go somewhere. Do something. Plus . . ." Bertie glared at me. "I needed to get away from your brother. He's spent the last week following me everywhere I go. Like he's afraid the baby's just going to fall out and he needs to be there to catch it."

"At least he's trying to be helpful."

Bertie didn't look appeased. "And then there's your aunt."

"What did *she* do?"

"Kept telling me that having a baby was no big deal. Just like delivering puppies. I got the distinct impression that if I went into labor, she wouldn't take me to the hospital. She'd just make up a whelping box, boil up some instruments, and go to work right there."

Now I was laughing in earnest.

"So I came to see you. You're my last chance for a little sanity and common sense."

"Good God, I should hope not. Not that I'm not glad to see you, but you know full well that my life hardly ever makes sense."

"I know." Bertie sat back and smiled. "That's what makes me feel better."

I wasn't quite sure whether I'd been complimented or insulted. Probably the latter.

"How would you feel about watching the kids for a few minutes after practice ends so I can go and talk to the director?" I asked. According to my watch, it was almost time.

"No problem. But last time I checked, you only had one child."

"Today I have three. Davey, plus Joey and Carly Brickman. Two Wise Men and a ballerina."

"Interesting casting choice," Bertie commented. "I don't recall my bible mentioning the ballet corps."

"Very funny."

I stood up, reached out a hand, and pulled Bertie to her feet. The classes had begun to let out; the lobby was filling with kids. I spotted Carly and motioned her over. After making introductions, I went to the auditorium to get Davey and Joey.

"Okay, guys," I said when I had the group assembled in the lobby. "I'll only be ten minutes or so. Listen to everything Bertie tells you to do."

The kids nodded. Above their heads, Bertie mouthed, *what should I tell them to do?*

"I'm sure you'll think of something."

I went to find Ms. Morehouse before she could make her escape.

# 9

The auditorium had emptied quickly when play practice ended. Only a few kids remained in the room as I made my way toward the stage. Ms. Morehouse was busy straightening the crates and cardboard boxes that served as a make-believe set until the actual scenery could be built.

"Excuse me," I said.

The older woman stopped what she was doing and looked up. "Can I help you?"

"I'm Melanie Travis." I hopped up onto the stage and extended a hand. "Davey's mother?"

"Of course." Smiling, Rebecca Morehouse looked much more approachable. Her handshake was firm. "Your son is delightful. I hope he's enjoying participating in the pageant as much as I'm enjoying having him."

"Thank you, he is. I think you're doing a wonderful job here."

She tipped her head in recognition of the compliment, but her smile had faded. Up close, I could see that Rebecca's eyes were rimmed in red and no amount of makeup could hide the lines of strain around her mouth.

"Do you have a minute to talk to me about your dogs?" I asked.

"Certainly. Though before we waste each other's time, I should tell you that all the puppies are spoken for and I won't be having any more until spring. My next litter will be Easter puppies if you're interested."

Easter puppies. I ground my teeth. "Do you always plan your litters to coincide with a holiday?"

"If possible. It makes placing the puppies so much easier. I don't even have to run ads in the newspaper. At holiday time there are puppy buyers lined up around the block. Who would want to get their children a silly old bunny when they could put an adorable Golden Retriever puppy in the Easter basket instead?"

Rebecca finally registered the expression on my face. She stopped abruptly. "Of course, bunnies make very nice pets too. Does Davey have a bunny?"

"No, actually we have two dogs . . . Standard Poodles."

"Lovely breed."

"We think so." I was *not* appeased. "Don't you ever worry that when you sell your puppies as holiday gifts, they might end up with impulse buyers who are looking for a cute present on the spur of the moment but haven't given any thought to the long-term commitment that dog ownership entails?"

"Well, frankly," Rebecca said slowly, "no. I don't think that's any of my business. If people want to purchase a puppy, it's certainly not up to me to tell them how and when to do it."

"I'm sorry," I said. "Maybe I misheard you. Did you say you don't think your puppies' welfare is any of your business?"

"No, not at all." She was beginning to sound annoyed. "Until my puppies leave my home, their care is of the highest standard. But eventually, of course, they have to go out into the real world. Only a fool would think that she could control what happens to every single puppy after that."

I guess that made Aunt Peg a fool then. And I was probably a fool-in-training. If I didn't change the subject soon, the chances of this conversation remaining civil were just about nil. And aside from the fact that Davey had to work with Ms. Morehouse for the next three weeks, there were things I needed to accomplish.

"As it happens," I said, "you do have an opportunity to have an effect on the life of a puppy you once bred. His name is Remington now and he belonged to a man named Henry Pruitt."

Rebecca took a step back. Her hand rose to her mouth. "What are you talking about?"

"Henry died earlier this week." I was sure I wasn't telling her anything she didn't already know. After all, the story had been in the newspapers. "At the time of his death, he had two dogs. One is a young Golden Retriever that Henry got from you. That dog now needs a home."

"I don't see why you think that has anything to do with me."

"Remington is a puppy you bred. That makes you responsible for him."

"What a perfectly silly idea!" Rebecca turned away and went back to cleaning up. "I sold that dog years ago. He belonged to Henry. I imagine his heirs will figure out something to do with him."

"They may," I said implacably. "Or they may want to have nothing to do with him. In that case, he could end up at the pound. That's why I wanted to let you know what was going on and give you the chance to take him back."

All right, so I was laying it on a little thick. Now that he was in Aunt Peg's clutches, there was no way Remington was ever going to end up at the pound. Worst case, Peg would get the dog hooked up with the local Golden Retriever club, whose rescue committee would take him in and place him. But Rebecca Morehouse didn't know that, and her complete indifference to the dog's plight was really beginning to get on my nerves.

"Take him back?" she said. "Why would I want to do that? The dog's been neutered. He's of no use to me."

"You could find another home for him. That way you wouldn't have to worry about what became of him."

Rebecca stopped working. She straightened, placed both hands on her hips, and stared at me in exasperation. "Maybe you don't understand. I don't have a big kennel; I'm just a small backyard breeder. I wouldn't have any place to put a dog like Remington. And nobody who comes to me is looking for adult dogs. Puppies are what sell—the cuter, the better.

"Believe me, that dog will be much better off going to the pound. They're the ones with the facilities and the means to find him a new home. A good-looking dog like Remington will probably get plucked up by some new family in no time."

Without waiting for me to answer, Rebecca turned away and strode to the back of the stage. A box of switches was on the wall. One by one, she shut down the lights.

"That's *it?*" I asked incredulously.

Glancing back over her shoulder, she seemed surprised to find that I had followed her. "I'm afraid I have no idea what else you expect me to say."

Suddenly I was feeling somewhat speechless myself. I spun around and recrossed the now dark stage. A half flight of steps led down to the auditorium floor. I'd reached the bottom when Rebecca called after me.

I stopped and looked back. "Yes?"

"Did you . . . ?" Her face mirrored her hesitation. "I didn't think to ask before . . . How did you know about Remington? Were you a friend of Henry's?"

"Henry drove Davey's school bus. When he didn't show up for work, a friend and I went to check on him. That's when we found his dogs."

"He was already dead, then," she said softly.

"Yes."

Rebecca's shoulders slumped. She nodded slowly.

Too annoyed to feel any sympathy, I left her standing on the stage in the dark.

It took me ten minutes to come to the realization that the children I was supposed to be in charge of were missing. By that time, I'd searched the lobby, the ballet studio, a half-dozen empty classrooms, and the parking lot. Of course Bertie, who was supposed to be in charge of the troops, was missing as well. I figured that had to be a good sign.

I called her on her cell phone. "Where are you?" I asked when she picked up. Noise in the background made her almost impossible to hear.

"Not speeding to the hospital, about to deliver a baby, more's the pity. We're at the Bean Counter. The kids got tired of waiting for you, so we came over here to see what kind of trouble we could get into."

The Bean Counter was Frank's coffee house, a business he co-owned with my ex-husband, Bob. Also located in North Stamford, it was only a mile or so away.

"Joey called his mom to tell her what was up," Bertie said. "She's on her way."

"Why? I was going to deliver Joey and Carly back home. Alice doesn't have to come and get them."

"The kids wanted to stay and eat dinner here, you know, sandwiches and stuff. It's Friday night so there's live music. The kids think that's pretty exciting. When Joey called Alice, she said Joe was working late—I gather that's not unusual—and that she would come join us. So get in your car and get over here."

That sounded like a perfectly splendid idea to me.

Of course, on the way to the coffee house I realized that I'd never gotten around to asking Rebecca the questions about genetic testing and puppy socialization that I'd meant to find out for Alice. Sad to say, she would probably be relieved by my omission. With her deposit already paid, if there was more bad news about Rebecca Morehouse's breeding operation, I was quite certain Alice didn't want to hear it.

The Bean Counter was every bit as crowded as it had sounded over the phone. The small parking lot was full; I was forced to leave the Volvo at the end of a long line of cars that snaked along the street. I had to give my little brother credit. In less than two years, the business he'd started under less-than-ideal circumstances was definitely thriving.

Originally, the coffee bar had been intended as a local hangout. But good reviews in area newspapers had started some buzz and positive word of mouth had done the rest. When Frank and Bob had hired a trio of musicians to come in and play on Friday and Saturday nights, receipts had shot up again. I knew Bertie had no intention of retiring from handling, but it was nice to know she could take a couple of months' maternity leave without worrying about who was going to put food on the table.

Frank was working behind the counter. He waved when I came through the door and pointed toward a back corner where Bertie and Alice had staked out a couple of booths. Threading my way between closely packed tables, I went to join them. Though the musicians were just starting to set up, the coffee house was already packed. By the time they began to play, there wouldn't be a single empty seat.

"Kids in one booth, adults in the other," Alice said when I slid in beside her. "This way we can talk about anything we want and they can feel very grown up, sitting by themselves."

"Unless they all order themselves cake for dinner," I said. With Davey, who had inherited Aunt Peg's sweet tooth, that was a distinct possibility.

"Don't worry, we didn't offer them that much freedom." Bertie nodded toward a waitress who was delivering three tall glasses of milk to the next booth. "This is great practice for me. I need to learn how to do kid things."

Alice laughed. "I hate to say it, but the only kid things you're going to need to know how to do for a while are go without sleep and wipe spit-up off your shoulder. When's that baby due anyway?"

"Any minute now," said Bertie. She had to sit sideways to wedge herself between seat and table. "Yesterday would have been good."

"Oh," Alice said sympathetically. "Been there."

"Go ahead. Tell me your horror story. I'm sure you have one—everybody does. As soon as I started looking pregnant, people I'd never even met suddenly felt obliged to tell me the story of their cousin Rachel or Aunt Debbie who was in labor for forty-eight hours and barely survived. Do your worst. I'm immune to it now."

"No, you're not." I reached over and patted Bertie's hand. "You're just feeling crabby because you're ready for it to be over."

"You can say that again." Her eyes lit up as the waitress arrived with our food.

Three sandwiches, I noted, and three drinks. "What'd I order?" I asked.

"Chicken salad on a croissant," said Alice. "We figured we were better off getting our food before things got too hectic. If you hate that idea, get something else. Bertie said she could probably manage to eat anything you didn't want."

Bertie, who'd just been delivered a Ruben sandwich and a side order of fries, looked at me and stuck out her tongue.

"No way." I pulled the plate close. "This looks great."

In the next booth, Davey had just been served a thick hamburger. Joey and Carly both had chicken fingers. All three attacked their food happily.

"Boy or girl?" Alice asked, nibbling at a Caesar salad. It was her life's goal to lose ten pounds. Nobody, including Alice herself, was holding their breath that this weight loss was actually going to take place.

Bertie's shoulders rose and fell. "We don't know."

"Don't you want to know?"

"Nope. We talked about it and decided we'd rather be surprised. Either way is good."

Alice looked at me. "Did you know with Davey?"

"No. Actually, I was quite convinced he was going to be a girl. I was utterly shocked when the doctor said I'd had a boy."

"I knew for both of mine," said Alice. "It was a big deal for Joe. He wanted to know."

"Why?" asked Bertie. "It's not as if finding out ahead of time lets you change anything."

"I know. But having a boy who would carry on the family

name was very important to Joe. Luckily, we got that out of the way right off the bat, which was great. With Carly, I could just relax and take what came. I was glad she was a girl, though. I wanted one of each."

"How about you?" I said to Bertie. "Do you have a preference?"

"Healthy."

"That goes without saying. But after that?"

She thought for a minute, then shook her head. "Each sex has a different sort of appeal, you know? Kind of like with puppies. You know the temperaments are going to be different, but both have their good points and their bad points."

"Really?" Alice fished a crouton out of her salad. "I didn't know that."

"Alice is shopping for a puppy," I told Bertie.

"Alice has *found* a puppy," she corrected me. We both glanced at the next booth. Aside from all the noise, the kids were totally absorbed in their own conversation. They weren't paying any attention to us. "A Golden Retriever."

"Male or female?" asked Bertie.

"Male," said Alice. "We're bringing him home for Christmas."

Bertie swirled a french fry through her mound of ketchup and popped it in her mouth. "That's a terrible idea. I can't believe any good breeder would sell you a Christmas puppy."

Alice sighed. "Not you, too."

"The puppy isn't coming from a reputable breeder," I said.

"Does Peg know that?"

I grinned at Bertie's horrified tone. "Luckily for Alice, she's my aunt and not hers."

"The puppies are very cute," Alice said firmly. "I'm sure he'll be fine."

"If you say so," Bertie agreed. "So why'd you pick a male?"

"Actually, I didn't," Alice admitted. "Ms. Morehouse told me that was what I wanted."

"It was probably what she had left," I said.

"Of course, I didn't realize it made any difference, so I just said fine. I figured that would be easier because I wouldn't have to get him spayed."

"Even a male should be neutered," Bertie said. "Aside from the whole accidental reproduction issue, they stay healthier that way. Is this the same Ms. Morehouse that's doing the play? She's a dog breeder, too? Busy lady."

Mouth full, I simply nodded.

"So which is better?" Alice asked curiously. "Male or female?"

"It depends," I answered.

"Males tend to be bigger," said Bertie. "And they usually have a more profuse coat. Think more hair in the house."

"Females are often smarter," I interjected. "At least in Poodles. And bear in mind that we're generalizing now. Though males can be sweeter and more affectionate."

"Boys can be harder to housebreak sometimes," Bertie offered.

"Now that I think about it," said Alice, "I've heard that boy dogs are more likely to roam, aren't they?"

Bertie and I shared a look. "Only if you let them run loose. Which I assume you won't."

"But dogs need to run loose to get exercise . . ." Alice's voice trailed away. Bertie and I were both shaking our heads.

"You don't want your puppy to get hit by a car," I said. "Or get lost."

"Or stolen," added Bertie. "Or run around the neighborhood barking and making a nuisance of itself. Owning a dog is a big responsibility."

"I'm beginning to get that idea." All at once, Alice looked glum. "It wasn't this hard when I was little. We had a dog that lived its whole life outside."

"Times change," I said.

"Yes, but this puppy is just going to be a pet. Your dogs are show dogs—"

"It makes no difference," Bertie said firmly. Case closed.

Alice went back to eating. A few minutes later she finished her salad and set her fork aside. "Speaking of running around the neighborhood, did you get a flyer in your mailbox recently asking if you want to hire someone to clean your house?"

"Yes," I said with a smirk. "From Merry Maids. What an idiotic name. As if we're supposed to think that a bunch of women are going to get all excited about the prospect of cleaning for us. It sounds like a group that Robin Hood might have put together. I threw the flyer out."

"I didn't," said Alice. "I was thinking of giving them a call. Maybe having someone jolly around sweeping things up might not be a bad idea. Especially if the new puppy is going to be making a lot of messes. Apparently, the business is based right in the neighborhood."

"It is?" Our area is strictly residential, but people had been known to bend the rules when it came to small operations like tax preparation or pet grooming. I wondered which house the band of merry maids had been hiding out in, and the thought made me smile.

"Finally," said Alice. "Something you approve of."

"Hey, I never said being my friend was easy."

Bertie leaned over and whispered. "You think that's bad, try being a relative."

# 10

When Davey and I finally arrived home, Faith and Eve were thrilled to see us. They spun in circles and danced with their paws in the air until we were both laughing at their antics. People who've never owned a dog have no idea what they're missing.

Even in this era of ubiquitous cell phones, people continue to leave messages on my answering machine. Of course, the fact that I rarely turn my cell phone on could be responsible for that. As usual, the light on the phone in the kitchen was blinking. There were three messages: one from Aunt Peg, one from Betty Bowen, and one from Stamford Police Detective Ron Marley, all requesting a call back. Why am I never this popular when I'm sitting at home waiting for the phone to ring?

Davey went out back with Faith and Eve, and I dialed Aunt Peg's number first.

"You've been out!" she said without waiting for me to identify myself. Aunt Peg now has caller ID.

"It's Friday night. Isn't that allowed?"

"Of course it's allowed. It's just unexpected."

A sad commentary on my social life, if ever there was one.

"I was with Bertie and Alice having dinner at the Bean Counter."

"Oh." Peg sounded disappointed. "I was hoping you were going to say you'd been at the hospital watching my newest niece or nephew arrive."

"Not yet. Besides, you just saw Bertie a couple of hours ago. Did she look like she was about to deliver a baby?"

"Of course she did. Bertie's looked like that baby was ready to pop out every day for the last month. The poor girl is as big as a house. I don't know why Frank lets her go out running around like that all by herself. It can't possibly be safe."

Knowing Bertie, I doubted whether my brother was allowed to have an opinion on that subject. "They're together now," I said to appease my aunt. "Davey and I just left them at the coffee house."

"And did you and Bertie together manage to talk some sense into Alice Brickman?"

Aunt Peg was ever predictable. Tell her you'd been out socializing with friends, and she would assume you'd spent the evening discussing dogs. Of course, in this instance, she was at least partly right.

"Not exactly," I admitted. "Alice is still planning to get a puppy from Rebecca Morehouse. She's already put down a deposit and I'm sure she doesn't want to lose her money."

"Rebecca is probably counting on just that very fact," Peg said huffily. "That's how those operations work, making sure they get some money up front so that people can't back out later if they change their minds."

"I'll tell you something else about how Rebecca's operation works. She couldn't care less about the fact that Remington is now homeless. She told me we should go ahead and send him to the pound."

Aunt Peg sighed. "I'm disappointed, but not entirely surprised. Anyone who's breeding to make money can't afford to keep an eye on the welfare of their older dogs. It simply isn't a cost-effective way to do business. Don't worry, when the time comes I'll find a good place for him. And by the way, thank you for contacting Cindy Marshall. She and I had an absolutely delightful conversation this afternoon. As soon as I get the go-ahead from Henry's relatives, we're going to make arrangements to meet."

"Thank Sam," I said. "That was his doing."

The back door flew open hard enough to bounce off the wall. Child and Poodles came bounding through the doorway. "It's snowing!" Davey announced gleefully.

In the glow of the porch lights outside, I could see the first flakes beginning to fall. With the temperature slightly above freezing, I doubted they'd last once they hit the ground.

"Close the door," I said to Davey. Cold air was wafting into the kitchen at an alarming rate.

"Nah, we're going back out. Come on, guys!" All three spun around and disappeared. I crossed the room and pushed the door shut myself.

"Was that my nephew?" asked Peg.

"And various assorted Poodle relatives. All now back outside trying to play in the snow."

"What snow?"

"Therein lies the problem," I said with a grin.

"They're not playing too hard? You're not letting Faith destroy Eve's hair?"

As if. I'd been pampering that hair for nearly a year and a half now. By Eve's first birthday in July she'd accumulated seven of the fifteen points necessary to complete her championship.

Once the Poodle was an adult, however, her trim had needed to be changed; much more hair was required to balance the new look. Accordingly, Eve had spent the last five months out of the show ring. Her adult debut was to take place the following weekend.

No way were there going to be any hair calamities now. Of necessity, both Davey and Faith were well versed in the proper procedure for playing with a Poodle in show coat. Nevertheless, I sidled over and had a look out the back window. So far, so good.

"Here's the reason for my call," said Peg. "I had a visit this afternoon from a Stamford police detective."

"Ron Marley?"

"He talked to you, too?"

"Not yet, but he left me a message. I was going to call him back when we were done."

"He must have gotten our names from Betty Bowen, or maybe that boy, Johnny. He asked me what our connection to Henry Pruitt was and what we were doing inside his house."

"I assume you told him about Remington and Pepper?"

"Of course I did. Though I must say he seemed rather skeptical."

I pulled a chair out from the table and sat down. Conversations with Aunt Peg tend to take a while. "About what?"

"I gather he didn't believe you and I would have taken over the care of two dogs belonging to a man that neither of us knew well."

"Someone had to," I said. Maybe that approach was simply too logical for someone who wasn't a dog person. "Did you take him out to the kennel and show him the dogs?"

"I offered to, but he said he didn't have time. Instead he asked me if they were valuable."

Only to Henry, I thought sadly.

"But listen to this. Then Marley asked if I knew any reason why someone would want to harm either one of them."

"That's an odd question. Did you find out why he wanted to know?"

"It took a bit of perseverance on my part, but eventually yes. Apparently, the reason Detective Marley was asking about Pepper and Remington is because Henry died after ingesting a rarely used poison, ethylene-glycol."

The name sounded familiar, but I couldn't quite place it. "What is that?"

"The chief component of antifreeze."

Aha, I thought. Now Marley's questions made sense. Most dog owners, even novice ones, knew that two things were toxic to their pets: chocolate and antifreeze.

"Does he think someone was trying to harm the dogs and poisoned Henry instead?" The notion sounded awfully far-fetched to me.

"I don't believe he knows what to think just yet. He's just asking around and seeing what turns up."

"I'll call him back after I see what Betty Bowen wants," I said. "Though I won't have any more to tell him other than what you already have. Still, if Henry was murdered, I'd love to see his killer brought to justice."

"Tell him that," said Peg.

The next number I dialed was Betty Bowen's. That call went more quickly. As soon as I identified myself, Betty got right down to business.

"Now listen," she said. "How are those two dogs doing?"

"Pepper and Remington are fine. They're at my aunt's house in Greenwich. We're making arrangements to get them placed in good homes."

"You can't do that." Betty's voice lifted. "You've got to bring them back."

"*Back?*" I repeated. Did she expect us to return the Goldens to an empty house? "Back where?"

"Henry's daughters are here. It's about time, if you ask me. Robin Pruitt and Laurel Johnson. They rolled into town this afternoon and the first thing they did was come right over here and get Henry's keys back."

That seemed reasonable to me.

"They wanted to know how I happened to have the keys in the first place." Betty sounded annoyed. "Like maybe they thought I was holding on to something I shouldn't have. So I explained about how Johnny and I had been the ones to call nine-one-one, that we were right here when Henry was taken away. I told them about the dogs being left behind to fend for themselves. Rather than being grateful that someone was here to care for their father in his time of need, these two got all upset when they found out that something that belonged to them had been removed from the house."

From the sound of things, Betty had gotten equally upset.

"Did you tell them that the dogs were being well cared for—"

"As if they gave a fig about that. Or about all the work that I did for those two animals out of the goodness of my heart. The girls said something about prosecuting me for theft and trespassing and God knows what else if I didn't get those dogs back, and quick."

I sighed. So much for our well-laid plans.

"Okay, we can do that. Are the sisters staying at Henry's house? Is that where they want Pepper and Remington delivered?"

"No, they're not at the house. They're at . . . just a minute, I wrote it down here somewhere." Paper shuffled in the background, then Betty was back. "They've got a room at the Hyatt Regency in Greenwich."

"And the sisters think I'm going to bring those two big dogs there?" I asked incredulously. "The doorman won't even let me in the door."

"They didn't mention anything about that." Betty finally seemed to be calming down. "All they said was that they wanted Henry's property returned. That I'd been the one to lose it so I was responsible for getting it back."

"You didn't *lose* Pepper and Remington, you put them in a place where you knew they'd be safe. You did the right thing." In actuality, Betty had been all too willing to abdicate responsibility to the first person who'd shown up on her doorstep and indicated an interest in the dogs. Not that I could see any benefit to pointing that out.

"How about this?" I tried. "Tomorrow morning, I'll go see the two sisters, tell them I have Henry's dogs, and ask what they want me to do with them. That should make them happy, don't you think?"

"I hope so." Betty sniffed. "I'll say one thing. Stuff like this sure teaches you not to try and be neighborly. Next time

I see something bad going on, I'll just stay inside my own house and mind my own business."

My last call was to Detective Marley. Predictably, since it was nearly nine P.M., he wasn't in his office. I left a message that I'd called and told him to try back at his convenience.

It occurred to me when I hung up for the third time that I hadn't heard from Davey or the Poodles in a while. While I'd been on the phone, the snow had begun to come down in earnest. There hadn't been enough time for much to accumulate but Davey was on his knees in the middle of the yard, pushing what little snow there was into a small mound.

"What are you doing?" I asked.

"Making a fort."

Ahhh, the optimism of youth. He'd already used up most of the snow that was on the ground. Sadly, so far his accomplishment looked less like a fort than like a medium-sized snowball.

"At that rate, it's going to take you awhile."

"I know." Davey shrugged. He didn't look unhappy about that prospect. He had time.

At moments like that I realized with singular clarity why motherhood is such a gift. In a world where it often seems as though everything needs to be newer, faster, and more expensive, it's nice to be reminded that patience is a virtue worth cultivating, and that the simple joys of childhood are important, too.

"It's almost your bedtime," I said. "If it snows overnight, you can finish building a fort tomorrow. Maybe your dad will come by and help you."

Now that Bob lived in the neighborhood, he and I shared a custody arrangement that was constantly evolving. Most weeks while school was in session, Davey lived with me. Most weekends he spent at least one day, and sometimes both, with his father. Eight years after our somewhat tumultuous parting, my ex-husband and I had actually turned out to be friends. Would wonders never cease?

Out in the yard, Davey stood up reluctantly. The Poodles

had already come up the steps while we were talking. Davey was bundled up from the top of his head to the tips of his fingers. The Poodles, especially Eve, whose hindquarter was clipped to the skin, didn't have nearly as much protection from the cold.

Faith's short black curls were covered with a light dusting of snowflakes. Eve must have laid down in the snow. Her long mane coat was thoroughly wet on one side. She was going to have to be brushed out and blown dry once I'd put Davey to bed or the hair would solidify into thick, impenetrable mats.

Both Poodles moved past me to the center of the room. Stopping side by side, they braced their feet on the tile floor and shook vigorously. Ice-cold beads of water sprayed up my back and down my legs. I should have seen *that* coming.

"How about some hot chocolate?" I said to Davey as he shut the door behind him. I was sliding around the kitchen floor in my socks, trying to soak up the water the Poodles had just brought in. Shortcut housekeeping, the only kind I generally practice.

"With marshmallows?"

"If we have some."

While I heated up the milk, Davey dug around in the pantry. Faith and Eve elected to help him look. The fact that both Poodles emerged with biscuits didn't come as a big surprise.

I prepared two steaming mugs. Davey plopped marshmallows on top, three for him, one for me. The dogs settled under the kitchen table to chew on their biscuits.

"There's something I've been meaning to talk to you about," I said. "You know how Henry hasn't been driving your bus all week?"

My son nodded. "We have Annie now. She's not as nice as Henry, but Joey and I like her okay. Is Henry coming back soon?"

"No." I reached over and took his small hand in mine. "He isn't. I'm afraid he won't be coming back at all."

"Did Henry die?" He seemed less shocked than interested. Children see so much on television, they've almost become inured to the small, everyday tragedies.

"Yes, he did."

Davey considered that for a moment. "He was pretty old," he said finally.

"Yes, he was."

"I liked Henry."

"I did too."

Davey tipped back his head, looking out the window and up into the sky. "Did Henry go to heaven?"

"I'm sure he did."

Davey smiled. "Henry used to give all the kids a lollipop on their birthday. Do you think he'll have one for Jesus on Christmas?"

"I bet he will," I said, and smiled with him.

# 11

To Davey's dismay and my relief, the snowstorm fizzled out overnight.

Saturday morning the air was crisp and cold, the sky a shimmering, cloudless blue. And instead of being able to enjoy such a fine winter day, I had to go to the Hyatt and meet with Henry's daughters. That visit would probably be followed by a session with the Stamford police. Why was it that my days off never seemed to have any more downtime than my workdays did?

The phone rang as we were eating breakfast. Oatmeal with cinnamon for Davey and me, several handfuls of dry kibble for Faith and Eve. Faith was pushing her food around the floor, Eve was scarfing up everything in sight. Judging by our bowls, Davey and I were following a similar pattern.

"That's for me!" Davey cried, jumping up. My son was an eternal optimist. Not only was he always sure that the call was for him, he was positive it was someone he wanted to speak to.

"Hi, Dad," he said gleefully into the receiver. The greeting was followed by a long laugh and a sidelong glance in my direction. "Okay," he said after another pause. "Great. See you then."

He hung up without even giving me the option of talking.

"Excuse me," I said as my son slipped back into his chair

and attacked his oatmeal with the renewed enthusiasm of someone who was in a hurry to move on to his next adventure.

"What?" So help me if this child did not have the most innocent brown eyes in the world.

"That was your father on the phone?"

Mouth full, Davey nodded.

"And he didn't want to talk to me?"

"Nope."

"How do you know? You didn't even give him a chance."

Davey shrugged. "He's coming to get me, you can talk to him then. Dad and I are going Christmas tree shopping. He wants me to help him get his house decorated for the holidays."

I sat back in my chair. That sounded like fun—fun I was going to have to miss. Not only that, but we had yet to put up a single decoration ourselves. It was a sad day when I found myself falling behind Bob when it came to domestic duties.

Since I was already feeling sorry for myself, I asked, "What did your father say that made you laugh?"

"He asked if you were making me eat oatmeal for breakfast." Davey stared downward intently. He scraped the last spoonful off the sides of his bowl.

"I thought you liked oatmeal."

"I do. But let's not tell Dad, okay?"

Bob arrived within the hour. When my ex-husband had first reappeared in our lives, he'd been living in Texas and driving a flashy cherry red Trans Am. A subsequent relocation to Connecticut, with its long, often snowy winters, had convinced him of the need for a more practical vehicle. Over the summer he'd traded his car in for a dark green Ford Explorer, perfect for carting home Christmas trees and any other large objects of desire he and my son happened to stumble upon.

Not content to blend in with all the suburban matrons driving similar SUVs, Bob had modified the Explorer's lights, bumper, and exhaust system. I heard the car's low, powerful rumble as he pulled in the driveway. I imagined the neighbors did as well.

The Poodles ran to the front of the house, recognized Bob, and declined to bark. They faded back as Davey opened the door and ran out to greet his father. Bob tries but he's just not a dog person. He doesn't understand the elemental connection I feel with Faith and Eve. To me, the two Poodles are members of our extended family. To Bob, they're just big, black animals that are often in the way.

"I hear I missed you last night," he said as he followed Davey back inside. Seeing the two of them together, it was hard not to be struck by the resemblance between them. They shared the same coloring—sandy brown hair and dark, umber eyes—as well as the same lithe, lanky frames. Even their mannerisms were similar. Bob and I waited in the hall as our son went to find his shoes and warm jacket.

"I stopped by the Bean Counter after you'd left," he said. "Bertie was still there. She said you'd had dinner together."

Bob is Frank's partner in the coffee house. My brother's in charge of day-to-day management; my ex-husband handles the accounts, the taxes, and most of the ordering. Recently, they'd decided that their joint enterprise had been successful enough to tempt them into thinking about expanding.

"We stopped by after Davey's play practice yesterday."

"Oh yeah, the Christmas pageant. I've heard all about it. *I bring a gift of incense for the Baby Jesus.*"

I grinned. "I guess Davey's had you running lines with him, too?"

"Both of them," Bob confirmed. "I think he has them down pat now."

Good luck with that, I thought. By my count, Davey was rehearsing his two lines at least a dozen times a day. No doubt Bob would discover that fact for himself as the afternoon went on.

"Davey says you're going Christmas tree shopping?"

"Right. Want to come?" Bob craned his head around and

looked into the living room. "We could pick up a tree for you, too."

"I'd love to, but I can't. Unfortunately, there are some people I need to see this morning in Greenwich."

"Listen," Bob whispered. He nudged Faith out of the way with his knee and leaned closer so he wouldn't be overheard. "What's the deal with Santa Claus?"

"What do you mean?"

"I want to make sure I don't say the wrong thing. Does Davey still believe or doesn't he?"

"No," I said with some regret. These small rites of passage only served to remind me how quickly time was going by, and how fleeting my son's childhood would be. "Remember all those questions Davey asked last year? How did Santa travel all over the world in one night? How did he know who'd been good or bad? And what about houses that didn't have chimneys? Even then, he had his suspicions, and this year the jig is up. The kids talked about it at school. One of the parents confirmed that there was no Santa and next thing you know, they all knew."

"How'd he take the news?"

"For a while he was really bummed. Apparently, he was afraid that if he stopped believing, that would be the end of Christmas. Once I explained that for adults the holiday was about the spirit of giving rather than receiving, he decided he could really get into it."

Davey had taken my little speech to heart and we'd already tucked away presents he'd chosen for both his father and for Sam. Later in the weekend, we were planning to go shopping for Bertie, Frank, and Aunt Peg.

"Good," said Bob. "I'll follow your lead, then. And speaking of leads . . ."

He paused as Davey came charging down the stairs. His boots were on and correctly laced; he was dragging his jacket behind him. Trotting down the stairs after him, Eve was carrying his gloves in her mouth. I wondered when he'd trained the Poodle to do that.

". . . I got this flyer in my mailbox."

"Merry Maids?"

"No. Franny's Dog-Walking Service." He pulled a crumpled pamphlet out of his pocket. "I thought this might be something you could try if you ever have to leave the Poodles alone for a long period of time." He smoothed out the sheet of paper and handed it over. "What's Merry Maids?"

"A neighborhood house-cleaning service. Alice was talking about them last night. They've put pamphlets in everyone's mailboxes too."

"I wouldn't mind having someone come in and clean my house once a week. Are they any good?"

"I have no idea. All I know is that they're advertising in the area."

"You should ask Annie," said Davey.

"Who?" Bob asked.

"My bus driver," said Davey. "She knows all about everybody."

"What makes you think that?" I asked curiously.

"Because Henry said so."

"Now you've lost me," said Bob.

"Henry was Davey's bus driver," I told him. "He was an older man and unfortunately he died last week. Annie is Davey's new bus driver." I turned to my son. "What did Henry say about Annie?"

"He didn't say anything about Annie." Davey rolled his eyes. It didn't take a genius to interpret that expression. *Mothers could be so dense.* "He was talking about himself."

"And?" Bob prompted.

"Henry used to tell us that we had to behave ourselves because if we didn't, he would know about it. It was his job to drive around the neighborhood, so he saw everything that was going on."

*How did he die?* Bob mouthed to me above Davey's head.

I turned away so Davey wouldn't hear and muttered under my breath, "He was poisoned."

Bob looked taken aback. As Davey darted after Eve, who still had his gloves and was heading for the kitchen, he said, "Do the police know about that?"

"Of course. A detective on the case called me last night. That's one of the stops I have to make today."

Bob shook his head. "I'd rather be Christmas shopping, myself."

Me too, I thought.

The Hyatt Regency Hotel is an imposing edifice on Route One in Old Greenwich, situated on property that belonged, years ago, to Condé Nast Publications. Large stone sign-posts still trumpet the names of the company's signature magazines.

Driving in, I bypassed the valet parking at the main door. There would be plenty of parking in the big lot in the back and I didn't mind the extra walk. It would give me time to consider what I was going to say to Henry's daughters. I'd called before leaving home, so Robin and Laurel were expecting me. Neither had sounded particularly happy at the prospect of meeting an acquaintance of their father's. Even one who was currently in possession of their missing property.

Declining to give me their room number, the women had opted instead to wait for me in the plant-filled atrium in the hotel's center. Compared to the cold, crisp air outside, the lobby felt warm and humid. I already had my coat and scarf off before I'd even reached the end of the wide hallway that led to the front of the building.

Midmorning on a Saturday, the area was mostly empty save for hotel employees. Two women sat side by side on a low couch flanked by leafy ferns. I turned and headed their way. As I approached, they exchanged a glance and rose.

"Are you Melanie Travis?" asked the taller of the two.

Judging by the warm, honeyed tone of her skin, I decided

she must be the daughter who lived in California. Tans were hard to come by in Connecticut in December. Her hair was styled in a sleek chignon; her clothing was crisp and creased. By comparison, her sister looked as though she'd just tumbled out of bed. Dark hair, shot through with gray, was barely contained by a rubber band at the nape of her neck. The bulky sweater she wore with her jeans was at least a size too big. Her smile looked genuine, however, as she stuck out a hand.

"That's right," I said.

The woman's palm was calloused. She pumped my arm vigorously. "I'm Robin," she said, then nodded toward her more elegant sister. "And this is Laurel. Where are Dad's dogs? We thought you'd bring them with you."

"This hotel doesn't allow dogs. If I'd brought them, I would have had to leave them outside in my car. Then you would have had to figure out some place to put them. I thought it was easier to leave them where they were for the time being."

"Maybe that was for us to decide," Laurel said frostily.

I sighed inwardly. This wasn't going to be easy. "Mind if I sit?"

Laurel looked as though she might. Two upholstered chairs opposite faced the couch. I ignored her, chose one, and sat anyway.

"I'm very sorry about your father," I said. "He was a kind and decent man."

"Thank you," said Robin.

Laurel waved a hand dismissively. "We're not here for condolences. We're here to retrieve our property, which was taken without permission from our father's house. You should know we're contemplating taking legal action."

"You must be joking," I blurted. "Over what? The fact that someone tried to be helpful and take care of two abandoned animals in your absence? Do you honestly think those two dogs should have been left to fend for themselves in your father's house until you chose to arrive?"

"I understand a neighbor had been feeding them."

"Yes, grudgingly. But she wasn't walking them. Surely you can imagine how big a mess they were making."

Robin's nose wrinkled. She got the picture, even if her sister didn't. "We would have come sooner, but both Laurel and I have obligations. It wasn't easy to drop everything on a moment's notice. And, of course, our father died very unexpectedly. Before we even knew what had happened, it was already too late. At that point, there didn't seem to be any need to hurry."

"That was before we realized that strangers had complete access to our father's things," Laurel interjected. "Had we understood the true situation, I assure you we would have been here sooner."

"Then you didn't know that your father had two Golden Retrievers that needed to be attended to?"

"Of course we knew about Pepper and Remington," said Robin. "We saw pictures every Christmas. Dad put them on the card, for Pete's sake. He loved those dogs."

"So that's why you're so anxious to get them back." I was being facetious. Robin didn't seem to notice.

"No, not really," she replied. "Dad may have been attached to the dogs, but we barely know them. I can't take them home with me; I already have two cats. And as for Laurel—"

"I live in an apartment." Tired of standing, Laurel finally sat down on the couch. She crossed her legs gracefully and placed her folded hands atop her knee. "So Pepper and Remington will have to be disposed of with the rest of our father's things. We intend to sell them to the highest bidder."

My brow lifted. They couldn't be serious. "The *highest bidder*?"

"Precisely," Robin confirmed. "Laurel and I have spoken about it and we've decided that's the best way to handle things. We'll place an ad in the newspaper and see what kind of offers come rolling in."

I cleared my throat. It was either that or laugh in their faces. "What makes you think any offers are going to come rolling in at all?"

"Perhaps you don't know much about dogs," said Laurel. "At any rate, I imagine you're unaware that these two are excellent purebreds. Our father was very particular about the things he owned. Pepper and Remington have papers and pedigrees."

So did nearly every purebred dog in the country, I thought. But a pedigree alone wasn't enough to confer value on an older dog. Rebecca Morehouse could have told them that; she hadn't wanted him back for free. And as for her puppies that presumably carried the same pedigree, she'd resorted to selling them out of the back of a car.

The notion that someone might actually pay a large sum of money for either of those two dogs was dizzyingly optimistic. And vastly untrue.

"That's not all," said Robin. "I remember Dad telling me that one of them comes from a famous breeding kennel. He has relatives that showed at Westminster. That's the big dog show in New York that they show on TV every year," she added helpfully, in case I wasn't familiar with the name.

"I know about Westminster," I managed to say.

"Then you should understand why we value these dogs so highly," said Laurel. "Westminster is the pinnacle."

"Well, yes, but . . ." There were so many things wrong with their logic, I scarcely knew where to begin refuting it.

"But what?"

"Lots of dogs come from the same stock as those that show at Westminster. It doesn't necessarily mean that they're worth money."

Laurel lifted her head back and gazed down her nose at me. "I see what this is about. You knew our father in his capacity as a school bus driver." She said the words distastefully and quickly moved on. "Obviously, this has colored your impression of his business affairs. Let me assure you that our father was very well situated financially. Living simply as he did was his choice; it was by no means a necessity."

"I'm aware of that—" I began.

"Then perhaps you take my sister and me for a pair of fools?"

"Of course not, but—"

"Yet somehow you believe that we are going to allow you to abscond with valuable property that rightfully belongs to us?"

I sighed and settled back in my seat. Good thing I hadn't brought Pepper and Remington and left them waiting in the car. It looked as though sorting this mess out was going to take some time.

# 12

In my experience, "abscond" is one of those fancy words people use when they want you to believe that their education is better than it really is. But since Laurel had used the word first, I felt free to toss it right back at her.

"No one wanted to abscond with your property," I said. "I was trying to look after it." Not that I'd cared one bit about the sisters' feelings in the matter; it was Pepper and Remington I'd been trying to protect. And judging by the way these two were acting, my job wasn't over yet.

"I'm curious," I said. "If you believed the two dogs were so valuable, why didn't you make arrangements for their care when you received the news about your father?"

"Naturally, we just assumed . . ." Robin shrugged as if the answer was obvious. It wasn't to me.

"What?" I asked.

"Our mother died ten years ago," Laurel said. Her tone clearly implied this was none of my business. "In the meantime, our father, being a man . . ."

"Hasn't lacked for companionship," Robin finished when her sister's voice trailed off. "For a while now, he's been seeing a woman who breeds dogs. In fact, she bred one of his dogs. So when something happened to Dad, we thought she would step in and take care of things."

Henry Pruitt and Rebecca Morehouse? On the surface,

they seemed like an unlikely couple. Henry with his baseball
cap and fingerless gloves, a warm smile always at the ready;
and Rebecca whose rigid demeanor and steely gaze could
freeze the laughter in children's throats. Then I remembered
the way she'd looked the day before, wan and unhappy.
Maybe this explained a great deal.

What it didn't explain was Rebecca's reluctance to get involved after the fact. Now that I knew Remington was more
to her than a puppy that had been sold at the first opportunity
and never thought of again, her callous refusal to help out
was even more inexplicable to me.

"Clearly," Laurel said coldly, "there's been no attempt on
our parts to shirk our duties."

"I never said—"

"No, but you were thinking it." Robin frowned. "Just like
Dad's neighbor who read us the riot act when we arrived.
Like it was our fault that something had happened to him.
Like maybe things would have been different if we'd been
here."

Laurel gave her sister a quelling look. Robin either didn't
notice or she didn't care. My guess was, she was feeling
guilty enough about her absence from her father's life to feel
the need to justify it.

"You knew our father," she said, "so I'm sure you understand. He could be . . . difficult."

"He was impossibly demanding," said Laurel. Now that
the topic had been broached, she wanted to be heard too.
"He was set in his ways and determined that everyone con-
form to them. Heaven help the person who had a different
idea."

"It didn't matter how old we got to be," said Robin. "In
Dad's eyes, we were still his little girls. He wanted to run our
lives for us." She snorted under her breath. "It's probably no
wonder that we ended up in Alaska and California. That was
how far we had to go in order to be able to make our own decisions and lead our own lives."

"Don't get us wrong," said Laurel. My head was swiveling back and forth between the two sisters like a spectator at a tennis match. "Of course we're sorry he's gone. But we weren't a touchy-feely sort of family. That just wasn't us. Not ever."

I clasped my hands together in my lap and stared calmly at two of the coldest bitches I'd ever seen. The kind of family life they were talking about was utterly foreign to me. I'd been close to both my parents until their deaths when I was in my early twenties. And even though I'd subsequently discovered that there were areas of their lives I'd known nothing about, that hadn't in any way diminished my wonderful memories of the time we'd spent together.

"I see," I said. "So you haven't come to Connecticut to mourn your father, you've simply come to claim his property."

Laurel smiled tightly. "You may think we're unfeeling, but the truth of the matter is, your opinion is immaterial to us. This afternoon we'll see our father's lawyer. His will will be read. Barring any last-minute surprises, everything he has will be divided between my sister and me—including his two dogs." She paused, then added, "And any other items of his you may have seen fit to remove from his house?"

I'd started to stand. That crack about my opinion being immaterial had pretty much done it for me. But now, incredulously, I sank back down into my seat. "Excuse me?"

"I think you heard me. Be assured that Robin and I will be spending the next few days doing an inventory of our father's possessions. If anything should turn up missing, we'll know where to come looking for it."

I opened my purse and got out a piece of paper and a pen. Leaning on my knee, I wrote *Two Golden Retrievers, Remington and Pepper. Approx. 20 pounds of Iams kibble, 2 stainless steel bowls.* Then I signed the bottom.

"There you go," I said, tossing the sheet onto Laurel's lap. "That's the sum total of everything I took from the house. I'll go get your dogs now. They're not far from here. I'll probably be back within half an hour, so that's how long you'll have to make other arrangements for their care. By the way,

I won't be allowed to bring them into the lobby so you'd better be prepared to meet me at the door." I stopped, then
smiled sweetly. "Unless you'd like me to check Pepper and
Remington with the parking valet?"

"Wait, please," Robin said quickly. "I know my sister's
offended you and I'm sorry. Much as she might like to think
that she speaks for both of us, she doesn't. Obviously, there
are things we didn't understand. You've gone out of your
way to be helpful and we appreciate that."

Robin must have thought I'd be dazzled by her apology.
Either that or she was hoping I was half-blind. Because
otherwise there was no way I could have missed the fact that
when Laurel opened her mouth to speak, probably intending
to repudiate what her sister had said, Robin kicked her in the
ankle. Hard. A bruise was going to mark that spot later. That
thought didn't distress me in the slightest.

"You're quite right to point out that we're going to need a
place to keep the dogs until we manage to dispose of them,"
Robin said. "Perhaps you could suggest something?"

I shrugged. If it weren't for those two lovely, innocent
Golden Retrievers, I would have already been long gone.
"The boys are happy where they are now."

"And that would be exactly where?" Laurel demanded.

"At my aunt's house. She breeds dogs on a very small
scale and had the facilities for taking in a couple of extras on
short notice. Remington and Pepper have been there since
midweek. They've settled in just fine."

"So you say. My sister and I would like to check out these
arrangements for ourselves. I assume there will be fees involved for their care?"

"I'm not surprised you'd think that," I said. "Since you've
obviously never done anything in your life out of the goodness of your heart. My aunt may have her faults but, bottom
line, she adores dogs. Big ones, little ones, all kinds of dogs.
Just the knowledge that these two were being neglected was
enough to make her want to help them."

Laurel's cheeks were bright with color. Robin looked like

she was ready to burst; whether with laughter or outrage, I wasn't quite sure. Nor did I intend to hang around and find out. I gathered up my things and stood.

"There aren't any fees," I said. "There aren't any conditions. Just someone who doesn't mind doing her share to make her part of the world a slightly better place. My aunt's name is Margaret Turnbull, you can find her in the phone book. I'm sure she'll be happy to show you 'the arrangements.' "

Aunt Peg was going to have a field day with these two, I thought. I debated calling to warn her, then decided against it. Better to let her form her own opinion on the spot; that way none of her anger would be mitigated by my advance notice.

I hoped she ate them alive.


Stamford police headquarters was located in a square, nondescript building downtown. Taking Route One east from Old Greenwich, I got there in no time. After checking in at the front desk, I then had to wait twenty minutes before Detective Marley was available to see me. Since I hadn't thought to bring along a book to read, I had nothing to do but sit and stew.

Belatedly, I realized that one thing that hadn't come up in my conversation with Robin and Laurel was the fact that the police believed their father had been murdered. Surely news like that must have come as a shock to them, no matter how distant their relationship with Henry had been. Nobody expects their lives to be touched by violent crime.

I wondered whether Detective Marley had already spoken to the two sisters. I wondered if they'd known enough about Henry's current life to have any ideas who might have been responsible for his death. Then I found myself wondering exactly how large the estate was that the two of them stood to inherit.

"Sorry about the wait."

Pulled from my musing, I looked up into a pair of inquisitive hazel eyes topped by bushy brows. Ron Marley wasn't tall but he was solidly built. His wiry brown hair was cropped close. His handshake was firm.

Working on a Saturday, he was casually dressed in jeans and a denim shirt. His tie sported a retro tie-dye design in eye-popping shades of mellow yellow, purple haze, and acid green. Like psychedelic, man.

The detective caught me staring and smiled. "My daughter's in preschool. This was their Father's Day project."

"It's . . . um . . . eye-catching."

"Good save. I've heard it called worse."

Taking my elbow, he guided me around the reception desk and into the back hallway that led to his office. The small room was sparsely furnished; a desk and credenza, two chairs, and a file cabinet filled most of the space. His window looked out over the mostly empty parking lot. Forced-air heat blasted into the room through two large vents along the floor. Quickly, I shed my coat. Detective Marley took it and hung it on a hook on the back of the door.

"Have a seat," he said. "And thanks for stopping by. I'm sure you realize this is just a formality. We're talking to everyone who had contact with the deceased, Henry Pruitt, in the last weeks of his life. Although you are a bit of a special case in that you entered his house after his death. . . ."

"For a very good reason."

"Yes," Marley said. I wondered whether he was agreeing with me or just encouraging me to speak. "Why don't you tell me about that?"

"Henry was my son's bus driver."

The detective opened his top drawer and pulled out a pad of paper and pen. "That would be the bus to Hunting Ridge Elementary, right?"

"Yes. Davey's in the third grade. We—all the mothers in the neighborhood—liked Henry. He's been driving the bus for years. So when he didn't show up for several days and the company assigned a new driver to the route, I wondered if something was the matter."

"And you decided to go see?"

"A friend and I wanted to check on Henry and make sure that he was okay."

"So you weren't alone when you went to Henry's house for the first time?"

"No."

I was sure he must have known the answer to that. So why was he asking? Surely he didn't expect me to lie?

"Your friend's name?"

"Alice Brickman. We knocked on Henry's door and of course there was no answer, though we could hear his dogs barking inside the house. Then his neighbor, Betty Bowen, called us over and told us that he had died."

"And it was at that point you decided to enter his house? A house where a suspicious death had recently taken place?"

I sat up straight, leaned forward, and braced my hands on the top of his desk. My fingers curled around the edge hard enough to make my knuckles whiten. "For one thing, at that point I had no idea that Henry had been murdered. All Betty told me was that he'd collapsed and been taken to the hospital. And for another, there were animals in distress inside that empty house. There was no way I was just going to walk away and leave them there."

"Even though you didn't know Mr. Pruitt very well, you didn't have a key to his house, and you'd apparently never met his dogs before. You still felt it was your responsibility to do something."

Ignoring the skepticism I heard in his tone, I said, "Yes."

"Besides," I added after a minute of silence, "Henry's neighbor had already been going in and out of his house to put food down for the dogs. So my going in really wasn't very different."

Marley glanced down at his notes. Since there was barely

anything written on the page, I couldn't imagine what he wanted me to think he was checking. "So you say."

"It's the truth."

"Except that you removed something from the house."

I sighed softly. My patience was beginning to fray. Hadn't I had this conversation once today already?

"Would you like the dogs back?" I asked. "Because at this point I am more than willing to go get them, bring them here, and tie them to your desk. They're big but they're friendly. Not terribly well trained, but well meaning. There's a twenty-pound bag of kibble that goes with them. I stole that from Henry's house, too.

"The dogs' names are Pepper and Remington. They don't always come when they're called, so you're going to want to walk them on a leash. Three or four times a day should do it. Oh, and they're Golden Retrievers, so they're shedding. You'd better tell your janitors to get more bags for the vacuum. . . ."

I paused for breath and looked over to find Detective Marley sitting back in his chair, smiling. "Done yet?"

"Not quite, because I haven't gotten to the part about Henry's daughters yet. They've finally arrived, and they want his dogs back, too. So you may have to fight for them."

"I have no intention of fighting for anything." Marley chuckled. "Any more than I had any intention of fighting with you when I walked in here. So I guess you're a dog lover, huh?"

"I guess so."

"I suppose that explains what you were doing in Henry's house."

"I would think so." I tried to sound huffy, but I was running out of steam.

"And your second visit?"

This time his question didn't sound accusatory, merely curious. I explained about the papers we'd been looking for, and the fact that Peg and I had hoped to place the two Goldens in good homes rather than having to take them to the pound. Detective Marley nodded at the end.

"Do you have any leads?" I asked.

"Some," he said guardedly. "Mostly we're still asking questions. If you have any thoughts, I'm open to listening."

"Have you interviewed Henry's daughters?"

"Not yet, but I will."

"Other than those two, everyone I know liked him."

"That's pretty much what we've found." Marley flipped his pad shut and capped his pen. "We haven't found a single person with anything bad to say about him."

"Then how did Henry end up poisoned?" I asked.

"That's what we'd like to know," he said.

# 13

It was early afternoon when I got home. While the Poodles were outside in the yard, I fixed myself a turkey sandwich on rye and ate it standing at the counter. When Davey's around, I make an effort to serve proper meals and we always eat at the table. When I'm by myself, expediency rules the day.

By the time Faith and Eve were ready to come back in, I was rinsing my plate in the sink. Briefly I considered putting the younger Poodle up on her grooming table, brushing through her coat, and unwrapping and rewrapping her ears and topknot. Done correctly, the entire process would take more than an hour.

Aunt Peg wouldn't have hesitated. I did, and the impulse petered out. Instead I helped myself to a handful of Oreos and called Sam. We'd made rudimentary plans to see each other over the weekend but never bothered to firm anything up.

No answer at his house. I tried his cell phone.

Sam answered fast. "Is it Bertie?" he asked.

"No." I cradled the receiver between my shoulder and ear. That left both hands free so I could refill the dogs' water bowl. "Not unless you know something I don't. Why would I be calling about Bertie?"

"Because you never call me on my cell phone. I thought maybe it was an emergency."

"No emergency," I said. "I haven't even seen Bertie since yesterday. I just missed you."

There was a beat of time before Sam answered. I could hear the sounds of traffic in the background. "I miss you, too," he replied. "Are we getting together tomorrow?"

"Or sooner." Bowl full, I turned off the tap. Water sloshed from side to side as I set it down on the floor.

"I'm on the New Jersey Turnpike. Heading south, stuck in traffic, and not moving. God knows when I'll be back."

"Why are you—" A horn blared. I heard Sam swear under his breath. "Never mind," I said. "You can tell me tomorrow."

The only answer I got to that was static. I clicked off and called Bob's house. Davey picked up right away.

"Did you find a Christmas tree?" I asked.

"A huge one," my son informed me gleefully. "And a wreath and tons of pine roping."

"What are you guys doing now?"

"As soon as Dad gets the tree in the house, we're going to start decorating."

"I'll come and help," I said. "Be there in five minutes."

Bob's house was a good-sized colonial on a landscaped two-acre lot. It was much too big for his purposes, but he'd made the purchase with an eye toward its potential as an investment. Once an accountant, always an accountant; and in Fairfield County, buying real estate was never a bad decision.

Bob's street was wide and quiet, and shaded by mature trees. Though families with children lived in most of the surrounding houses, the road had neither sidewalks nor curbs. Unlike my neighborhood, where something always seemed to be going on, here it was unusual to see anyone outside at all.

When the Poodles and I arrived, the Christmas tree was inside the house. It was even somewhat upright. Bob was down on the floor underneath it, grappling with the intricacies of the stand.

"Anything I can do?" I asked.

"Yeah. Keep that hound from licking my face, would you?"

Since Bob was down at her level and had his hands otherwise occupied, Eve had seen her chance to try and make friends, doggy-style. My ex was not amused by her greeting.

"She's not a hound." Davey giggled as I shooed her away. "She's a non-sporting dog."

"Of course," Bob muttered. The tree tilted precariously. Both Davey and I leapt to catch it. When it was straight once more, Bob went back to tightening the screws. "Whatever that means."

"It means that Poodles show in the non-sporting group," said Davey. Showing off his knowledge for his father, he ticked off the names of the groups on his fingers. "There are seven different ones: sporting, hound, working, terrier, toy, non-sporting, and herding. But the non-sporting group is the best."

I looked at Davey curiously. "What makes you say that?"

"Because that's where the Poodles are." *Of course.*

"Well, it sounds pretty dumb to me." Bob slithered out from beneath the tree. Davey and I released our holds and stepped back cautiously. It swayed briefly, then held. "Anyone can tell just by looking at a Poodle that they're not a sporting dog. But to have a whole group of dogs named for their deficiencies? Why don't they just call it the misfit group and leave it at that?"

"Because that would be insulting," I said. "In England, they call it the utility group, which *is* a better name. But since you brought it up, Standard Poodles actually do very well as sporting dogs. Some people use them with great success as retrievers of birds and game."

"I know. That's where the trim came from, right?"

"Right." I grinned. "Have you had this lecture before?"

"At least twice," Bob said, wincing. "And every so often Peg feels obliged to give me a refresher course. By now, I probably know the drill as well as you do." He held out a hand and beckoned Eve to him. Tail wagging, the Poodle complied happily.

"Okay," he said, cupping one hand under Eve's muzzle, and using the other to showcase her profuse mane coat. "So the Poodle was a dog bred to retrieve. Since the waters were cold, the French developed a dog with a long, thick coat—"

"Germans," I said. "The Standard Poodle was developed in Germany."

"Whatever." Bob looked at Davey and rolled his eyes. His son giggled on cue. "Then they discovered that that big coat wasn't such a good idea. When the dogs jumped in the cold water, it soaked into their hair and weighed them down. They sank like stones."

Bob threw himself down on the floor and flopped dramatically. He looked less like a wet dog than a dying fish. Eve, however, must have appreciated his efforts because she began to race circles around him, barking uproariously. That brought Faith running. Rounding the corner, she skidded on the hardwood floor. Feet scrambling for purchase that wasn't there, the big Poodle went barreling right into Bob.

The impact sent both of them flying. Eve jumped out of the way and remained on her feet. Davey wasn't so lucky. Caught in the cross fire, he joined the tangled heap on the floor.

Shrieks emanated from the pile. Faith extricated herself first, followed a minute later by Davey. Left alone on the floor, Bob groaned as he righted himself.

"Serves you right," I said, "for making fun of my dogs like that."

"Hey, I wasn't done." He hopped to his feet, grabbed Eve, and resumed his explanation. "Okay, the water's cold. The hair's wet."

"Like you, Dad," said Davey. "You're all wet."

Bob snaked out a hand. Laughing, Davey dodged away.

"So the hunters cut off all the coat they didn't think was necessary. They left this big pile of hair in the front—"

"The mane coat," I interjected.

". . . to protect the heart and lungs. These froufrou items over here—"

"Those would be the hip rosettes."

"Cover the kidneys. While the puffy things around the legs . . ."

Close enough, I thought, and declined to interrupt.

". . . serve as protection for the joints and keep them warm." Finished and proud of himself, Bob bowed with a flourish. In spite of myself, I was impressed. All this time, Bob must have been paying more attention than I'd thought.

"You forgot something," said Davey. "What about the tail?"

"What about the tail? Why don't you tell me?"

"The pom pon on the tail was like a flag," said Davey. "When the Poodle dove under water after a bird, the hunters would see it sticking up and know where he was."

"Very good," said a voice from the doorway. "Davey, you're a child after my own heart."

Belatedly, the two Poodles noticed we had a visitor they hadn't announced. As one they spun around and went to remedy the situation. Aunt Peg shushed them with a stern look. She has that effect on people, too.

"Some watchdogs you are," I said to the abashed pair. "Aunt Peg, what are you doing here?"

Peg ignored the question. She stood in the doorway and took in the scene. Bob lived like a bachelor. After a year in residence, he had yet to hang curtains and his living room still held more entertainment equipment than furniture. The walls were bare and the magazine pile on his battered coffee table probably wouldn't reveal anything creditable about his character.

Cardboard cartons filled with ornaments and Christmas trimmings, dragged up from the basement before my arrival, were scattered around the room. The tree was upright, but just barely. At least Bob wasn't still flopping around on the floor.

"Most people lock their front doors," she said to my ex-husband. He had never been one of her favorite people, and Aunt Peg missed no opportunity to remind him of his shortcomings.

"What can I say?" Bob spread his hands. "I'm a friendly kind of guy. Come on in, make yourself at home. Want a cup of coffee?"

"Tea," I prompted under my breath. Aunt Peg only drank tea. Anyone who paid attention would know that. Of course, Bob might simply have been trying to bait Peg right back.

"No, thank you," she said primly. "I needn't bother you at all. As it happens, I was looking for Melanie."

"And you came here?" Interesting. Maybe I'd been spending more time with my ex than I'd realized.

"I tried your house first, but obviously you weren't home. Since I was already in the neighborhood, I took a shot."

"Is something the matter?"

"Nothing that couldn't be solved by access to illegal weaponry. I've met the daughters."

"Oh." I should have known.

"That's all you have to say?"

"What daughters?" asked Bob. He was leaning into a box, bent on untangling a long skein of white lights.

"Henry Pruitt's daughters. I told you about him this morning." I glanced toward Davey. Busy unpacking the cartons of decorations, he was happily oblivious. "I guess they called you about Pepper and Remington?"

"They not only called, they came to visit. They *inspected* my kennel." Her voice quivered with barely suppressed outrage. "They asked me to present them with an itemized bill."

"They're not the brightest pair."

"Idiots," Peg corrected. "Complete nitwits. Did they tell you they expect to sell those two dogs for lots of money?"

"They did mention something about the highest bidder. I imagine you set them straight?"

"How could I when neither one seemed capable of logical thought? Five minutes in their company and I was sorely tempted to bang both their heads together."

Too bad she hadn't followed through, I thought.

"Did you give them Pepper and Remington?"

"To do what with?" Peg's brow lifted. "The only thing they *did* seem able to understand is that the dogs are better off with me until they figure out what to do next. Of course, that put the kibosh on the plans we'd made to send them on to new homes."

"Think of it this way," I said, "at least they're paying you board."

"Very funny," Aunt Peg snapped.

Bob and Davey now had a stepladder propped open beside the tree. The first string of lights was going on. Since the two of them seemed to be managing just fine without us, Peg and I withdrew to a leather couch on the other side of the room.

"Did you speak with Robin and Laurel about their father's murder?" Aunt Peg asked.

I shook my head. "It never came up."

*"I* brought it up. They're horrified by the thought that Henry didn't die a natural death. Now that they're here, they're planning to stay until their father's murder is solved."

"Is that a bad thing?"

"You wouldn't dream of asking such a ridiculous question if their dogs were living with you. Not only that, but the longer they stay, the more time that will give them to come up with something truly stupid to do with Pepper and Remington."

"Or the more time it will give *you* to convince them of the wisdom of doing things your way."

"Trust me, I have no intention of spending any more time than necessary with those two. In fact, I wouldn't mind at all if I never saw them again. That's why I've made a plan."

"Oh no."

"You haven't even heard what I was going to say yet."

It didn't matter. Whatever it was, it wouldn't be good. Take my word on this, I've been around a while.

"It's very simple," said Aunt Peg. "Henry Pruitt's murder needs solving, and the sooner, the better. I thought I would look into it."

"You?" I sputtered.

"Not what you expected me to say, was it?" Her eyes gleamed with satisfaction. "I guess this old dog still has a few new tricks left to play yet."

Trust me, that particular old dog was nothing but a continuing source of new tricks.

"You?" I said again.

"Why not me?"

"Why not the police? You didn't even know Henry Pruitt."

"Neither do the police."

As if that was a salient point. "It's their job to find murderers."

"You of all people should know they're not always particularly good at it. Sometimes they overlook the most obvious things."

What Aunt Peg meant was that, due to our background in dogs, she and I had sometimes been able to interpret clues differently than they looked on the surface. Occasionally, we'd been known to beat the police to the punch. But while Aunt Peg had often been the instigator, she usually seemed to think that poking a nose into other people's business was my job, not hers.

"That's the craziest thing I've ever heard," I said.

"What is?" Bob, passing by with an extension cord, had stopped to listen in.

"Aunt Peg wants to investigate a murder."

"Hey, great idea." Bob held up my aunt's hand and slapped her five. "Way to go, Peg!"

"That," I said sharply, "was not the appropriate response."

"Oh, I don't know." Aunt Peg was smiling. "For once, your ex-husband and I seem to be in complete agreement."

Somewhere in the world, I thought, pigs were flying.

"What about me?" I asked.

"You needn't feel left out."

"I don't!"

"Then what's the problem?" Peg asked reasonably.

Bob moved on. He and Davey had all the strands of lights in place. When he plugged in the cord, hundreds of small white bulbs began to glow. The magic of Christmas was coming to life right before our eyes.

"I know you're busy," said Aunt Peg. "That's the beauty of this. I'll handle everything myself. You won't have to worry about a single thing."

Right. Like that was *ever* going to happen in my lifetime.

# 14

"All I need from you," said Aunt Peg, "is a little information to get me started."

"There's probably a book," I mumbled. *"Solving Mysteries for Dummies."*

I knew I sounded surly and my own reaction surprised me. It wasn't as though an investigation into Henry Pruitt's murder was anything that I needed to be involved in. But still, Aunt Peg should have asked for my help. Aunt Peg *always* asked for my help.

What was the world coming to when she didn't feel a need to poke around and rearrange my life?

All right, so maybe I was slightly miffed.

"What kind of information?" I asked.

"You know, like who might have had a reason to want to see him dead?"

I sputtered a laugh. "If I knew that, I'd have told Detective Marley this morning, and he could be wrapping up this whole thing right now."

"Good point," said Peg. "What did you tell him?"

"About Robin and Laurel, for one. Beyond that, I didn't have much to offer. Although here's something interesting. According to Robin, Henry was romantically involved with the breeder of one of his dogs."

" 'Romantically involved,' what a quaint way of putting it. You mean they were shacking up?"

"That's my guess," I said primly, "though I wasn't told any details. All I know is what Robin said. That for some time now, Henry had been seeing a woman who bred one of his Goldens."

"Not Cindy Marshall," said Aunt Peg. "She's married."

"These days, that's hardly enough to rule her out. Though I agree that Rebecca Morehouse seems the more likely candidate. It's odd she didn't mention anything about that when I talked to her about Remington yesterday."

"Nothing?"

I shook my head.

"Well, then that makes her a suspect, doesn't it? And here I thought solving a mystery was going to be hard. I'll have this sorted out in no time." Aunt Peg was almost giddy with satisfaction. "Don't forget, Henry died after being poisoned with ethylene-glycol. There probably isn't a dog person any-where who doesn't know about antifreeze's sweet taste and toxic properties."

I really hated to rain on her parade, but it had to be done.

"Motive?" I mentioned.

"Pardon me?" Aunt Peg was so busy patting herself on the back that she didn't hear what I said.

"What about a motive? What reason did Rebecca have for wanting to kill Henry?"

"There could have been any number of reasons," Peg said blithely. "Especially now that I know they were a couple. Maybe they had a lovers' spat."

"After which she convinced him to drink a half gallon of antifreeze she just happened to have around the house?"

Aunt Peg's hand waved through the air, brushing away my objections. If I hadn't gotten out of the way in time, it would have slapped my cheek. The near miss was, no doubt, inten-tional.

"Maybe they had a disagreement over Remington," she said.

"People don't kill each other over dogs."

Aunt Peg's deadpan look told me what she thought of *that* statement.

I didn't care; I was sticking to my guns. Though we'd both seen a number of people in the dog show world come to grief, in nearly every instance the arguments that seemed to have started over a dog had been symptomatic of larger issues. Usually much larger issues.

"Work with me here," said Peg. "I'm just throwing out ideas. Maybe she didn't like the fact that he drove a bus, or that he didn't get along with his daughters. Maybe he tried to break up with her."

"And so she killed him? That would stop him all right. Though it wouldn't do much for the relationship. I think you need to consider other options. The daughters stood to inherit, and apparently Henry had some money."

"Not to mention two very valuable Golden Retrievers," Aunt Peg snorted. "Believe me, I've heard all about their prospects. But you're probably right, I should do some more digging. What we really need to do is talk to other people who knew Henry. People who could tell us what was going on in other facets of his life . . ."

Her voice trailed away. She gazed past me at Davey and Bob. I turned to see what had caught her attention.

While we'd been talking, they'd finished decorating the Christmas tree. Red ribbon bows, shimmering ornaments, and strands of cranberries and popcorn hung from every branch. Set beside a picture window and framed by the gathering dark outside, the tree sparkled and glowed. I sighed with appreciation.

What can I say? I'm a sucker for a holiday.

Aunt Peg, however, was frowning.

The tree complete, Bob and Davey were now draping several yards of evergreen roping over the mantelpiece. The ends hung down to frame the natural brick fireplace where a fire had been laid but not yet lit. This being Bob's house, there were twice as many logs in the andirons as there should have been, and no precautionary screen.

Abruptly, Peg rose from the couch and strode over to help. "Give me that." She held out a hand and Bob obeyed without comment. It was easy to see why *her* marriage had lasted so many years.

"Davey's a child, but you should know better," she told him. "You can't hang pine boughs right next to the fireplace. You're going to set your house on fire."

It wouldn't be the first time, I thought.

"Honestly," Peg muttered, but she didn't look entirely unhappy to be called upon to rearrange the decorations.

Once Aunt Peg and I were up and moving around, the Poodles came to see what was going on. Eve grabbed the dangling end of the roping and teased a pinecone loose. Prize clenched between her teeth, she dashed away with the other dog in pursuit.

That pinecone would tear Eve's tongue to shreds, I realized. Not to mention upsetting her stomach.

Davey must have read my mind. "I'll get it!" he cried. Dropping his end of the roping, he fled from the room.

I grabbed the long strand of pine branching as it fell, lifting quickly before the garland could swing free and dislodge everything on the mantel. Kneeling on the hearth below me, oblivious to the fact that half the decorations had just nearly landed on his head, Bob was poking at the kindling.

"Since you two have taken over my job, I'll go ahead and light the fire," he said.

"Wait!"

Too late. Bob had already flicked a long wooden match against one of the stones. A small burst of flame appeared. He touched it to the kindling before glancing up to see what I wanted.

"Did you open the flue?" I asked, as the fire caught and flared.

"Damn," Bob muttered.

Davey shrieked in the other room. Eve began to bark. I wondered who was winning that engagement.

Beside me, Aunt Peg arranged the last of the roping with

a flourish. Then she raised her hand to her mouth and began to cough. "Is it just me or it is smoky in here?"

Family; you know what I mean.

"She's going to do *what*?" Sam asked.

"You heard me." At least I thought he had. Considering how loudly Davey had the CD of Christmas carols playing, it was hard to hold a conversation without shouting.

It was Sunday afternoon, and Davey and I, along with the Poodles, were in Redding. Having decorated Bob's house the day before, we were now doing the same for Sam's. This, too, was a bachelor pad, but other than that the two houses had little in common. Sam's place was a soaring contemporary, all clean lines and sheer glass. Perched on a hillside, surrounded by trees, its cedar shingles blended perfectly into the stark winter tableau.

Inside the differences continued. This house wasn't an investment, it was very much a home. Recently Sam had come into a bit of money. He hadn't moved, but he had redecorated. Rich oriental carpets covered the hardwood floors; butter soft leather furniture was grouped around a fireplace whose stone chimney took up an entire wall.

There was a cedar dog bed on the floor next to the fireplace. One of Sam's Standard Poodles was curled up inside. After a frenzied initial greeting, the five dogs—two of mine, three of Sam's—had helped themselves to the most comfortable spots in the room and settled down to sleep.

Sam had already hung a wreath on the chimney. There was another on his front door. Fresh greenery twined with twinkling lights swagged the doorways. Only the tree remained to be trimmed, and we were working on that.

Was I the only person, I wondered, who wasn't yet ready for Christmas? And when had everyone decided that no holiday was complete without acres of ribbon and garland and roping? As far as I was concerned, Martha Stewart had a lot to answer for.

"Peg thinks she's going to track down Henry Pruitt's murderer," I said again, just in case he hadn't heard me. Davey, perched on a sturdy stepladder around the back of the tree, wasn't paying the slightest bit of attention, so I felt free to elaborate.

"Why would she want to do that?"

Good question. That was one of the things I enjoyed about Sam. He always asked good questions. Unfortunately, I didn't always have equally good answers.

"She wants the daughters to go home and leave Remington and Pepper's fate up to her." I explained about the plan to sell the two Golden Retrievers to the highest bidder.

Sam knows plenty about dogs; he understood right away the lunacy of that idea. "I can't believe Peg didn't set them straight."

"She did. And so did I. But they didn't believe either of us. And neither is leaving until they find out what happened to their father."

"The police . . . ?" He let the thought dangle.

"Interviewed Aunt Peg and me both. Apparently, they didn't take kindly to the fact that we'd been walking around their crime scene."

"I can't imagine why not." Sam's tongue was planted firmly in his cheek.

"If there was any evidence in the house, we certainly didn't tamper with it. The police don't have any leads. Aside from his family squabbles, Henry seems to have been universally liked."

I selected a shiny golden bell from the box of ornaments. Last year's hook was still attached. Though Sam had already secured a satin-draped fairy to the top of the tree, there was still plenty of room left on the upper branches. I walked around to where Davey was standing on the ladder and handed him the bell. He took it and considered his options carefully.

"I was thinking you might want to try talking some sense into Peg," I said a minute later to Sam.

"You were, were you?"

"Yes." The *dammit* I added silently. Clearly Sam—who'd been known to try and talk sense into me—was enjoying my discomfort.

"You've already tried yourself?"

"Of course, but she didn't listen to me. Aunt Peg never listens to me, you know that. She respects your opinion."

"She respects yours, too."

"Only when it agrees with her own," I grumbled.

"Amazing," said Sam. "Does that sound like anyone else we know?"

Taking the high road, I declined to rise to *that* bait.

Instead, I continued fishing through the Christmas cartons that were scattered around the room. Sam had enough holiday supplies to festoon a fleet of department store windows. Boxes of ornaments and trimmings abounded, as well as bells, Christmas candles, and several different kinds of tinsel. An oddly shaped wreath, fashioned of twigs, colored string, and glitter, was probably a contribution from his two nephews.

Nestled in one carton I found three stockings, all carefully packed in tissue paper. The first, well worn, looked as though it dated from Sam's childhood. The second depicted a trio of appliquéd Poodles dancing in the snow. A raffle prize from a Poodle specialty, I was guessing.

The third stocking, made of velvet, was heavy and ornate. Its needlepoint design was intricately conceived; a golden-haired Christmas fairy lounged in indolent splendor against a plush, royal blue background. As I opened it up, Sam made a choking noise under his breath.

He reached for the stocking. Curiosity piqued by his response, I angled it away and had a closer look. The fairy wasn't your typical holiday sprite. For one thing, her features had a distinctly modern look; for another, her shimmering gown was nearly diaphanous. Only the careful positioning of her long golden curls kept her modesty mostly intact.

"Anyone you know?" I asked.

"It was a gift from an old friend," Sam said unhappily.

"Blond?"

"How'd you guess?"

There wasn't a woman in the world who would have asked *that* question.

"She posed for a Christmas stocking?"

"She needlepointed it herself. Chris was quite handy."

"So I see. Also rather well endowed."

"Yes, well—" Sam started, then stopped. He saw my smile. "You're kidding, right?"

I nodded. "I can't believe you kept this. Got any other mementos lying around?"

"Maybe. I haven't really kept track." Sam hung the ornament he was holding and came around to my side. "Until I met you, there wasn't any reason to."

Oh.

"Hey!" said Davey. "Look what I found."

He'd come down off the ladder and was digging around in another box. When he raised both hands they were filled with strands of white beads. Linked together like pearls, they sparkled as he lifted them out, reflecting the lights from the tree.

"These can go on next," I said. "You're in charge."

"Cool," cried Davey. He ran back to the tree.

"About Aunt Peg," I said to Sam. "I'm afraid she doesn't know what she's getting herself into. People who have killed someone are desperate. They have secrets they don't want exposed."

"You never worried about that when you were the one doing the poking around."

"When it was me, I knew I'd be careful. You know Aunt Peg. She thinks she's invincible."

Sam laughed at that. "I've never seen anything stop Peg yet. For all I know, she may *be* invincible."

Superwoman to the rescue? As if *that* would solve our problems.

# 15

Sometimes it seems as though Aunt Peg calls me on the phone every other minute. Now that I was on the other end of the equation, however, wondering what sort of trouble she might be getting herself into, I found I had to resist the temptation to do the same. The least she could have done was check in every so often and let me know what she'd found out.

"Nothing," Peg said huffily when I finally broke down and called her Wednesday during lunch break. "Not a blessed thing."

Well that was a relief.

Apparently Aunt Peg didn't think so. "It's rather depressing when you think about it. I had such high hopes for myself. Then Monday my septic system backed up. And Tuesday I had three baths to give."

Heaven forbid Aunt Peg's Poodles ever look anything less than perfect.

"I did manage to put a call in to Cindy Marshall," she said. "Cindy got back to me yesterday."

"And?"

"I discovered that, over the phone, it's nearly impossible to ask someone you barely know whether or not they were having an affair with a dead man."

No surprise there. "You think that would be easier in person?"

"I'm about to find out," Aunt Peg said with some satisfaction. "Cindy and I are having lunch tomorrow."

"I thought you and I both agreed that Rebecca Morehouse was more likely to have been involved with Henry."

"Yes, but from what I've heard about Rebecca, I can't imagine I would like her at all. Why on earth would I want to eat lunch with her?"

Okay. What we had here was a totally different animal than I was used to. Murder investigation as social event.

"But since you've called," said Aunt Peg. "There's something you could do for me. Remember the office lady from Davey's school who was quoted in the article about Henry?"

"Michelle Raddison."

"She's a friend of yours, right?"

"I knew her when I used to work at Hunting Ridge."

"Perfect. Stop by and have a chat with her, would you? She seemed to know plenty about Henry. Perhaps she could put us in touch with some of his friends."

"Why would she want to do that?"

"Because you're going to ask her very nicely," said Peg.

Put that way, I supposed I was.

Which was how I came to find myself ducking out of school early that afternoon just after my last tutoring session ended. I raced from Greenwich back to Stamford and dropped off the Poodles. From our house, Davey's school was only a five minute drive. With luck, I'd reach Hunting Ridge Elementary before the last bell.

Two years had passed since I'd been employed as a special education teacher at the neighborhood public school. Still, the minute I drove up the sloping driveway, bypassed the front of the low brick building where a fleet of buses was already lined up at the curb, and parked in the teachers' lot on the side, I felt right at home. Hunting Ridge Elementary had given me my start as a teacher; I'd worked there for nearly a decade. Much as I enjoyed being at Howard Academy, it was hard not to feel a tug of nostalgia for the place, and the people, who had shaped my early career.

Hurrying along the wide front sidewalk on the way to the door, I gazed through windows into familiar classrooms, their walls adorned with colorful posters and artwork. It didn't look as though much had changed in the time I'd been gone. A round clock situated next to a doorway informed me I had only a few minutes to get to the office before the school day ended.

Still staring in the window, I picked up my pace and barreled right into someone heading the other way. "Oof!" I grunted at the impact, then stepped back quickly. "My fault. Sorry."

"Yeah, it was." The surly voice belonged to Davey's bus driver, Annie Gault. We stared at each other in surprise. "Hey, I know you," she said after a moment.

"Melanie Travis. We met last week. You drive my son's bus."

"That's right." She nodded toward the big yellow vehicle parked at the curb. "You here picking him up?"

"No," I reached up and rubbed my shoulder. The girl packed quite a wallop. "He'll ride with you to the arts center like he usually does on Wednesdays. I'm here to see someone."

Annie popped the wad of gum in her mouth. "Really, who?"

I couldn't imagine why she'd care. Nor why she wanted to prolong the conversation. Maybe since school had yet to let out, she had nothing better to do.

"Michelle Raddison," I said. "In the office. Now if you'll excuse me—"

"Is it about Henry Pruitt?"

I'd started to walk around her. Now I stopped. "What makes you think that?"

"I got told some of the mothers think I don't drive the bus as well as Henry did."

"There's a reason for that," I said bluntly. "You don't."

"Hey, I'm new around here. Cut me some slack, okay?"

"Being new should make you more careful, not less so. Those are our children you're transporting. Did you think we wouldn't be watching how you drive?"

Annie rolled her eyes. "That was my first day. I didn't know where I was going and I was trying not to mess up the schedule. I've slowed down some since then."

"Good," I said.

"So what's the big deal about Henry?"

"What big deal?" I asked curiously.

"You know, like all the mothers think he was some sort of saint or something. He was just a guy who drove a bus, that's all."

Considering the care with which he'd treated our children, Henry Pruitt had been a great deal more than that to every mother on the route. I thought about trying to explain, then decided Annie was probably too young to understand. Someday she'd have children of her own. Then she'd know why we'd treasured him.

"Did you know Henry?" I asked.

"We'd met, like a few times." Annie shrugged. "He was all right for an old guy. He liked to talk. He liked to ask questions."

She made that sound like it was a bad thing. "He was a friendly person," I said. "He liked to connect with other people."

"Yeah, well, look where it got him. Look, I gotta go."

She slipped past me, grabbed the pole that ran along the door to her bus, and swung nimbly up the stairs. As I started to turn after her, she sank into the driver's seat and snapped the door shut.

Inside the school, the bell rang. Perfect, I thought. Now I was late.

It turned out that it didn't matter. Michelle Raddison was not only still in the office, she was still seated at her desk with a mountain of paperwork piled on her blotter. Michelle had always been a bundle of frenetic energy, well suited to the demands of her busy job. We'd been friends as well as coworkers; seeing her again now, I was sorry I hadn't done a better job of keeping in touch.

"I'm glad I caught you," I said, pausing in the doorway to the glass-walled office.

"Caught me?" Michelle looked up and smiled. "You're joking, right? If you actually think I leave when the bell rings, that private school of yours must be staffed by dilettantes. Get yourself in here, Travis, and grab a seat. It's been entirely too long. What's new with you?"

I glanced over my shoulder at the bustling outer office. Like most schools, Hunting Ridge thrived on gossip. Quarters were tight in the administrative area; things could be easily overheard. As I shrugged out of my coat, I nudged the door-jamb free with my toe. The door swung shut as I sat down. The gesture wasn't lost on Michelle.

"And here I was hoping this was a social call," she said.

"It is. With a bit of personal business thrown in at the end. It's good to see you, too."

We took a few minutes to catch up with one another. Michelle brought me up-to-date on changes at Hunting Ridge: one teacher I'd taught with had gotten divorced, another had had a baby. I filled her in on some of the idiosyncrasies of my ritzy private school job; she came right back with stories of her own. We had a good laugh at each other's expense, then settled down to business.

"Is it Davey?" she asked. "You know I try to keep on top of all the kids, but with nearly two hundred enrolled here, sometimes things get past me. Is he having trouble in school?"

"No," I said quickly. "No, Davey's fine. He loves being in Miss Cooke's class. Third grade suits him to a tee."

"I'm glad to hear that." Michelle leaned forward, rested her elbows on the desk, and steepled her fingers. "So tell me what else I can do for you."

That was one of the things I'd liked best about working with Michelle. Her office was strictly a no bullshit zone.

"Tell me about Henry Pruitt," I said.

For a moment she didn't react at all. Then Michelle smiled slowly. "You surprised me with that one," she said. "And I don't surprise easily. What do you want to know?"

"The newspaper quoted you after he died, so I figured you must have known him. . . ."

"They could have quoted any one of us. Most of us knew Henry, some better than others. I'm the vice-principal. It fell to me to make a statement. Henry was a good guy. We were all sorry about what happened."

"Me too," I said. "He's driven our bus for years, and when Davey was with Henry I always knew Davey was in good hands."

She looked at me shrewdly. "Not quite the same with Annie, is it?"

"Not yet. But I have hopes for improvement. When you said some of you knew him better than others, what did you mean?"

"Exactly that. Henry was a sociable man. He got around. No harm in that. His wife had been dead for a long time, and we're all consenting adults around here."

"You mean he dated some of the women who work here?"

"Sure. Henry was a really sweet man. Because he drove the bus, he was around a lot. We all got to know him. The thing about Henry was that he was charming in an old-fashioned sort of way. I saw women who weren't even looking, look twice at him."

Food for thought there, I decided. "I read in the paper that before Henry started driving a bus, he'd worked for a commodities brokerage firm?"

"That's right. One of the big companies in Greenwich. He did well, too, from what I hear, but Henry got tired of being 'a suit.' That was the phrase he used. His wife had died, his children grew up and moved away. He couldn't see the point of holding on to such a big high-pressure job anymore. He opted for early retirement and then discovered that being home all day bored the hell out of him."

"So he ended up driving a bus?"

"Pretty much," said Michelle. "I know he wanted to do something that put him in touch with kids. I think he felt he'd missed out on a lot when his own children were growing up. Plus—and maybe you'll think this sounds dumb, but if you knew Henry, you'd understand—he had these two dogs. Golden Retrievers. Those guys just meant the world to him. And driving the bus, the hours worked out perfectly. He never had to leave the dogs alone at home for too long a stretch."

"That doesn't sound dumb to me at all," I said.

"Oh yeah, how could I forget? You have Poodles, right? The large size?"

"Standards. I had one when I worked here, now I have two. Faith and Eve are mother and daughter. One of the better perks of working at Howard Academy is that they get to come to school with me."

"Two big dogs like that?" Her eyes widened. "Wouldn't happen around here. Last year one of the kindergarten mothers complained about Hammie the Hamster. Said he was giving her daughter allergies. Bye bye, Hammie. I figure the parakeet in the music room will go next."

I winced at her tone. "That's the difference between public and private. We don't have to please everybody. Russell Hanover runs a pretty tight ship. Parents can either get with the program or go elsewhere."

"Lucky you."

"Lucky for me, I'm not in administration."

We both nodded at that.

"You still doing the dog show thing?" she asked.

"All the time. I'll be showing Eve this weekend up in Massachusetts."

"Speaking of which, I think I remember hearing that one of Henry's dogs came from some important dog show kennel."

"Pepper," I replied. "In a roundabout way, that's why I'm here. Because of Henry's dogs. After he died, I ended up with custody of them."

I told her about Alice and my visit to Henry's house. About meeting Betty Bowen and volunteering to care for the Goldens. Outside in the main office, people were packing up their desks and preparing to head home. Oblivious to their departures, Michelle listened, rapt, as I concluded with the story of meeting with Henry's two daughters over the weekend.

"Geez, you couldn't make this stuff up," she said when I was done. "You're like a magnet for trouble, aren't you?"

"I hope not," I said, though her assessment wasn't far from the mark. "The problem is, my aunt has decided that she wants to get involved in the investigation. She wants things wrapped up so that Robin and Laurel will go back where they came from and she can place Pepper and Remington in good homes."

"The police have been here twice already," said Michelle. "A Detective Marley and a couple of other guys, too. We told them everything we know. I mean, why wouldn't we? Everybody liked Henry. We'd like to see his killer brought to justice just as much as anyone."

"Who did the police talk to?" I asked.

Michelle tossed out several names—her own, the principal's, and the school secretary's among them.

"What about the women on the staff that he'd been involved with?"

Her look was stern. "It's not like that came up."

"How come?"

"Let's just say there are things you'd discuss with a friend that you wouldn't mention to a stranger. And certainly not to the police."

"They didn't ask?"

"No, not even once. Funny, isn't it? You'd think they would. But they knew he drove a bus. In fact, that was the way they kept referring to him—not Henry, not Mr. Pruitt, but as 'the bus driver.' It put us off pretty good, let me tell you. It was like they'd never looked much beyond that, and it didn't seem to occur to them that we might have."

I might have made that same mistake myself in the past, but I knew better now.

"If you could give me a couple of names, I'd appreciate it," I said. "I'm not looking to make trouble for anyone, I just want to find out a little bit more about Henry's life and who he hung out with."

"Sure," Michelle replied. "I don't think they'll mind. Besides, as far as I know, anything he had going around here is old news now. Unless someone's awfully good at keeping secrets—which, trust me, none of us are—he's been sowing his oats elsewhere for a while now. Talk to Jenna Phillips and Carrie Baker. You know them, right?"

I did. Jenna taught fifth grade; I'd worked with her frequently. Carrie had taken over Michelle's old job as office manager.

"Thanks," I said, standing up. "I appreciate the help."

"Anytime. Give Davey a hug for me, okay? I hear he and Joey Brickman are going to be Wise Men. Good going. I made my son do Cotillion. He's in high school now and he still hasn't forgiven me."

I walked out with a smile. It was nice to know I made the right choices at least once in a while.

# 16

The rest of the week sped by, helped along by the fact that my Eve, Aunt Peg's Zeke, and Sam's Tar were all entered in a dog show in Worcester, Massachusetts, that Saturday. Preparations for all three Standard Poodles began midweek and would continue right up until the moment we entered the ring to be judged. Of necessity, any time that wasn't devoted to my job or to Davey was spent grooming.

I began the process by clipping Eve. Black Poodles have white skin; conversely, most white Poodles have black skin. In clipping for the show ring, a surgical blade is used, and the unwanted hair is removed entirely. Black Poodles are always clipped early to allow time for a sheen of dark hair to grow back so that the dog appears to be one continuous color. White Poodles are clipped late so that the flashy contrast between light hair and dark skin is highlighted.

Eve's feet were done on Wednesday. Thursday evening, I clipped her hindquarter and face. The former was an exacting job, as this was the first time Eve would be shown in the continental trim, and although I'd set the lines in July when she turned a year old, Eve had been away from the show ring since. This was the first time my efforts were going to be judged.

And if my results weren't perfect, I would hear about it from Aunt Peg. Endlessly.

Friday night was bath night. First Eve's coat needed to be thoroughly soaped and rinsed in the tub. Then each section of her hair had to be painstakingly blown dry. From start to finish, the process took three to four hours.

Davey, no surprise, opted to spend Friday night at his father's. I knew they had an outing planned for Saturday. And considering that their recent phone conversations had come to a precipitous halt whenever I entered the room, I suspected their plans had something to do with Christmas shopping.

To tell the truth, it wouldn't have been a bad thing if mine had as well. Christmas was fast approaching. Aside from the fact that I had yet to hang a wreath on the front door or put up a tree in the living room, I also still had more presents to shop for. That's the thing about showing dogs; if you let it, it can take over your life.

Saturday morning, the Poodles and I were up and out before the sun rose. Worcester was a two-hour drive, and the downtown building where the show was being held was notoriously short on both parking and grooming space. Early arrivals got spots; later ones had to make due with whatever dark corner they could find.

In the parking lot I piled crate, grooming table, and tack box on a dolly. Pulling that with one hand, I held Faith and Eve's leashes in the other. The two Poodles surged on ahead, tails high with excitement. Neither had been to a show since summer, and it looked as though they'd missed the experience just as much as I had.

"Melanie! Over here."

Arms waving above the throngs of exhibitors that had already gathered in the grooming area beckoned me over to Crawford Langley's setup. Crawford was one of the most-respected professional handlers in the Northeast. Due to the size of his string and the number of dogs that had to be prepped to go in the ring, he and his partner, Terry Denunzio, had probably been at the show since before I'd even gotten out of bed.

"Come set up with us," Terry said, blowing me an air kiss. "We saved you some room."

Terry was one of my best friends. He was also annoyingly good looking and flamboyantly gay. He had sharply styled hair, a wicked sense of humor, and always knew the best gossip. Terry was utterly irresistible, and well aware of his own appeal. Spending the next two hours grooming beside him would be a pleasure.

"Crawford's in the ring with a Yorkie," he said as he helped me unload. "Peg is outside taking Zeke for a run around the block. I hear Sam is due any minute. There, that's everything I know. What's new with you?"

I stopped and thought for a moment. That was probably about as much time as Terry would give me before launching into another topic of his own. "Bertie hasn't had her baby yet."

"We *know* that," Terry sniffed. "Good Lord, the whole world knows that. I suspect when the big event finally does come to pass we'll see beacons shooting an announcement into the sky. You know, like the Bat Signal?"

I shoved Faith's crate into line with the others and piled my tack box on top. Terry unfolded my portable grooming table and helped Eve up into place.

"Bat Signal?"

"Tell me you didn't read comic books as a child."

"Archie and Veronica," I said. "With a little Superman on the side."

"Your education was sorely lacking."

"You should talk." Crawford appeared, Yorkshire Terrier tucked handily under one arm. He was holding a purple and gold rosette indicating that the little dog had taken Best of Breed. "He thinks reality TV is the height of good drama."

"You mean it's not?" Terry clutched at his heart. There's nothing he loved more than a good dramatic moment.

Crawford grunted in reply and returned the tiny Toy dog to its crate. The older handler was, as always, a model of composure. His silver hair glinted in the lights from above; his tie was crisply knotted at his throat. In an era where informality was the norm, Crawford was a throwback to an earlier age. His posture was impeccable, as was his reputation in the dog show world. It had taken us a long time to get comfortable with one another. But once we had, our friendship had grown quickly.

"I hear Peg's planning to solve a murder." Crawford straightened and turned to look at me. His gray eyes twinkled.

"Did she tell you that?"

"As soon as she got here," Terry said happily. "Babe, you've been holding out on us. Luckily, Peg filled us in on the whole sordid story. Everything from Golden Retrievers to Christmas pageants to school bus drivers gone bad. Frankly, it put reality TV to shame."

*Golden Retrievers and school bus drivers gone bad?* Terry's description sounded like a come-on for a sleazy internet porn site.

"Aunt Peg may have put a little spin on things for your benefit," I mentioned.

"Who cares? If the story's good, I'm in." Like that was news. Terry and a strict interpretation of the facts did not always have the closest of relationships.

"And didn't anything bother you about this?"

"No. Should it?"

"Doesn't Aunt Peg strike you as a little old to be playing Nancy Drew?"

As soon as the words had left my mouth, I knew they were a mistake. Crawford, Aunt Peg's contemporary as well as her friend, turned around and nailed me with a hard stare. "And just what would you consider to be a good age for getting mixed up in things that are better off left to the police?"

He had me there. I knew it and so did Terry. Tamping down a grin, Crawford's assistant patted my arm and backed away. "You're on your own with that one, doll." Then he gazed past me and his expression brightened. "Look, Sam's here. I think I'll go help him unload."

Sam, carrying tack box and table and leading Tar, stopped, looked around, and took in the situation in a glance. "I know you just got here," he said to me. "Don't tell me you're in trouble already."

"It was an accident," I said. "A slip of the tongue."

"She called Crawford old," Terry said, just to fan the flames.

"I did not!"

"Didn't what?" Peg asked, returning from walking Zeke.

Now the gang was all here. And I was, in all likelihood, dead.

"Call Crawford old," I mumbled.

"I should hope not," Peg said roundly.

"Quite right," said Terry. "It wasn't actually Crawford she was referring to. It was—"

"Terry!" Fortunately for me, Crawford's peremptory tone stopped that runaway train in its tracks.

"Yes, sir?" A man with lesser acting skills couldn't have pulled that off. Terry made it sound almost respectful.

"Shouldn't you be putting in topknots?"

"Probably."

Among their other entrants, their string of dogs for the day included six Poodles, two in each of the three varieties. Judging by what I could see of the Poodles who were sitting out in the setup on tables and crate tops, there was still plenty of work to be done.

"That's what I thought," said Crawford. He glanced at a schedule taped to the top of his tack box, opened a crate, pulled out a Chinese Crested, and headed back toward the rings on the other side of the room.

Aunt Peg hopped Zeke up onto his matted grooming table, which was right next to mine. The two Standard Poodles, littermates from the first—and so far only—litter I'd bred, reached across the expanse between tables and touched noses. While I kept an eye on the pair to make sure they didn't mess each other's hair, Aunt Peg leaned down and said hello to Faith, who'd been tucked inside my crate.

Sam, who was busy getting his stuff arranged, got Peg's second greeting. Like me, he was used to that.

Amenities aside, Aunt Peg turned back to me. "What was that all about?"

"You probably don't want to know."

"On the contrary, I'm quite sure I do."

"I was um . . . questioning the wisdom of your looking into Henry's murder."

She snorted under her breath. "I suppose you think you ought to be the only detective in the family."

"If my vote counts for anything," said Sam, "I don't think there ought to be *any* detectives in the family."

Peg turned slowly. "Luckily," she said, "no one asked you."

That should have put Sam in his place. Instead it made him smile. With an attitude like that, it was no wonder he'd recently managed to handle Tar into the top spot among non-sporting dogs in New England. The man had absolutely no fear.

"Michelle Raddison," Peg said, as the three of us pulled out brushes, combs, and spray bottles and went to work. "What did she have to say for herself?"

"Plenty." I related the gist of our conversation, speaking loudly to ensure that Terry, who was eavesdropping shamelessly, wouldn't miss a thing.

"I gather Henry must have cut quite a swath among the ladies," I said at the end. "Apparently, almost everybody at Hunting Ridge knew him and liked him, which is unusual when you stop to consider that he didn't actually work for the school, he just passed through there a couple of times a day."

"Yes, but Henry wasn't your typical bus driver," said Peg. "Everything we've learned about him so far certainly supports that."

"Poison," said Terry, "is a woman's murder weapon. Passive, nonviolent, nonconfrontational. Everybody knows that."

Hands still flying through Zeke's coat, Aunt Peg looked over at Terry. "Where did you hear that?"

"He's been watching forensic shows on TV," I said.

"Scoff if you like, but they get their facts straight. I think you ought to check out those women who were involved with your bus driver. Odds are, he's got a disgruntled ex-girlfriend or two running around."

"He's also got two disgruntled daughters," Sam contributed, just to show he was paying attention. "Not to mention a woman he's involved with currently, and a nosy neighbor with a surly son."

"That's right," I said. "Johnny Bowen said that Henry's retirement had cut into the profits of his lawn mowing service." I snuck a peek at Peg. "Maybe you should look into that."

"And maybe you shouldn't be so fresh," she retorted. "Let's not forget, you were the one who saddled me with Remington and Pepper in the first place. If it wasn't for you, I wouldn't care a whit whether this business got resolved or not. I'd simply be sitting home in Greenwich, reading about it in the newspaper like everyone else."

"Want to bet?" asked Sam.

Aunt Peg frowned. Terry snickered. As for me, I got busy grooming. We'd all arrived at roughly the same time and we all had big black Poodles to prepare for the ring. From ample experience, I knew who was going to get the job done slowest.

Moi.

By the time I had Eve thoroughly brushed out, Sam was unwrapping Tar's ears and Aunt Peg was already putting in Zeke's topknot. The entry in Standard Poodles was large enough to provide a major in dogs. Peg and I both wanted it. If we were really, really lucky, there was a possibility that both of us could have it. Bearing that in mind, we weren't about to skimp on our preparations.

The first thing Aunt Peg had taught me about showing

dogs was that the judges you exhibited under had to be chosen wisely. The American Kennel Club recognizes thousands of judges. Their names are printed in a fat little book which is updated every year. Of the several hundred of those that are approved to judge Poodles, not all are necessarily competent to render an opinion on the breed.

Aunt Peg, like most experienced exhibitors, kept a fat little book of her own. It was filled with notes on judges she'd shown to: her opinion on how much their opinion was worth.

Peg was broadminded enough to give almost anyone at least one chance. Poodle breeders or ex-handlers, plus those judges who exhibited a special interest in the breed, were preferred. Judges with rough hands or an inattentive attitude toward their job were dismissed from future consideration. Those who were merely ignorant about the breed were tried again after a decent interval had passed, in the hope that they might have learned something.

Today's judge, Val Homberg, fell into the first category. A former handler who'd bred Toys on the side, she'd made no secret of her admiration for the Poodle breed. She knew what she wanted in a dog and she fully expected her exhibitors to bring it to her. Val judged quickly; she had no time for specimens that were dirty, poorly groomed, or untrained. But give her what she was looking for and she didn't play politics. An owner-handler was just as likely to win under her as a pro. Knowing that, we'd all turned out to support her, which accounted for the major entry in dogs.

Because of the variations in trims, Poodles are one of those rare breeds where puppies often beat the adults to take the points. For that reason, both Zeke and Eve had been shown quite a lot as puppies. Zeke, who'd had the benefit of having Aunt Peg at the end of his leash, had already managed to amass almost all the points he needed to complete his championship. One more win would "finish" him.

A championship title is attained by winning a total of fifteen points in breed competition. The classes are split by sex—both one dog and one bitch will take home points in each breed at each show. The number of points awarded varies between one and five and is based on the amount of competition. Along the way, each dog must also secure two major wins, meaning that at least twice he must defeat enough other dogs to be awarded three or more points. Fifteen single points do not add up to a championship.

Eve had been to as many shows as Zeke had during her puppy career, but the competition she'd faced had been stiffer. So far she had seven points to her credit, all of them singles. Today's three-point major, if she could get it, would round out her current resume nicely.

Our third entry was Sam's specials dog, Tar, a.k.a. Champion Cedar Crest Scimitar. Specials are exactly what the name implies—the best of the best. These are dogs that have finished their championships in style and are now being campaigned in the hopes of amassing the coveted Best of Breed, Group First, and Best in Show wins. Tar had been showing as a special since spring. In that time, his record had grown to include eight non-sporting group wins and his first all-breed Best in Show. In short, he'd become a factor to be reckoned with.

Crawford Langley, who was known for the quality of the Poodles he exhibited, had lately contented himself with specialing only a Mini and a Toy at most venues. His Standard special went only to carefully selected shows where he knew Tar wouldn't be present. No professional handler shows to be beaten. The fact that Crawford left his Standard special at home was a sign of his respect for Tar's quality.

By the time Crawford reappeared with the Chinese Crested, Terry had both their Toy Poodles ready to go. The two of them headed up to the ring. Sam went with them to pick up our armbands. Topknot finally in, I finished spraying up Eve's neck hair. Aunt Peg was scissoring Zeke's trim.

Eve's littermate looked wonderful standing on his table. He was tall, well muscled, and beautifully masculine. His eyes were dark and expressive; his coat, an inky black.

"He could finish today," I commented.

"Shhh!" Peg glared in my direction. She's a great believer in jinxes.

"He would be my first homebred champion."

"Not if you keep talking about it," she grumbled. "Don't you have some scissoring to do?"

The question was rhetorical. If we were twenty minutes away from going into the show ring, there was always scissoring to do. I picked up a pair of curved shears and went to work.

Sam returned and we got ourselves organized. Crawford lost with his Toys, then won with his Minis. Seemingly only seconds passed before it was our turn. Time to go do what the Poodles did best.

It was show time.

# 17

Dogs always show before bitches. For some reason, which I have yet to figure out, they also always wear odd-numbered armbands, while bitches are assigned even numbers. Aunt Peg, with Zeke, would be the first of us to go in the ring. She stood near the gate as the Standard Poodle judging started with the Puppy Dog class.

Summoned by the steward, four rambunctious puppies filed into the ring. Two were black, two were white; none, thankfully, looked mature enough to give Zeke a run for his money. Nevertheless, I was delighted to see them. Their numbers, added to those in the other classes, supplied the total that had come up a major.

Aunt Peg had Zeke entered in the Open class. Usually she shows in Bred by Exhibitor; however, since I was Zeke's breeder Peg was ineligible for her favorite class. Instead she would face four other opponents all presented by professional handlers in Open.

As Peg entered the ring, Sam and Tar came to stand beside me.

"He looks good," Sam said in a low voice. At ringside, everybody listens in. Those who don't want the whole world to know what they're thinking whisper compliments and insults alike.

"I just told Aunt Peg that. She thought I was jinxing her."

"You probably were. That's how superstitions work. If you believe, you're done for."

We both watched as Val made her first pass down the line of four. First impressions count for a lot in dog shows. The judge has only a very limited amount of time, usually less than two minutes, to devote to assessing each dog.

Savvy handlers try to grab the judge's attention right away. The really talented ones never relinquish it.

"Good," Sam said as Val paused for a second look at Zeke. "She knows he's there."

The judge lifted her hands and sent the entry around the matted ring. Called in catalog order, Zeke was leading the parade. Trotting smoothly, Aunt Peg raised her hand, let out her leash, and hung back ever so slightly. Zeke, striding out in front of her, looked as though he was showing himself and towing her along behind as an afterthought.

A subtle point, well made. Aunt Peg's actions indicated her feelings to the judge: *this dog has so much presence and ability, he can do it all by himself.* Val, a former handler herself, was well able to appreciate the effort. Nor would the effect be lost on her.

"That's it," Sam whispered when the Poodles had completed a circuit of the ring. "He's got it."

I reached over and punched him in the arm. "Not so fast. At least give the judge a chance to put her hands on him before you go ahead and make up her mind for her."

Sam shut up then, but it didn't matter. He was right, just as I'd hoped he would be. When the judge had completed her individual examinations of all four entries, she left Zeke standing at the head of the line and shuffled only those behind him. A minute later, Val Homberg handed Aunt Peg the narrow strip of blue ribbon.

"Almost there," I said under my breath.

Eve, all but forgotten, waited patiently at my side. One of my hands supported her head; the other lifted her tail. I scratched under her chin absently and watched as the handler of the Puppy class winner brought his Standard Poodle back into the ring. This competition was called Winners Dog, and would decide which of the previous class winners got the points. And the major. Three important and oh-so-coveted points.

For Aunt Peg, Zeke would simply be another in a long line of beautiful Poodles that she had escorted to their titles. For me, however, his championship would be a first. Though I had finished Faith, I hadn't had the distinction of being her breeder. Zeke was a homebred, and that made all the difference.

I'd been there when he was born. I'd broken the sac and dried him off, then helped him find the nipple and take his first drink. I'd seen his eyes open, and watched him take his first wobbly steps. I was the one who'd planned his breeding and brought him into the world. It was an awesome responsibility, one I knew I would never take lightly.

Win or lose, Zeke was my baby. He would always make me proud. But now, watching as the judge once again placed him at the front of the line, my heart began to pound.

"He *is* going to do it," I whispered incredulously.

"Told you," said Sam.

As Val sent the two dogs around the ring for the last time, Sam was already beginning to clap. Though the judge hadn't pointed yet, it was probably just a formality. Nevertheless, I waited, breath caught in my throat, until Val raised her hand and made it official. When she did, I think I might have screamed; thankfully, the moment remains somewhat hazy in recollection.

I wasn't just a fledgling breeder anymore, I realized. Now I was the breeder of a champion. My first, and hopefully, the start of many more to come.

Catching my excitement, Eve bounced up into the air beside me. Only Sam's quick reflexes kept her from landing on Tar and laying waste to the hours of grooming we'd both done.

Aunt Peg was all smiles as she ushered Zeke over to the marker. She had a few words with the judge and accepted the purple Winners ribbon graciously. Zeke stood like a statue, basking in the smattering of applause from ringside.

"One down," Peg said happily as she exited the ring and came to join us. "Now it's your turn."

"My turn?" In all the excitement, I'd almost forgotten that Eve and I were due to show ourselves in just a matter of minutes. "You must be kidding. She won't put both of us up."

"Why not?"

"Two owner-handlers in a row? I don't think so."

"Make that three," said Sam. "Because Tar and I are planning on winning Best of Variety. Besides, she's already indicated that she likes the family."

Val Homberg had done that, I considered. Faced with a major entry that had some quality to it, the judge had wasted little time in finding Zeke and awarding him the points. Good judges are consistent. They know what they like in a dog, and they look for it time after time. So if Zeke was Val's kind of Standard Poodle, it made sense that his littermate, Eve, would be too.

Inside the ring, the judge was making short work of the puppy bitches. The entry was smaller in bitches than it had been in dogs. With a total of six bitches entered, only two points were at stake.

However, after Winners Bitch had been awarded, Best of Variety would be called into the ring. The three champions in that class would be joined by the Winners Dog and Winners Bitch. Since both were still undefeated in the day's competition, they were also contenders for the higher award. Not only that but the judge would choose between them for Best of Winners. Whichever Poodle received that designation would take home the higher number of points awarded in the classes that day. So if the Winners Bitch beat Zeke for BOW, she too would be credited with a three-point major.

Every handler showing at Worcester understood the way the point system worked. Every single one had come to the show with a covetous eye on that major. They all wanted it just as badly as I did.

I should have been watching the Puppy Bitch class and scoping out the competition. Instead I was busy making hasty repairs to Eve's topknot, combing through her tail, and patting my pockets to make sure they held both a squeaky toy and several pieces of dried liver.

Sam watched my harried and mostly unnecessary preparations with amusement. Cool as ice himself, he'd resigned himself to the fact that last-minute nerves always sent my stomach fluttering. "She looks great," he said.

I nodded in reply as the two puppies filed from the ring. Now it was my turn.

Eve was the only Bred-by Bitch entered. Some judges rushed summarily though a single entry, since awarding the blue was usually a foregone conclusion. That could work against a nice dog, as it put them in the weaker position of having to go into the Winners class without having beaten any previous competition.

Fortunately, Val took her time and paid attention. Eve showed like the pro she was fast becoming. Her stack was solid. Her movement was straight and correct. When I stopped in front of the judge at the end of the gaiting pattern, Eve looked past the liver I was holding, caught Val's eye and wagged her tail.

The judge was smiling as she motioned us to the marker. Always a good sign.

Then we were back outside the ring again, waiting in the gate as the bitches in the Open class were judged. Aunt Peg studied the entry with a critical eye. An experienced Poodle judge herself, she could determine a Poodle's quality, or lack thereof, at a glance.

"I've seen better Open classes," she muttered under her breath. "The brown's the best of that lot, but that isn't saying much."

The brown bitch was in the ring with Crawford. She wasn't the soundest Poodle I'd ever seen. Nor, with her unbecoming light eyes, the prettiest. But Crawford presented her to the judge with all the flourish of an escort at a debutante ball. It was a handler's job to highlight his entry's good points and downplay her faults, and Crawford was a master at it.

Nobody was surprised when he won the class, least of all Crawford. He accepted the blue ribbon, slipped it into his pocket, and then hurried the brown Poodle back to the head of the Winners lineup. I was behind him with Eve, and the cream bitch who'd won the Puppy class followed me.

Val walked to the other side of the ring and stood, feet braced wide apart, hands clasped behind her back. She studied her choices for a long minute, her patient stance serving notice to those who were watching from ringside: this wasn't going to be a quick decision, they'd better be prepared to wait.

Speaking objectively—assuming that was possible under the circumstances—I had to say that Eve was the best of the three Standard Poodles in the ring. Unfortunately, there were other factors the judge would take into consideration. For one thing, she had just put an owner-handler up over the pros for Winners Dog. Did she dare do so again? For another, it was readily apparent that Crawford could handle circles around me. What *was*, and what he might be able to convince the judge to think, could be two entirely different things.

And then there was the puppy, a pretty cream with a cute face, a nice way of going, and another professional handler at the end of her leash. Remember what I told you earlier? In Poodles, you never discount the puppy.

All of which meant this wasn't going to be easy. Possible, certainly. Doable, maybe. But easy? No way.

Val lifted her hands and motioned for Crawford to lead the line around the ring. Since all of the entrants in a Winners class have just been seen by the judge in earlier classes, picking the winner can often be a cursory effort. Not this time. Val Homberg judged the three Poodles in front of her like she'd never seen them before; examining each and re-gaiting it, comparing it to the others and considering.

When she sent us around a final time, she hadn't changed our order. Crawford was still at the head of the line. My shoulders slumped ever so slightly. I assumed she'd made her choice and the brown bitch was it. Then I glanced over and realized that Val hadn't taken her eyes off of Eve.

And when she raised her hand and indicated the Poodle she wanted, her finger was pointing straight at us.

"Yes!" I said under my breath.

There was no time to stop and celebrate the win. Nor to recomb Eve. Instead, as the three specials came striding into the ring, I slipped her a piece of liver as a reward. Then we dropped back to take our place at the end of the line. Aunt Peg with Zeke, the Winners Dog, was just in front of us.

"Pay attention now!" she said just loud enough for me to hear. "You've got two points, but you can have three."

Instead of stacking Zeke and holding him at attention as the other handlers were doing, Aunt Peg stepped away and let the Poodle stand naturally. The pose was more casual than those he'd be compared to, and slightly less eye-catching. Zeke already had the major and he wasn't going to beat Tar for Best of Variety. So if Aunt Peg took the edge off his performance, making him look less like a star than he had in his own classes, nothing would be lost and much might be gained, especially if the judge could be convinced to put his sister up over him for Best of Winners.

Val Homberg had been around. She knew how the game was played, and she could count points every bit as well as we could. She took her time judging the three specials one by one, but when the time came to compare the two littermates, she simply walked to the back of the line and motioned Eve forward. She didn't have to call us twice.

Tar, who looked magnificent, every inch a champion and a worthy representative of the Poodle breed, was standing at the head of the line. I slipped Eve into the spot behind him. A champion bitch held the third position.

Val Homberg sent us all around the ring one last time and pinned it just that way. Tar won Best of Variety, Eve was Best of Winners, the champion bitch was Best of Opposite Sex.

Showing dogs is often an exercise in frustration. Most exhibitors lose more often than they win, and I was no exception. But a day like that was one to savor. Two major wins, a new champion, and BOV for Tar. In the dog show world, it simply didn't get much better than that.

# 18

"Well," said Aunt Peg, hopping Zeke up onto his table back at the setup. "We had ourselves quite a day."

We had indeed. Even though twenty minutes had passed since the Poodle classes had ended—we'd waited and had win pictures taken with the judge before making our way back to the grooming area to begin the process of taking the dogs' elaborate hairdos apart—I was still feeling quite giddy with the excitement of it all.

"I can't believe it," I said.

"I can," Terry announced from the other end of the aisle. The man had ears like a bat. "It was like watching the Cedar Crest show out there. None of the rest of us stood a chance."

Aunt Peg wasn't having any of it. "So you lost in Standards, big deal. You got yours in Toys and Minis. Suck it up and act like a man."

"Oh please," said Terry. "Are you ever barking up the wrong tree."

He gazed unhappily at the grooming tables in his setup, all holding Poodles that Crawford had shown earlier. Each now needed to be undone and rewrapped. The handler, as usual, had picked up another dog and headed back to the rings.

A nicer person might have worked up a modicum of sympathy for Terry, but for me it just wasn't happening. I knew how he felt; I'd been beaten by Crawford plenty of times in the past. Many more times, in fact, than I'd ever beaten him. But instead of feeling sorry for Terry, I was hosting my own private celebration.

Eve, who should have been returned to her table as Zeke and Tar had been, was still on the floor. Taking advantage of the unaccustomed freedom, she'd chosen to dance rings around my legs. In less than a minute, we'd both become hopelessly entangled in the leather show lead. On a normal day, that would have been cause for great concern. The slender leash, twisting through a thick mane coat that had been hairsprayed into place, was bound to cause mats and tangles.

Somehow I just couldn't bring myself to care. I was standing there grinning like a happy fool when Sam came to the rescue.

"Here, let me." He took the looped end of the leash from my hand and began the convoluted process of trying to separate dog from handler, a task made all the more arduous by the fact that neither Eve nor I was unduly upset by our dilemma.

"I have a homebred champion," I said to no one in particular.

"We know," Aunt Peg replied. She watched with some amusement as Sam wound his hands first one way around my legs, then the other, trying to unravel the leather strip. Eve had stopped twirling now; there wasn't enough play left for either of us to move. "Sad to say, you seem to have gone daft on account of it. I'd have to think back—it was many, many years ago—but I don't think my first champion had that effect on me."

"Nor me," said Sam, still working diligently.

"I also have a Poodle with a new major," I mentioned.

"Hard to miss that." Sam blew out a frustrated breath. "Since you seem to have attached her to your hip."

"Oh for Pete's sake," said Peg, watching Eve's coat being twisted into tight knots.

She reached into her tack box and pulled out a pair of

sharp scissors. Holding Eve's ear hair carefully to one side, Aunt Peg slipped one edge of the scissors under the collar and snipped. A quick tug and the constricting band snaked loose. Pressure released, the Poodle immediately stepped away and shook her head.

Before Eve could think of what to do next, Aunt Peg had slipped a confining palm around her muzzle. She spun the Poodle in place. An experienced show-goer, Eve knew what was expected. With a movement that was half hoist, half jump, she bounded up onto her table.

"I trust"—Peg aimed a fulminating look my way—"that you can deal with the rest of the problem."

"You cut my show leash," I said in disbelief, holding up the snipped fragments as evidence. Now that there was nothing attached to the other end, the coil slid down my legs and pooled innocuously at my feet.

"I did indeed. Somebody had to do something, considering that you were content to stand there looking like an idiot. Be glad I didn't slap you. I considered that option as well."

Well, yes, I supposed that was something to be thankful for. Small favors and all that.

Sam, damn him, was looking as though he was trying not to laugh.

"Buck up, Melanie," Peg said sternly. "Show leads are a dime a dozen. You can get another at the concession stand. You were entirely too happy for your own good."

Too happy for my own good? That was a new one. I glared at my ruined leash. "You've fixed *that* now, haven't you? I'll have you know that was my lucky show lead."

All right, in the same way that I don't believe in jinxes, maybe I don't set much store by lucky talismans either. But my aunt, the queen of high-handed tactics, needed to be taken down a notch. And considering that Eve had just been wearing that leash on the occasion of winning her first major, I figured I had a pretty good shot of making my case. Judging by Aunt Peg's suddenly stricken look, I was probably right.

"Oh dear," she said.

Sam was laughing in earnest now.

Magically, Terry appeared at Aunt Peg's side. He was drawn to trouble like a moth to a flame. I wondered why he was holding a stainless steel dog bowl in his hands. I didn't have long to speculate.

"I could throw a bowl of water over her if you like," he offered.

"You're not helping," I said.

"What on earth makes you think I'm trying to be helpful?"

There was that.

"Okay," said Sam, stepping in between us. "Back to your corners, everyone. We all have work to do."

"And some of us," I said pointedly, "need to go shopping."

"Don't be such a crybaby," said Terry. "We must have twenty leashes in our tack box." He walked back to his own setup, dug around in a drawer, and came up with a small plastic pouch holding a new black lead. "Catch," he said, tossing it in my direction.

I snatched it out of the air and examined the bag. The leash looked exactly like the one I'd just lost.

"Not so fast," said Aunt Peg. Now she was the one holding the tattered remnants of the sliced leash. "Maybe this one could be fixed. What if that one isn't a lucky leash?"

"Too bad." I tossed it into my tack box. "Thanks, Terry."

"No prob."

*"Yes,* there's a problem." Aunt Peg was grinding her teeth now. She hated it when no one paid attention to her. Especially since it happened so seldom.

And may I be the first to mention that in this particular instance it served her right?

"Don't worry," Terry said blithely. "All our leads have major mojo. That's why Crawford wins so much."

Sam was past laughing now; he sounded as though he

might be choking. Thank goodness Crawford hadn't been there to hear *that* assertion. I doubted any of us would have survived the fallout. And although I was quite certain Terry hadn't meant for us to take him seriously, Aunt Peg seemed to be considering it. She retrieved the leash from my tack box and gave it a look.

"Major mojo," she said. "That might make a good name for a Standard Poodle. I'll have to give it some thought."

There was still an hour to wait before the start of the non-sporting group. In the interim, Eve and Zeke were brushed out, rewrapped and—after all four Poodles had gone outside for a long walk—put back in their crates. Tar, who would be showing again in the group, rested atop his table where his hair wouldn't get mussed.

The Poodles had been to enough shows to know the routine. Once crated, Faith and the littermates immediately flopped over on their sides and went to sleep. Tar, knowing he couldn't relax just yet, kept a watchful and curious eye on the activity in the surrounding area. The big black Poodle was the first to spot the slender, middle-aged woman making her way purposefully through the crowds and heading in our direction.

Sam had gone to get lunch while Aunt Peg and I held down the fort. As I scanned the crowds waiting for his return, my gaze, too, fastened on the woman that had caught Tar's eye.

The dog show world is actually a rather small community. Exhibit enough and after a while everyone begins to look at least somewhat familiar. I couldn't remember seeing this woman before, though.

Dressed in a workmanlike suit—skirt loose enough to run in, jacket with plenty of pockets for holding brushes and bait, and all in a dark, murky plaid that wouldn't show the dirt—she bore the same look as any number of exhibitors on the grounds. As she drew near, a gold pin fastened to her lapel and winking in the overhead lights, announced her breed affiliation: Goldens. I was about to point her out to Aunt Peg, who was rooting around in her bag for a granola bar, when the woman announced herself.

"Finally!" she said, skirting expertly around the last row of crates and wending her way through the tables to our setup. "I knew if I kept looking, I'd find you sooner or later."

Aunt Peg straightened and immediately smiled. "Cindy! I'm so glad you made it. Let me introduce my niece, Melanie."

Cindy turned out to be Cindy Marshall, Pepper's breeder from New Jersey. The mention of her name reminded me that the two women had been planning to have lunch together at the end of the week. I'd forgotten to ask how that had gone.

"I had to cancel," Cindy said when I asked. "Something came up at the last minute. Isn't that always the way? But then Peg said she was going to be showing here, and I was entered, too. I'd told her if I got a free moment, I'd stop by and say hello."

To nobody's surprise, the talk turned immediately to dogs. Peg and Pepper's breeder didn't know one another well, but once they started discussing the day's activities, they became as chummy as a pair of old friends. Cindy leaned down, peeking inside the crates to say hello to Faith, Eve, and Zeke, then greeted Tar with the utmost care.

"I won't even touch," she said with a little laugh. "I've been around dogs my whole life but it's hard not to be intimidated by all that hair. I don't know how you Poodle people do it."

"It's not so bad once you get the hang of it," Peg replied. "I can't imagine coping with shedding."

She walked over to Tar and placed a hand on his flank where the hair had been shaved to the skin. "Right now, when he's all sprayed up and waiting to go back in, you want to confine your patting to the clipped areas. Later, when he's done, you just treat him like any other normal dog. That's all they are, really. The hair is just a giant sleight of hand.

"It's one thing for you to be reticent about it; you're trying to be polite. But there's nothing more annoying than a judge who doesn't want to put his hands down inside the coat. How on earth do they expect to feel what the exhibitor is trying to hide? If a judge can't deal with hair, they should only be doing breeds they can eyeball."

"Like Dobermans," Cindy said in agreement. "Or Whippets."

"Or Siamese cats," Terry piped up. Shiba Inu tucked under his arm, he walked down to our end of the aisle and placed the dog on an empty table next to our setup where he could join in the conversation.

He leaned in and kissed Cindy on the cheek. Terry, a newer face in the dog show world than I was, nevertheless managed to know just about everybody.

"Where's Brad today?" he inquired after Cindy's husband.

"Playing golf," Cindy sighed. "In December. Probably freezing his buns off and loving every minute of it. The man's an addict."

The three of us glanced at each other guiltily. And we weren't?

"Besides," Cindy continued, "he's never really enjoyed the whole dog show scene. Years ago, when we were newlyweds, he used to come just to humor me. But devotion like that wears off. It's really just a matter of time."

Cindy turned to Peg. "I've found that dogs are really more a woman's thing, haven't you? So few men seem to get the same enjoyment. If I ever found one that did, I think I'd be tempted to hang on to him with both hands."

Interesting. I wondered if Brad the golfer might have something to say about that.

"I didn't expect to see you here today," said Terry. "You're quite a long way from home."

"Three states, to be exact. And shows in Allentown this weekend, too. But of course you know the good judges would be all the way up here."

That was the story of an exhibitor's life. We lived and died by the judging assignments.

"How did you do?" asked Aunt Peg.

"Points on a puppy," Cindy said with satisfaction. "You can't ask for better than that. It will make the long drive home feel worthwhile. How about you? I see this one is headed for the group. Were your others as successful?"

The catalog was brought out; the major entry and our wins exclaimed over. Cindy congratulated us on our good fortune. Then she apologized once again for missing lunch with Peg and said, "I really did want to talk to you about Henry Pruitt. I'd been thinking about what you said about his two dogs. The first time we spoke, I told you I'd be happy to come and get Pepper. Then I believe you said there was some sort of problem with Henry's daughters?"

"They've inherited the dogs as part of their father's estate," I said. "And they seem to feel that as purebred Golden Retrievers, Pepper and Remington should be worth money. Rather than simply finding them good homes, the daughters are determined to try and sell them."

"To the highest bidder," Peg added with a wink.

"I see. Well, in that case, my offer won't do you much good. But I thought since I was taking one boy, I might as well have them both. Remington didn't come from me, but I feel as though I know him from Henry's pictures. At my house there's always room for another Golden. And if I'm lucky, I might be able to come up with a home where the two of them can stay together."

"That would be wonderful," I said.

"And much appreciated," Peg added. "We're hoping to get Henry's daughters dealt with and out of our lives as soon as possible. The minute that happens, I'll let you know."

"Do," said Cindy. "I'm sure the police must be working on solving this case. Do you know if they've made any progress? In New Jersey, we don't hear a thing, but as it's local news for you . . ."

"All they'll say is that they're exploring a number of options," I told her. "I don't think they really know anything."

"Probably just as well," Cindy said under her breath.

I stared at her, surprised. "It *is*?"

"Oh, you know," she said quickly. "Sleeping dogs and all that. I've never seen any good come of stirring things up too much."

Things were already stirred up, I thought. And letting Henry's killer go free certainly wouldn't help any. I'd have said as much, but I never got the chance. Cindy was already turning away.

"I guess I'd better be getting back to my own dog," she said. "Good luck in the group."

"Now that was odd," said Aunt Peg, watching Cindy walk away.

I had to agree.

# 19

"What did I miss?" Sam asked, reappearing with lunch for three, balanced precariously in a flimsy cardboard container. Since Aunt Peg, Terry, and I were all standing there looking perplexed, it wasn't an odd question.

"Cindy Marshall stopped by," I said.

I leaned over to have a look in the box. Dog show food is notoriously poor, and the meal Sam had procured from the concession stand didn't look terribly appetizing. At least the french fries appeared edible. I snagged one and popped it into my mouth. All that winning had given me an appetite.

"She and I were supposed to have lunch last week but she had to cancel," said Peg. "So she came looking for me here instead."

"That was nice of her." Sam slid the box carefully onto an empty grooming table and we all dug in.

"Maybe . . ." I said.

"She offered to find a home for Remington as well as Pepper," Aunt Peg added.

"Except that at the moment, you can't let her have either dog." I slit open a packet of ketchup. "Which I'm assuming you'd already told her."

Mouth full, Aunt Peg nodded.

"So why bother?"

"Why indeed?" Terry lowered his voice mysteriously.

"Maybe that was just an excuse to come and pump you for information. Maybe Cindy Marshall is a suspect!"

Let's be honest, it wasn't as though the thought hadn't occurred to me. Except that, sad to say, we didn't have much information to be pumped for.

"You did say that Henry was having an affair with a woman dog breeder," Sam pointed out.

"We assumed that was Rebecca Morehouse," I mused. "Maybe we were wrong."

"You'll have to add Cindy to your list," Terry said to Aunt Peg.

"What list?"

"Your list of suspects, of course. Don't you watch TV? Don't you read books? How do you expect to solve a mystery if you're not keeping a list?"

"Don't encourage her," I said to Terry.

"Yes, do," said Peg. "Sadly, it's beginning to look as though I'm not a very good sleuth after all. I have no idea who killed Henry Pruitt, nor even why anyone would even want to have done so."

"The police—" I began.

A look from Aunt Peg stopped me. "Have had ten days to figure something out," she said. "Meanwhile, I'm stuck with Henry's nitwit daughters still breathing down my neck. It's time to move things along. If this were your problem, what would you do next?"

I thought for a moment. "Talk to Jenna and Carrie, the two women Henry dated at Hunting Ridge. Try to find out what was going on in his life that doesn't seem apparent on the surface. Maybe there's something there that could have led to his murder."

"Good choice," said Peg. "Let me know what you find out."

I must be getting slow in my old age. To think, I never even saw that one coming.

*       *       *

Watching Sam take a dog in the ring is always a pleasure. He's shown Poodles for years, and although the sport is a hobby for him, his handling technique would put many of the pros to shame. On top of that, Sam and Tar make an excellent team.

When the two of them entered the ring and walked to the head of the long non-sporting group line, I couldn't take my eyes off them. Nor was I the only one. Usually the ringside waits until after the individual examinations to pick their favorites. Not that day. As soon as the judge sent the line around for the first time with Tar leading the way, spontaneous applause followed their every move.

Anyone who felt that Poodles were a silly breed, deserving of bows and painted toenails to go with their stylized trims, needed only to have been watching the big black Poodle that day to learn differently. Tar was stunningly, ruggedly masculine and totally in control of his surroundings. Muscles rippled across his hindquarter as he gaited down and back. His stride was fluid and effortless, each of his pieces working in harmony with the others.

Newcomers often ask how it's possible for a judge to compare dogs to one another in a group, since each breed has a different, distinctive look. Actually, the judge doesn't compare the dogs to each other, he compares each to its own standard of excellence. That day, standing majestically in the center of the ring and surveying all with an aristocratic arch in his neck and a twinkle in his eye, Tar was the embodiment of the Poodle standard come to life.

He won the group, and two hours later garnered his second Best in Show. And each of us, Aunt Peg, Sam, and I, floated home that night on clouds of pure contentment.

Monday, it was back to real life. And once again back to school, the last week before Christmas break. Nobody had their mind on their studies, including me.

After a blissfully successful Saturday, I'd rounded out the

weekend by spending most of Sunday at the mall. The day was an exercise in shopping hell. Errands that should have taken a couple of hours took twice that. The end result was that by Sunday evening, Davey and I still didn't have a tree or any decorations up. On the plus side, at least I'd finally gotten a handle on most of my Christmas shopping.

Monday morning, sitting in my classroom between tutoring sessions, I pulled out my cell phone and gave Bertie a quick call to see how things were going.

"What?" she snarled by way of a greeting.

"Good morning to you, too."

"What's good about it?" Bertie demanded. "Tell me one damn thing."

"Maybe if you try jumping up and down," I said, "the baby will fall out."

"Right. Like that didn't already occur to me."

Oh. I'd been kidding.

"Let's talk about something happy," I said. "Have you and Frank settled on names yet?"

"We had, but now I've changed my mind. I told Frank last night. Now the little stinker's going to be named Godot. As in *Waiting For . . .*"

I covered the receiver to muffle my laugh. "I'll bet that went over well."

"Frank just nodded and smiled and said, 'Anything you want, honey.' "

Smart man, my brother.

"I heard you had yourself quite a weekend," said Bertie. "I'm sorry I missed it."

"You'll be there next time."

"Let's hope so." She sighed. "Either that or I'll be in the *Guinness Book* for the longest human pregnancy on record."

"Come on now, you're not *that* far overdue."

"Easy for you to say. You're not the one wearing a watermelon strapped to your waist. What about when Davey was born? Was he early, on-time, or late?"

"Late," I said. "By three days."

"And were they the longest three days of your life?"

I answered without hesitation. "Yes."

"See? I rest my case."

"Maybe the doctor would like to think about inducing you," I said.

"That's what I thought. He said no, everything seems friggin' normal to him, except of course for the fact that the baby isn't here. He's thinking maybe we had the due date wrong. And damn it all, he could be right. You know I've never been any good in math."

"Have you noticed you're swearing a lot more than you used to?" I mentioned. "You're going to have to clean that up when the baby arrives."

"After the baby arrives," Bertie snapped, "I won't have anything to swear about."

Little did she know, I thought. Motherhood was a joy, but still. Bertie's frustrations were only beginning.

That afternoon, with Davey booked for play practice, I headed back to Hunting Ridge Elementary. Wouldn't you know it, the first person I ran into was Annie Gault. She didn't look happy to see me.

"What are you doing here again?" she demanded, hopping down out of her bus to confront me as I walked by. "Checking up on me?"

Interesting, I thought, that Annie should think she needed checking up on.

"I'm here to see an old friend," I said. She didn't deserve an explanation, but there was something about her unexpected belligerence that made me want to keep her talking. "How are things going with you?"

"Fine." Her tongue pushed a wad of gum around her mouth. "Good. Pretty good. Anyway, I'm still here, aren't I?"

I looked at her curiously. Something looked different; it took me a moment to figure out what. The hoop that had pierced her eyebrow was gone. Also her fingernails were clean and her spiked blond hair seemed to have been toned down a shade or two. Annie Gault was getting her act together.

"Did you expect not to be?" I asked.

"You never know, do you?" Her shrug was careless but the expression in her eyes made me think she cared more than she was willing to let on.

"Enjoying your job?"

"Sure, I guess. It pays pretty good money. As jobs go, I've had plenty that were worse."

Annie didn't look old enough to have been in the work force that long. The girl was a bundle of inconsistencies. Not the least of which was how she'd gotten to be so cynical so young.

"Do you remember the first time we met? I asked you where Henry was and you said you didn't even know who he was. Then last week, you talked about him as if the two of you were friends."

"So?"

"So I'm wondering why you lied to me in the beginning."

"I didn't lie, I just didn't feel like talking about him. Plus, I had a schedule to keep."

"So it's not like you had anything to hide?"

"Like what?"

Annie's pugnacious posture was back. She took a step toward me, clearly hoping I would retreat. I didn't.

"I don't know," I said. "That's why I'm asking."

"Well quit asking about me. My life is none of your business."

We were almost nose to nose now. I could feel her breath on my cheek and smell her spearmint gum. And I was damned if I was going to back up.

"How old are you?" I asked.

The question surprised her. Annie considered a moment before answering. "Nineteen. What's it to you?"

"Most nineteen-year-olds are in school."

"Let's just say I'm taking a break from education. You

know, like those British princes did. I read about them in *People* magazine. They had something called a gap year, and I guess I'm having one, too." The idea seemed to amuse her. She stepped away, shaking her head.

"Everything okay at home?"

Annie spun back around. "Yeah, everything's just fine. But you know what? People like you just irritate the crap out of me. Suppose I told you everything wasn't okay? Suppose I told you I was in deep shit? Then what would your answer be?"

Inside the school the bell rang, ending the last class. Any minute now, the doors would fly open and students would come racing out toward the buses. I only had another few seconds to try and reach her.

"I'd ask how I could help," I said quietly.

Annie stared at me, her expression hard. "Then I guess it's lucky for you that you don't have to worry, isn't it? I'm getting along just fine."

Behind me, I heard the door bang open. The sound of excited voices mixed with that of running feet. School was out for the day.

Annie turned and headed toward her bus and I thought we were done. Then unexpectedly she stopped and looked back. "You know what?" she said, lifting her voice so it carried back to me over the waves of chatter that suddenly engulfed us. "Thanks."

"You're welcome." I smiled.

Her gaze left mine and went to the kids. "Hey, no running!" Annie yelled. "Form a line and NO pushing. There's plenty of room for everyone."

I wouldn't say that the kids leapt to obey, but they didn't entirely disregard her authority either. From a mother's point of view, it looked as though Annie might be turning into an asset after all. I made my way purposefully through the melee and headed into the building.

\* \* \*

Michelle Raddison had given me two names: Jenna Phillips and Carrie Baker. I'd have been happy to talk to either woman but I knew Jenna better, having worked with her on numerous occasions when I was a teacher at Hunting Ridge. Accordingly, I continued walking past the school office and headed down the wide hallway that led to the fifth grade rooms. As I'd hoped, Jenna's students had already dispersed but she was still there, tidying up.

Jenna's classroom, like mine, had been decked out for the holidays. A papier-mâché wreath hung on the wall behind the teacher's desk. Ornaments fashioned of cardboard and glitter decorated the bulletin board. There was a menorah on the bookshelf and a banner reading "Happy Kwanzaa" had been strung across the window frame.

I paused in the doorway and knocked.

Jenna looked up. Surprise widened her dark eyes, followed quickly by a smile. "Melanie! Don't just stand there, come on in. Geez, knocking on my door like you have to wait for permission or something! I thought for a minute you were a parent. What are those, your private school manners? Get over it, girlfriend, and give me a hug!"

Jenna crossed the room in quick, graceful strides. She had the long legs and slender build of a marathon runner, which she'd been for as long as I'd known her. Her skin was the color of milk chocolate, and her black hair was worn close cropped above a face whose features were regal and distinctive. Her easy smile and ready laugh only added to her appeal.

"Long time, no see," she said. "It's like I told the others. Put that girl at Howard Academy and she'll turn into a snob on us. That's the last we peons will hear of her."

"Sorry," I said guiltily. Jenna was right. The last time we'd seen each other had been at least a year earlier at a school function. "It's just that things kind of keep getting away from me. I'm sure you know how it is; I've been so busy—"

"You got that right!" She laughed. "Like we don't read about you in the paper every now and again. It sounds like you're in and out of trouble every other minute. Girl, I think you've forgotten how to keep your head down."

"That's for sure. Do you have a few minutes to talk?"

"Now that school's out for the day, I've got all the time you need." Jenna pulled out a chair and motioned me to another. "What's up? You're not having problems with Davey, are you?"

"No, thank God. Davey's great."

"I'm glad. Shirley Cooke is pleased as punch with that class. Sometimes I stop Davey in the hallway and give him a hug. I tell him, pass that along to your mom. I bet he doesn't, does he?"

"No," I admitted.

Jenna only shrugged as if she expected as much. She'd always been a hugger. In the course of a school day, probably half the kids she came in contact with found themselves folded into her welcoming arms. Jenna was the best kind of teacher; the sort who genuinely cared about every one of her students.

"So what's this about?" she asked. "You haven't been back to my classroom in a couple of years, at least. So I figure it must be something important. Spill, girl. I'm sitting here waiting to hear."

"It's about Henry Pruitt." I watched her closely, gauging her reaction. I liked Jenna too much to want to tread on any toes. "I was hoping you'd be willing to tell me a little bit about him."

"Little bit?" Her brown eyes sparkled. "How much time do you have? Honey, I'll tell you everything."

# 20

"Everything?" I waggled my eyebrows like Groucho Marx.

Jenna laughed out loud. "That too, if you're interested. Hey, for a guy his age, Henry had it going on."

I held up a hand. Now I was laughing, too. "Please. Spare me the gory details. That's not the kind of information I'm looking for. I just want to know—"

"How he ended up dead?" Jenna finished for me.

I nodded soberly.

"I wouldn't mind knowing that myself," she said. "It's a real shame, a nice guy like that. Henry wouldn't hurt a fly. It's hard to imagine someone wanting to harm him like that."

I wriggled around in the small, child-sized seat until I was comfortable. "How long were the two of you together?"

"Probably three months, give or take. This was a year ago, pretty much old news if you know what I mean. Though we still saw each other around school and stuff. Henry was the kind of guy you'd stay friends with afterward." Jenna stood and began to move around the classroom. "Listen, you don't mind if I work while we talk, do you?"

"Not at all." I watched as she began to erase the blackboard. A garland of silver tinsel was draped around the top and sides. "Want some help?"

"Not on your life. You just sit there and keep me company."

I could do that. In fact, my next question seemed easier to ask when her back was turned. "If you don't mind my saying so . . . you and Henry don't seem like the most likely couple."

"Black and white, you mean?" Jenna finished erasing and turned to face me.

I shook my head. "Actually, I was thinking about the age difference. Henry must have been thirty years older than you."

"You'd think it would matter, wouldn't you?" She began to straighten a stack of books on the window sill. "Are you still with that same guy, what was his name? Sam?"

"Right." I held up my left hand. "Still together. Now we're engaged."

"Good for you!" Jenna strode over, leaned down, and treated me to another hug. "And when were you going to mention *that*?"

My cheeks grew warm. "When it came up in conversation, I guess."

"Girl, that is some diamond." She lifted my hand and had a closer look. "Your guy got a brother?"

"No, sorry."

"So when's the date?"

"We haven't set one yet."

Jenna rolled her eyes. "And what are you waiting for?"

"It's . . . complicated."

"So when isn't it? If you're going to let that one slip away, give him my number, okay?"

"Will do." I was lying through my teeth. Jenna and Sam would make a gorgeous couple. Just the thought of them together was enough to make my hackles rise. "Back to Henry?" I said.

"Right, Henry. So what I started to say was about dating. I guess you're not doing much of that these days, but I'm sure you remember what it's like. Men, good men that you want to spend some time with, are not a dime a dozen out there. And most of the younger guys . . . guys my age?"

Jenna stopped and sighed. "Forget it. Either they're still

into going out with the guys and getting drunk, or they're so wrapped up in their careers that they can barely remember your phone number, or they're taken but the thought of settling down makes them panicky so they're out there looking anyway."

Been there, I thought. Though thankfully not for the last couple of years.

"Plus," said Jenna, "those guys are busy all the time. They're at work, they're at the gym, they're talking to their broker, they're having dinner with Mama . . . I mean, give me a break! How the hell am I supposed to fit my fine self into a schedule like that?"

"Good question."

"Well, Henry," said Jenna, "was the answer. He was nice, he was available. He liked to talk. Even better, he liked to listen. Being with Henry was just . . . easy. You know what I mean?"

"Yes." I could see that.

"And fun. Don't get me wrong. That man was smart; he'd been places. You know he hadn't always been a bus driver, right?"

"COO," I said. "Sterling Management. I read about it in the newspaper."

"Then you know what I'm talking about. Henry was living life on his own terms and nobody else's. He retired because he wanted to, drove a school bus for the same reason. Henry wasn't going to let anybody push him around or tell him how they thought he ought to behave. Not even his daughters."

"You met them?" I asked.

"Once. That was plenty. They weren't around much, thank God."

"They're back in town now. Sorting out their father's estate and driving my Aunt Peg crazy."

"Those two could drive a Mormon to celibacy. Not that Henry paid much attention to their complaining, but they sure made it clear that they didn't approve of me."

"Race?" I asked. "Or age?"

"Both. Either." Jenna stalked around the classroom, neatening supplies and slamming cupboards shut. She stopped to straighten the Christmas wreath on the wall behind her desk. "Mostly I think they were just pissed he was involved with someone who wasn't their mother."

"I thought their mother was dead."

"She is."

Jenna took once last look around the now pristine room. She'd been generous with her time but I knew she'd be anxious to be heading home, or wherever it was she needed to be next. Men weren't the only ones who were busy all the time.

"So with you and Henry getting along so well," I asked, "what was it that broke you up?"

"Oh, you know. It was just time. Henry was the sweetest man in the world, but he wasn't someone I was going to be serious about long-term. I want to get married and have a family. Henry'd already done all that. Plus, the race thing wasn't making life any easier. He didn't care what his family said, but I cared about mine. I never introduced him to any of my relatives, and there was a reason for that. I just knew there was going to be a big hassle."

Jenna smiled wistfully. "Henry was a nice break for me, you know? Someone to hang with while I charged up my batteries before jumping back into the dating wars."

"So as far as you were concerned, he was just a fling. Did he feel the same way about you?"

"Sure. When we moved on, there were no hard feelings on either side. Henry never had a problem hooking up with women. Right after we called it quits, he started seeing Carrie Baker. You know, Carrie from the office?"

"Another fling?" I asked curiously. I'd spent so long with Jenna that I imagined Carrie would have already left. I wondered if it was worth my while to make another trip back to school.

"Not exactly." Jenna replied.

"Oh?"

She glanced around, as though looking for eavesdroppers. "I wouldn't want this to go any farther, you know? But when Carrie and Henry got involved, she got all wound up about it really fast. Like maybe she thought she'd found the man of her dreams, the man she was going to marry."

I pictured Carrie Baker in my mind. Mid-forties, slightly overweight, beautiful blue eyes, kind smile. We'd worked together in the same school, but I'd never known her particularly well.

"How did Henry feel about that?" I asked.

"Remember those panicky guys we were talking about earlier?" Jenna grinned. "Like one of them. Carrie started pushing him pretty hard for a commitment and he wasn't having any of it. Carrie always said differently, but I think in the end he just dumped her flat."

"How long ago was that?" I asked.

"Sometime last spring, I guess."

"And did Carrie get over it?"

"You'd think she would, wouldn't you? But last time I saw Henry pass by the office, she was still glaring daggers at him."

Interesting. It looked as though I was going to have to talk to Carrie after all.


I left Hunting Ridge and drove straight to the arts center where play practice was just letting out. Faith and Eve, who'd had to wait in the car while I spoke with Jenna, were delighted to see Davey come running out the front door as we pulled up next to the curb. The two big Poodles bounced up and down in the backseat, barking excitedly. Every few seconds Faith would look over and try to catch my eye, as if she were afraid that without her guidance I might miss seeing my own son.

No chance of that. Davey was already skipping toward the car before we'd even rolled to a stop. He could have opened the passenger-side door and climbed in next to me. Instead he went to the back, threw his backpack on the floor, and squeezed himself onto the already crowded seat with the two Poodles.

Glancing back over my shoulder, I saw only brief flashes of child. His small frame was enveloped by big black dogs, not to mention a surfeit of hair. There were giggles emanating from somewhere back there, though. I took that as a good sign.

"Seat belt?" I said.

"Got it." Davey's voice was muffled. Also choked with laughter.

His small hands came up and pushed Eve's hindquarter out of his face. As I pulled out into the lines of traffic, Faith was already moving to the other side of the seat and settling in for the ride home. Eve, looking for room, turned a tight circle and lay down across Davey's lap. If he held his head up really high, I could almost see his face over her topknot.

"How was play practice?"

"Great. We got to try on our costumes and wear them while we were saying our lines. Ms. Morehouse said it was almost like a dress rehearsal."

Davey's costume consisted of a sheet with an opening cut out for his head and a hem on the bottom so it wouldn't drag on the floor. My sewing skills are limited, and this new effort looked suspiciously like a ghost costume I'd made for him several Halloweens ago. We'd found a piece of tasseled rope to tie around his waist as a belt, and a pair of sandals to complete the outfit.

"That sounds pretty exciting."

"It was. Especially when one of the shepherds stepped on Mary's veil and yanked it off her head, except that it was fastened to her hair which made her scream and she dropped the Baby Jesus. Joey went to pick him up, but he tripped over his costume and knocked two sheep off the stage."

The Baby Jesus, thankfully, was only a doll. The sheep

hadn't been so lucky. My gaze flickered to the rear view mirror. "Anybody hurt?"

"Jamie Prescott lost a tooth, but he said it was supposed to come out anyway. His mom's going to be mad, though, because when he flipped off the stage, he swallowed it."

Like I said, never a dull moment around this family.

When we reached home, it turned out that the day wasn't over yet. A vintage Volkswagen Beetle was parked out front. The quickly gathering dusk obscured the driver's identity.

"Who's that?" Davey asked as we pulled up the driveway and parked in front of the garage.

"I don't know. Why don't you take the Poodles inside and I'll go see?"

It didn't take long to find out. As Davey and the Poodles disappeared inside, Betty Bowen was already climbing out of the small car. She stalked over to the front walk and stood with her fists propped on her hips.

"I need to talk to you," she said.

"Is something the matter?"

"Yes, something's the matter." Her glare went to the door Davey had just closed behind him. "Aren't you going to invite me in?"

"Yes, of course," I said without thinking.

So in we went.

Davey, who'd been watching the exchange through the front window, stuck out a hand and introduced himself. His good manners are like variable weather patterns. You never know when they're going to appear, and when they do it's usually at the most inconvenient time.

"Hi, I'm Davey," he said. "Would you like some cookies?"

"Cookies?" Betty's frown softened ever so slightly.

Davey nodded. "Oreos and maybe some shortbread cookies. There's milk, too."

"Cookies would be nice," said Betty. "Thank you. Your mother and I will be in the living room."

It was like being relegated to minor character status in my own play. But since Davey and Betty seemed to have the situation under control, I took my cue and walked into the living room where I cleared the usual debris off the couch and a chair so we'd have some place to sit.

"What a nice child," Betty said.

"Thank you. He is." I waved her toward a seat. "Now, why don't you tell me what's wrong?"

"It's that woman."

"What woman? Robin? Laurel?"

"No, not them. Peg something . . . The one you brought to my house the other week. The trouble maker. Johnny told me all about her."

Considering the brevity of our visit, I couldn't imagine there'd been much to tell. Then I clicked on what she'd said. *Aunt Peg had been making trouble?* That was just what I needed.

"Peg Turnbull is my aunt," I said. "She's the one who's been taking care of Pepper and Remington until Henry's daughters figure out what they want to do with them."

"So I gather." Betty's thin lips were pursed. "She told me as much when she came to see me earlier."

"Aunt Peg came to see you? Why would she do that?"

"That's what I would like to know!"

Was it just me, or was this conversation beginning to travel in circles?

"Did you ask her?"

"As if I could get a question in. That woman walked into my house, sat down on my sofa, and began to interrogate me."

"She walked in uninvited?" That didn't sound like Aunt Peg. Well, on second thought, it did but—

"No, not uninvited!" Betty's voice rose. "She rang the bell and I asked her in. Just like any neighborly person would do." Her glare went to my front door, reminding me that I'd been remiss earlier. "I thought maybe there was something she needed, something I could help with. That was before I knew she was on a mission."

Aunt Peg on a mission. Those were words to strike fear into even the most intrepid heart.

Oh lordy, lordy. We were all in trouble now.

# 21

"Umm," I said, scooting forward to the edge of my seat. "What exactly was her mission?"

"She said"—Betty's voice quivered with outrage—"that she was investigating Henry's murder. As if that woman looks like any sort of detective. Who hired her to do that? That's what I'd like to know."

Wouldn't we all? I thought with a sigh.

"What did Aunt Peg want from you?" I asked.

"Information. All sorts of information. And answers to hundreds of questions. She had a list."

Hundreds, I doubted. Dozens? Probably.

Thankfully, I was saved from having to reply. Davey reappeared; the Poodles were with him. He'd also brought along a bag of Oreos. No napkins, no plate, no drinks. But hey, he's only eight—at least he'd offered the cookies rather than eating them all himself.

"What's the matter with that dog?" Betty was staring, rather rudely, at Eve.

Eve, on the other hand, was staring rather rudely at the bag of Oreos Davey had placed on the table. Somehow I didn't think that Betty was referring to my Poodle's bad manners.

"What do you mean?" I asked.

"Has she had surgery? Is that why she's clipped like that?"

"It's called a continental trim," Davey said around a mouthful of cookie. "Eve wears her hair like that so she can go to dog shows. Pretty soon she's going to finish her championship and when she does, Mom will cut her coat off so she can look like a normal dog again."

"I see." Betty reached for the bag. "Can she have a cookie?"

"No." Quickly I moved between them. "It will only encourage her to beg, and besides, the chocolate isn't good for her. Davey, why don't you take the Poodles back to the kitchen and give them a biscuit?"

"That means you want to talk like grown-ups, right?" Davey grumbled.

"Right." Not much gets past that kid.

"One of Henry's dogs was a show dog, too," Betty said as the entourage filed out of the room. "I can never remember which one."

"Pepper. He came from a breeder named Cindy Marshall whose Golden Retrievers have done lots of winning."

"That's right. I never actually met the woman, but I remember seeing her around."

That made me sit up and pay attention. "Seeing her around?" I repeated casually.

"You know, in the neighborhood."

"I think you might have her mixed up with someone else. Cindy lives in New Jersey."

Betty didn't look happy to be corrected. "It's not like New Jersey is the other end of the world. She has a car, doesn't she? Skinny lady, brown hair, kind of tweedy? Henry told me about her once, seeing as how Pepper had come from such a famous place and all. He was absolutely dotty about those dogs."

I had to admit, that did sound like Cindy.

"She used to come and visit Henry sometimes. Not a lot, mind you, but every so often. Enough so that someone who was paying attention might notice."

And I was guessing that Betty had been paying attention.

"Did you tell Aunt Peg about this?" I asked.

"Nope."

Aunt Peg must have asked. With her long list of questions, I couldn't imagine she hadn't. "How come?"

"For one thing," Betty said with a snort. "She didn't offer me any cookies. And for another, I didn't like her attitude. Trying to pump me for information. Telling me that as Henry's neighbor I was in a good position to see what was going on over at his house. She made me feel like some sort of Peeping Tom."

"I'm sure she didn't mean for her questions to sound insulting," I said, feeling faintly amused. Aunt Peg was accustomed to bulldozing her way through opposition; in Betty Bowen, she'd finally met someone her scare tactics had failed to impress.

"You wouldn't say that if you had been there. What I see or don't see around the neighborhood is my own business."

She reached in the bag and came out with two more cookies, one for each hand. Who knew that Oreos would be such a big hit?

"Of course it's your business. I'm sure Peg just assumed that you would want to help catch Henry's killer."

Betty frowned. "Don't get me wrong. I'm as civic minded as the next person. But this whole episode has me all shook up. I haven't seen this much excitement in years, and frankly I don't think too much excitement is good for a person."

I pulled the bag of cookies over and helped myself. Betty just kept talking.

"First there was the ambulance. Then the police started asking questions. Then you and your friend came knocking at my door. With all the activity going on, you'd have thought my house had turned into Grand Central Station."

"I can see how that might have been upsetting for you."

"And that was only the beginning. The police have been back a couple of times. Not to mention the reporters that have been sniffing around. And there's been extra traffic on the road, too . . . ghouls driving past to have a look at the 'murder house.' " Betty shivered in her seat. "It's enough to give anyone the shakes."

"I'm sure Henry would have been sorry for all the trouble he's caused you," I said.

Not that I knew any such thing, but it seemed like what Betty wanted to hear. I'm always surprised when people treat someone else's death as a personal inconvenience. Like the murder victim should have been more considerate of everyone's feelings.

"Tell you the truth," said Betty, "it's not me I'm worried about, it's Johnny. He can be a little . . . antisocial, if you know what I mean."

"Peg and I met Johnny the other week," I said. He wasn't the friendliest teenager I'd ever run across, but he hadn't behaved horribly either. "He lent us the key to Henry's house."

"Johnny's a good boy. It's just that with his father gone, he feels as though he has to be the man of the house. Like it's his job to protect me and make sure nothing goes wrong. All those people nosing around, they begin to make him nervous. My Johnny's a bit on the nervous side anyway, so none of this is good for him. I keep telling him it doesn't matter, that sooner or later all these people will go away, but he doesn't want to listen."

"And Aunt Peg's second visit didn't help."

"You can say that again."

No need. I figured we'd both gotten the point. Betty must have as well, because she gathered up her coat and stood. "I tried to tell your aunt that I was grateful for what she's done. Those dogs needed a place to go, and she was a safe haven in a storm of trouble. But beyond offering my thanks, there's really nothing else Johnny and I can do for her. You'll be sure and pass that message along, won't you?"

Me, tell Aunt Peg to butt out? What a novel concept.

Betty's confidence in my abilities was touching. Misplaced, but touching nonetheless. She was still munching cookies as she let herself out.

*   *   *

So you might be thinking that after a visit like that I might immediately call Aunt Peg and tell her to leave the business of investigating Henry Pruitt's murder to the police. I considered doing that, honestly I did. For about a minute and a half. Because, really, what would have been the point? Aunt Peg never listens to anything I say. Unless it's something she wants to hear; in that case, she's all ears.

Instead I did what any self-respecting mother of an eight-year-old would do two weeks before Christmas—I got on with my life. Tuesday after school, Davey and I finally went out and bought a Christmas tree. The one we chose wasn't big but it was perfectly formed and lush with pine needles. Best of all, it smelled divine. We brought the tree home strapped to the top of the Volvo and left it sitting outside in a bucket of water until we'd have time to decorate it over the weekend.

At least I managed to get some roping twined around the mailbox and the wreath fastened to the front door. In a neighborhood where most houses twinkled with lights, and several had oversized Santas or herds of reindeer decorating their porches and lawns it didn't look like much, but it was better than nothing.

Wednesday afternoon found me once again sitting in the back of the auditorium, watching the end of play practice. Nearly two weeks had passed since I'd seen a rehearsal and things really seemed to be coming together. At least none of the sheep fell off the stage.

As things were wrapping up, Alice slid into a seat beside me. "I've been thinking," she whispered as she unwound her scarf and pulled off her gloves. "Maybe you're right."

"About what?"

She shot me an exasperated look. "How can you even *ask* that?"

Easy, I thought. And if Alice had had any idea how much of a juggling act my life currently was, she'd have understood. Alice was busy too, but having a husband who was the sole breadwinner had to take some of the pressure off. As did not having an aunt who liked to get mixed up in mysteries. I'd be willing to bet the Brickmans' tree was up and their house fully decorated. She'd probably even managed to bake several batches of cookies for the third grade Christmas party, while I'd be reduced to running out and buying fruit punch at the last minute.

But rather than mentioning any of that, I cast my thoughts back to Alice's and my last conversation, which had been about . . . oh right, puppies. Specifically, the puppy she was planning on getting from Rebecca Morehouse to surprise her kids on Christmas day. How could I have forgotten that?

"I talked to Rebecca again," Alice said in a low tone.

"And?"

"Since you were being all pissy about me getting a puppy from her—"

"I was *not* being pissy."

"You were so. Don't even bother to deny it. So I began to think maybe you had a reason. After all, you'd brought up some good questions. Like about socializing young puppies and genetic testing for the parents. And I figured if that was the kind of thing that reputable Golden Retriever breeders were doing, then Rebecca ought to be doing it, too. So I asked her about it."

That must have been interesting, I thought.

"And what did she say?"

"Frankly, she wasn't too pleased. At first, she just kind of tried to brush me off. But I persisted. I mean, this is going to be my kids' pet, so I want to get the best puppy I can find."

So Alice *had* been listening. It was nice to know that some of the things I'd said had made an impression.

"Rebecca said of course her litters were well socialized. Her puppies got to go for rides in the car and get handled by all sorts of kids. . . ."

"As a selling tool," I muttered.

"Yeah, I know. When I really stopped and thought about

it, it didn't sound like the greatest idea to me either. So I checked on the other stuff you talked about. I asked about the sire and dam and what sort of testing they'd had done."

"Was there any?"

"No." Alice sighed. "Though Rebecca had a good reason for that. She said she didn't do any genetic testing because she'd never had any problems in her line. Like x-rays for hip dysplasia. Apparently they're hard to do, and on top of that they're uncomfortable for the dog. So most breeders don't bother with them unless they think there's something wrong."

"That's a lot of bullshit," I said.

Alice folded and unfolded her hands in her lap. "I was afraid you might say that. So I called Dr. Harrison at the animal clinic and I asked him. He gave me a whole list of tests that he said anyone considering buying a Golden Retriever should be aware of. I ran the list past Rebecca and her dogs hadn't had any of them. Ever."

No surprise there, I thought. It was nothing short of amazing how many lazy or unscrupulous breeders tried to get away with the "not in my line" defense. How did they know what genetic problems might or might not be lurking in their breeding program if they refused to test for them?

That would especially be the case with a breeder like Rebecca who sold all her puppies at a young age and promptly lost track of them. By the time the dogs were old enough for problems to develop, they would be out of her sight and, presumably, her thoughts. Then it would be up to the poor, uninformed puppy buyers to spend untold amounts of time, money, and emotion dealing with the health problems Rebecca had created. The thought of that kind of carelessness just made my blood boil.

"Good for Dr. Harrison," I said. "And good for you for checking with him."

"Yes, well . . . I probably should have listened to you sooner. It was just that the puppies were *so* cute and the thought of having one for Christmas day made me feel like I was doing something really special for the kids."

Just what Rebecca had been counting on, I thought.

"And besides, I'd already put down a deposit. Changing my mind after the fact would be like throwing that hundred dollars away."

I was quite certain Rebecca had considered that in her marketing plans, too. No doubt a fair portion of her puppies were sold to impulse buyers who had no recourse if, upon reflection, they changed their minds about adding a puppy to their households.

"But then I decided that was just stupid," said Alice. "Any dog I get for the kids is going to be a member of our family for a long, long time. So why shouldn't I make the extra effort to do things right? I want our puppy to come from a breeder who knows what they're doing, someone who can guarantee that their puppies get the best possible start in life."

"Aunt Peg would be happy to help you find someone like that," I said, feeling relieved for both our sakes. Now Alice would end up with a better pet for her family, and I wouldn't have to hold my breath wondering what was going to go wrong first. "There's a breeder in New Jersey, the woman who bred Henry's dog, Pepper. I have no idea if she has any puppies available but we can call and find out."

"Thanks." Alice smiled. "I was hoping you'd say that. Actually, I kind of figured you would. Which solves one of my problems . . . but not the other. I'm hoping you might want to help with that one, too."

"What problem is that?"

She nodded toward the stage. "I told Rebecca I was taking a puppy. I even gave her money to hold him for me. So now I've got to go tell her that I'm backing out of the deal. You'll come with me when I do it, won't you? If I go by myself, I'm afraid she'll convince me to change my mind again. With you there for moral support, I'll be able to stick to my guns."

"Of course I'll help," I said.

What choice did I have? I was the one who'd convinced

Alice to renege on the sale. No matter how unappealing the prospect, I supposed I ought to accompany her to deliver the bad news.

"I was thinking we should talk to her this afternoon," said Alice. "As soon as rehearsal's over. No time like the present, right?"

Sometimes it's just like they say: no good deed goes unpunished.

"Right," I agreed.

# 22

Luckily, we were saved by the bell.

Or, in this case, the first six bars of "Flight of the Bumblebee." As we got up to go confront Rebecca, my cell phone rang. I dug through my purse and told Alice to go on ahead backstage without me. No surprise, she didn't.

"Hey, Mel, it's Frank," my brother said when I clicked on. Like I wouldn't recognize his voice.

"What's up?"

"We're having a baby!"

I knew that. I'd known it for months. Then my brain reprocessed the information correctly. "You mean *now*?"

"Right now," Frank crowed. He swore under his breath and I thought I heard a horn honk.

"Where are you? Why aren't you at the hospital?"

"We're on the way. Bertie made me call you. Hang on a minute, here she is."

There was a pause during which I was quite sure I heard Bertie say, "Don't sideswipe that truck, honey, I want to get to the hospital in one piece," then her voice came through the phone, directed to me. "Your brother's a madman, you know that, don't you?"

"Have for years," I confirmed cheerfully. "But he was born into my family so I didn't have a choice. You're the one who married him."

"Yeah, well, I'm beginning to rethink that whole arrangement. Contractions are a real bitch, how come nobody mentioned that?"

Bertie had been to natural childbirth classes. She'd seen the video and been thoroughly briefed. So I was pretty sure she'd been warned. No sense in bringing that up now.

"How far apart are they?" I asked instead.

"Three minutes, give or take."

"Three minutes? And you're just on your way to the hospital now? At rush hour?"

Okay, so the last part wasn't strictly necessary, but *come on.* Bertie and Frank lived in Wilton. The hospital was in Norwalk, at least a twenty-minute drive under the best of circumstances. They were cutting things pretty close.

"I know." Bertie sighed. "It's all my fault. I did one of those hospital tours—you know, where they show you around so you know what to expect? And I kept seeing those pregnant women you hear about, the ones who go running to the hospital at the first twinge and then twelve hours later they're still pacing up and down the hallways. There was no way that was going to be me."

I could understand that.

"So the first couple of contractions I kind of ignored, in case they were just wishful thinking. Then when I realized it was the real deal, I called Frank and he had to get home from Stamford. Which was okay because the contractions were still ten minutes apart and I didn't think we were in any great hurry. So I was just sitting there watching *Dr. Phil* because, really, when you're more than nine months pregnant what else is there to do besides watch cheesy television shows?"

Bertie was rambling now. Maybe she was trying to take her mind off of Frank's driving. Or the intensity of her contractions. Far be it from me to interrupt.

"But then Frank got home and I got up and started to get ready to go and—here's another thing nobody told me—when you start moving around, the contractions speed up. Like a lot. So next thing I knew they were five minutes apart and we were in the car. And now they're closer than that, and we're stuck in traffic."

"We are *not* stuck in traffic," my brother yelled in the background. The assertion was punctuated by the loud blast of a horn. "Get out of the way, dammit! We're trying to have a baby over here."

"So as you can see," Bertie finished up, sounding surprisingly upbeat under the circumstances, "everything is going according to plan."

"What do you need me to do?" I said. "Have you called the doctor?"

"Before we even left home. He's meeting us at the hospital."

"I'll tell Aunt Peg," I said. "And Sam. What about your family?"

"With the baby being so late and all, they didn't want to come ahead of time and have to wait and wait. So now they're on their way up from Pennsylvania. They'll be here in a couple hours."

"Anything else?"

"Just get in your car and get the heck over here. I'm thinking someone's going to have to hold Frank's hand and if these contractions get much worse, it sure as hell isn't going to be me . . . ooohh!"

"Breathe!" I said automatically. It had been eight years since Davey was born. I couldn't remember whether, at this point, she was supposed to be taking deep breaths or panting. Hopefully, Bertie would know. "Breathe through it! Everything all right?"

"Ahh . . . I'm back," Bertie's voice sounded strained. "Hurry up, okay?"

"On my way. Hang on to little Godot until I get there."

"Godot." Bertie chuckled mirthlessly. "Who would give a baby an idiot name like that?"

I snapped the phone shut and looked over at Alice.

"You have to go," she said.

"My brother and sister-in-law are having a baby. They're on their way to Norwalk hospital."

Alice nodded briskly and cut straight to the chase. "Do you want to take Davey or would you rather leave him with me?"

Good question. In all the excitement, I'd forgotten all about him. No point dragging him to a hospital waiting room where he'd probably have to entertain himself for several hours. Not only that, but I had no idea what the hospital policy was about young children visiting the nursery. Better to leave him with Alice and bring him back to see his new cousin tomorrow.

"Do you mind?" I asked.

"Are you kidding? Of course not." Her hands shooed me away. "Go. Make your phone calls and get on the road. I'll keep Davey until whenever you show up. And if you're going to be really late, call, and I'll go get Faith and Eve, too."

I gathered Alice close in a quick hug. "You're the best."

She grinned in reply. "As if you ever doubted it."

I called Sam and Aunt Peg from the car. Sam got the message, hung up quick, and hit the road. Aunt Peg wanted to talk.

"Don't you want to head to the hospital?" I said. "We can talk when you get there."

"When I get to the hospital, there'll be all sorts of other important things to do. Besides, I can talk and drive at the same time. Isn't that what you're doing?"

Well, yes.

"Not only that, but I've been reading up on things. First babies usually take a long time to be born."

"Not this baby. It's in a bit of a hurry."

"It's about time it got with the program."

I imagined Bertie felt the same way. At least she seemed to be reconsidering the whole Godot thing.

"So tell me what you've been up to," said Peg. "Something useful, I hope."

"For starters, I've been placating Betty Bowen."

"Oh?" she said innocently. "Why would you need to do something like that?"

I'd driven south on High Ridge to the Merritt Parkway. There was a line waiting to get on the entrance ramp. I flicked on my turn signal and joined it. "Maybe because you marched yourself over to her house and called her a Peeping Tom?"

"I did no such thing!"

Fingers drumming lightly against the steering wheel as I waited for the light to change, I simply waited her out.

"Well, maybe I did. But it was for a good cause."

"So you could figure out who murdered Henry," I said. "How's that coming, by the way?"

"Slower than you might think," Aunt Peg grumbled. "It's not as if I have a lot of spare time for all these extracurricular activities."

And I supposed, by inference, that I did?

"You were supposed to be checking out his ex-girlfriends. Since I haven't heard anything, I assume that didn't happen?"

Now she sounded wounded; as though, once again, her unreliable relatives had let her down. I followed the line of cars up onto the parkway and accelerated quickly.

"I spoke with one," I said. "With luck, I'll get a chance to see the other in the next day or two. Jenna spoke very fondly of Henry."

"Of course she spoke well of him! She was talking to an investigator. If she murdered the man, she'd hardly want to come right out and say she hated him, now would she?"

The thought made me laugh. "Nobody thinks of me as an investigator, Aunt Peg. And that certainly includes Jenna. She and I are friends."

"Even so. It makes sense that she would want to deflect suspicion away from herself and onto someone else."

"Yes, it would, *if* she were guilty. Which I'm willing to bet she isn't."

"Well, someone has to be," Aunt Peg muttered. "Otherwise this perfectly nice older man who was, by all accounts, universally liked, wouldn't be dead. And I wouldn't be checking the classified section of the *Greenwich Time* with trepidation every morning to see whether Robin and Laurel have made good on their promise to run an ad for the boys."

*"The boys?"*

"These two really are a couple of sweethearts. No wonder Henry was so besotted with them. I've always thought you could tell a great deal about a person by looking at his dogs. Even though I never met Henry, having lived with this pair for the last two weeks, I'm quite certain he and I would have gotten along like gangbusters. These Goldens are lovely, both of them; it's obvious they had a wonderful upbringing. I couldn't see the point of leaving them in the kennel all by themselves so I brought them up to the house to live with my dogs."

"Have you spoken with Cindy Marshall since we saw her at the show?" I asked.

"No, but she emailed to say that she has several very good prospects for homes that would keep the two of them together. She'll be conducting interviews this week. Now if only I could convince Henry's daughters to let them go, I think we'd be all set."

I'd used the connector to join up with 95. Now the exit for the hospital was fast approaching. "There's something I've been thinking about," I said to Peg.

"What's that?"

"Nearly everyone I've spoken to has mentioned that Henry was the type of person who was very involved in everything going on around him. Even Davey said that his bus driver knew all about what was happening in the neighborhood. What if Henry saw something he shouldn't have and that's what got him killed?"

"Like what?" Aunt Peg sounded interested.

"I don't know, I'm just thinking out loud. Throwing another idea into the pot."

"Another mixed metaphor, you mean." Still, she didn't sound displeased. "Remember those photographs we found in Henry's desk? As I recall, they were pictures of the neighborhood."

"I know, I was thinking the same thing. Unfortunately, I don't remember what was in them. It couldn't have been anything sinister, or I'm sure we would have noticed."

"I imagine we would have," said Peg.

"Listen, you think about that. I'm almost at the hospital, so I'm going to park, go inside, and see if I can find out what's happening with Bertie."

"I'm ten minutes behind you," said Aunt Peg. "See you soon."

Inside the hospital, I was directed upstairs to the maternity wing. A nurse at the desk sent me down the hall to one of the birthing rooms. Standing outside, I paused and knocked.

Almost immediately the door flew open. Frank came barreling out. He was dressed in green scrubs and looked positively elated.

"It's about time you got here," he cried. "This is the most amazing thing. We have a baby. I'm a father!"

"Congratulations!" I wrapped my arms around him. "That was quick."

"Tell me about it. We almost didn't make it in time. They had a stretcher waiting for us at the door, and we were barely off the elevator before it was time to push." My brother was shaking with emotion, like he wasn't sure whether to laugh or cry.

"So?" I asked.

Frank looked at me blankly.

"Boy or girl?"

"Oh. Oh. Right. She's a girl. Eight pounds, seven ounces. A beautiful baby girl. She's going to look just like her mother." Frank gave me a loopy smile. "I still can't believe it."

"Can we go in and see Bertie?"

"In just a minute. They're just getting things cleaned up in there. They told me to come back in five."

He and I strolled down the hallway toward the elevator. "How's Bertie doing?"

"Fine. Perfect. Absolutely amazing. She was great."

The elevator door opened and Sam stepped out. "It's a girl," I said. "She's already here."

Sam looked back and forth between my brother and me. I realized our faces probably featured the same goofy grin.

"What's her name?" he asked.

"Oh God," said Frank. "I don't know. People are going to ask that, aren't they? And I won't know what to tell them. Bertie and I never made a final decision. She said she wanted to see the baby first to make sure the name matched."

"I think he's suffering from reaction," I said to Sam.

"Not surprising, under the circumstances."

We turned Frank around and walked him back to Bertie's room. A doctor and two nurses were just leaving. "You can go in now," the doctor said. He looked at Frank, then reached out and patted him gently on the shoulder. "You and Bertie both did a great job. And you have a beautiful baby daughter."

"I have a daughter," Frank repeated. He stared at the doctor as if he were hearing the news for the first time.

Happiness bubbled up inside me; I laughed out loud. "Don't worry," I said, wrapping an arm around my brother. "We'll take care of him."

"Him?" Bertie called from inside the room. "What about me? Come on in here and see the newest member of the family."

She didn't have to ask us twice.

# 23

Bertie was sitting up in the hospital bed, looking flushed and radiant. One of the nurses had combed her auburn hair off her face and tied it back with a velvet ribbon. Her arms were curled protectively around a tiny bundle, swathed in a pink blanket.

As we drew near, Bertie nudged the edge of the blanket aside and revealed her daughter's face. The baby's eyes were closed in a blissful sleep but she had her mother's creamy skin and high cheekbones. I thought I could see Frank's contribution in the pink bow lips and strong chin. Both tiny hands were fisted and pressed against her cheeks.

"Oh my," I whispered. "She's perfect."

"I told you," said Frank.

"I can't believe it." Bertie sighed happily. "I can't believe I really have a baby."

"You had nine months to get used to the idea," I pointed out.

"I know, but it didn't seem real until she was actually here."

"It seemed real enough in the car," Frank muttered.

Sam punched him in the arm. Good call, I thought.

"Isn't she just the sweetest thing?" asked Bertie. The question didn't seem to need an answer, but we all nodded in unison anyway.

"Look how tiny she is." Sam reached out and touched the baby's fingers with one of his own. Her hand opened, then curled closed again around the tip of his finger. I could see Sam's heart melt.

"I can't believe she's asleep," Frank said, gazing down at his child adoringly. "She just got here."

Sam chuckled. "If my sister's kids are any indication, there will be plenty of times to come when she'll be up and you'd give anything if she would just fall asleep and let you do the same."

"Besides," I said, "getting here was the hard part. She probably wore herself out."

"Tell me about it," Bertie agreed.

Despite her words, she didn't look tired. She looked . . . serene, blissful, even Madonna-like. It took me a minute to readjust the image I'd always had of my sister-in-law. Bertie was one of the smartest, busiest, most competent people I knew. There was always something going on in her life; it was unusual to see her sit still.

Marriage to my brother had gone a long way toward unwinding Bertie's tension. It had softened some of her hard edges. But now, seeing her looking like she never needed to move again, as though everything she wanted was right within her reach, I realized that Bertie had finally found the peace she'd always sought.

Good Lord, I thought, drawing in a sniffling breath. I was about to cry.

Sam slipped an arm around my shoulder and pulled me close. When he turned his head, his lips grazed my hair. "There's nothing like a new baby to put everything into perspective," he said.

With a sudden spear of intuition, I realized how badly he wanted a child of his own. Sam made a wonderful surrogate father for Davey and I knew he doted on his nieces and nephews. But he and I had never spoken about having children. In the beginning our mutual desire for them had simply been assumed. Then our marriage plans had gotten derailed and the subject seemed moot.

Maybe it was time to reawaken it. Not right now necessarily . . . but soon.

"She needs a name," said Frank. He looked at Bertie expectantly. "We have to make a decision. The bracelet on her wrist says Baby Girl Turnbull."

"Not Godot?" I asked innocently.

Sam grinned as Frank shot me a look. "I think they were kidding about that, Mel."

"Just checking."

"We wanted a family name," said Bertie. "Something that came with some history. Your grandmothers' names wouldn't do."

Agnes and Ethel, I thought. I could see why not. "What about yours?"

"Lavinia and Charlotte," Bertie admitted.

"Maybe Charlotte . . . ?"

We all looked down at the baby. One by one, we shook our heads.

"But then I remembered Great Aunt Emma," said Bertie. "She lived at the beginning of the last century, and when I was little my mother was always telling me stories about her adventures. She was way ahead of her time, fiercely independent, and probably a bit of a wild woman."

Frank rolled his eyes. "And of course anyone would want to have a daughter with *those* traits. I was thinking of something demure, maybe Sarah or Rosemary."

"Sorry, honey, but I don't think so," Bertie said with a smile. "Between your genes and mine, that die is already cast in the other direction."

"Emma's a great name," I said.

"I like it," Sam agreed.

"Emma." Frank let the name roll of his tongue experimentally.

He reached down, took the baby from Bertie's arms, and

lifted her up to cradle her gently in his own. Frank dipped his head until he and the sleeping infant were almost nose to nose. "Little baby Emma," he said on a soft breath. "Welcome to the world."

"Now you are going to make me cry," I said, fighting back another sniffle. Even Sam was looking a little teary eyed.

There was a discreet knock at the door, then Aunt Peg's imposing frame filled the doorway. She seemed to be holding an entire gift shop's worth of helium balloons in her hand. There were smiley faces, and bunny rabbits, and silver latex orbs bearing the message "Congratulations!" The balloons bounced and bobbled at the end of their strings, vying for space in the opening with my aunt.

"Am I too late?" she asked. "Did I miss all the excitement?"

"You're just in time," I said. "Come in and meet Emma."

Peg released the strings she held fisted in her hand and a dozen balloons floated up to rest on the ceiling. Eyes never leaving the bundle in Frank's arms, she crossed the room with cautious steps. Hesitantly, she reached out a hand toward the tiny infant. Then abruptly she pulled back and laughed self-consciously.

"I know everything in the world about puppies," she said. "And not a single thing about babies. Can I touch her?"

"Of course," Bertie said from the bed. "The doctor told me she's very sturdy. You can even hold her if you like."

"Oh no . . ." Aunt Peg said quickly, then stopped to reconsider. The tip of her finger traced the shape of the sleeping baby's face. "Well, maybe if I sit down."

A chair was brought forward. Aunt Peg settled into the seat. I thought of all the times I'd watched her show Poodle puppies to prospective families. How she always made the children sit on the floor before she placed the puppy in their arms. Babies were babies, I decided. And Aunt Peg wasn't as ignorant as she thought.

She raised her arms and Frank, the proud papa, handed

Emma over. Aunt Peg sat back and nestled her close. "Little Emma," she whispered. "What a lovely name."

Frank cleared his throat. He and Bertie exchanged a look. "That's not her whole name," he said. "Bertie and I were still thinking about first names, but we always knew what her middle name would be."

Bertie looked at Peg and smiled. "We're going to name her Emma Margaret Turnbull. I hope that's all right with you."

"All right?" Aunt Peg lifted her head; her eyes were shining. "I'd be honored."

Now I was crying. Tears slid from my eyes and down my cheeks. I brushed them away, took the handkerchief Sam held out to me, and gave myself up to the moment.

The next afternoon I drove back to Davey's school for the third time in little more than a week. This time I didn't run into Annie Gault; the buses were loaded and gone before I arrived.

I'd called ahead earlier in the day and spoken to Carrie Baker. She said she had some work to finish up after school but if I could drop by around five, she'd be happy to chat. I arranged for Bob to pick up Davey, dropped the Poodles off at home, and went to see what she had to say.

The parking lot at Hunting Ridge was just about empty when I pulled in. Most times of the year, the school would have still been busy at that hour, but two days before the start of Christmas vacation, nobody wanted to work any harder than they had to.

The only car in the lot was an older model Toyota sedan with a slightly dented fender and a bumper sticker that read "Have You Hugged Your Teacher Today?" I parked beside it, got out, and let myself in the side door to the building.

The lights in the outlying hallways and classrooms had already been shut off. Only the dim emergency lighting remained. Familiar with the layout from my years of working at Hunting Ridge, I strode through the darkened building toward the front lobby where I expected to find Carrie. The tap, tap, tap of my shoes on the slick linoleum floor echoed in the silence around me.

There wasn't any cause for concern; even so, I felt my heart beating faster as I made my way through the labyrinth of corridors and intersections. At one point in my life, this building had been as familiar to me as my own home. Now, in the shadowy gloom, everything looked different and slightly off-kilter.

Finally rounding the last corner, I saw the lights of the lobby up ahead. Feeling foolish, I expelled a shaky breath and headed toward them. Then I reached the edge of the reception area and stopped.

The school office was visible on the other side of the expanse. Lights were on in the office, but from what I could see through the windows, the outer room where Carrie worked appeared to be empty. Surely she wouldn't have left without speaking to me, I thought. And wasn't that her car I'd seen parked outside? But if she wasn't waiting for me at her desk, where was she?

Something . . . not a sound exactly, more a change in the air around me made the hair on the back of my neck quiver. Acting on instinct, I shrank back into the shadows and pressed my back against the cold corridor wall. As my eyes readjusted to the darkness, I looked around and saw . . . nothing. The portion of the lobby still visible to me appeared silent and empty. I'd lost my view of the office, but there hadn't been anyone there anyway. Or had there?

My heart was beating wildly now; adrenaline pumping into my veins. I clutched my purse strap with cold fingers and wondered if there was anything inside I could use as a weapon. Quietly, sliding on my toes so as not to make any noise, I inched back toward the corner. I had to find out what was going on.

All at once I heard a door slam, followed by the sound of

running footsteps. For a moment I stood paralyzed, unable to tell whether the runner was heading in my direction or the other way. Then the footsteps began to fade; whoever it was was getting away. I leapt out into the now empty lobby.

The office was directly across from me. To my right was another corridor much like the one I'd just left. A shadowy figure, moving quickly, had nearly reached the end. Without stopping to think, I took off in pursuit. Only a moment earlier, I'd felt like a target. Now with my quarry in sight in front of me, I was the hunter.

In the time it took me to cross the lobby, the runner disappeared from sight. Either he'd turned at one of several intersections or else ducked inside a classroom. I stopped and strained my ears, listening for the sound of muffled steps. After a moment, I heard them. He was still moving. And then so was I.

My loafers slipped and slid on the linoleum as I raced after him. Days are short in December; night had already fallen. If I didn't see the intruder before he reached the outer door, I'd lose him in the darkness outside. I knew he had to be counting on that.

I wasn't gaining ground, but I was pretty sure I wasn't losing any either. Maybe I'd get lucky, I thought, and the door on this end of the building would be locked. Then that thought brought me up short. If the exit was barred, the intruder would be cornered. He wouldn't have any choice but to double back in my direction. . . .

The moment of inattention was fractional, but it was enough. Chasing around the last corner, I felt my shoes slip on the slick, shiny floor. When my feet went flying out from under me, I was moving much too fast to hope to regain my balance. My hands grabbed for purchase; my fingers grazed briefly over a smooth concrete wall.

Then I was spinning out and going down. I landed sharply on my hip. Pain shot up through my side then into my shoulder, as my elbow crunched on the hard, unyielding floor. Momentum sent me flying across the corridor and into the wall opposite where I bounced off of a bank of metal lockers.

A dizzy, disorienting minute passed before I realized that I was finally still. At the end of the hallway, the outside door flew open, rebounded off the outer wall, then swung shut. My quarry vanished into the night.

"Oow!"

It was a wail born partly of pain, and partly of frustration. I let my head fall back down on the floor. My knee and elbow stung, the rest of my body just seemed to ache all over. The linoleum floor felt cold and hard beneath me.

In pain or not, I couldn't just lie there. I needed to find out where Carrie was, and what she'd been doing during my wild chase through the darkened school.

Slowly, painfully, I hauled myself to my feet. My purse was on the floor beside the wall where I'd flung it as I fell. Scooping it up, I reached inside and pulled out my cell phone. Under the circumstances, it felt good to have a connection with the outside world resting in my hand.

This time, as I made my way back to the front lobby, I heard nothing at all. No sign that there was anyone around but me. Quickly, I crossed the lighted expanse and reached for the office door. I half expected it to be locked, but instead it opened easily. It must have been the door I'd heard slam earlier.

I hesitated in the doorway. "Carrie?"

The office was a square, workmanlike space, crowded to capacity with four boxy, metal desks, matching chairs and credenzas, plus several banks of gray file cabinets. My eyes skimmed over the room, going first to the desk near the window that had been Carrie's when I'd worked at Hunting Ridge. The other desk tops were mostly clear, but that one held what I first took to be a dark, bulky envelope. Then I looked again and realized it was a leather clutch purse. Carrie's purse.

"Carrie?" I said again.

I was already striding toward the back of the room when I

heard the moan. Low and throaty, it sent a shiver up my spine and quickened my pace. I skirted the last row of files and saw her.

She was on the floor, lying in the aisle, half beneath her desk. One arm was outstretched as if reaching for help, the other curved protectively over her head. Only the slightest movement of her body indicated that she was still breathing.

Carrie's face was white; her eyes were closed. I saw that all in a glance. But what stopped me in my tracks was the blood. Thick and red, it was matted through her hair, smeared on her fingers, and splattered on the floor around her.

So much blood. I hoped I'd gotten there in time.

Fingers shaking, I punched nine-one-one as I knelt on the floor beside her.

# 24

"Carrie?" I said softly. There was no response.

I'd already spoken to emergency dispatch. The police and an ambulance were on the way. Someone would be there in less than ten minutes, they'd told me.

How much good would that be, I wondered, when Carrie desperately needed help now?

My hand reached out to stroke the older woman's arm. Lying on the chilly floor, she felt cold and clammy to the touch. I didn't dare try to move her. Then I remembered there was a first-aid station next door. There'd be blankets there. It wasn't much, but it was something.

When I returned a minute later, Carrie was moaning again. She shifted her weight and her head tipped back, revealing an ugly gash above her right eye. Blood oozed from the wound in a steady stream.

Head wounds always bled like crazy; I seemed to remember reading that somewhere. Lots of blood didn't necessarily mean that the wound was serious. I leaned down and spread the blanket I'd found over her. Maybe Carrie would be lucky; maybe she'd simply been knocked out.

Even as I covered her, Carrie's eyelashes began to flutter. Her hand came up from beneath the blanket, reaching reflexively for the jagged cut on her forehead. I caught her cold fingers in my own and squeezed gently.

"Don't," I said. "You've been hurt. Just lie still. Help is coming."

"Whaaat . . ." The word seemed to be dragged from her unwillingly; her voice sounded as though it was coming from a long way away. ". . . happened?"

"I don't know. It looks like somebody hit you."

Carrie's eyes opened slowly. She stared at me for a long minute. "Melanie?" she said finally, sounding drowsy and confused.

"Yes."

"What are you doing here?"

"We were supposed to meet, remember?"

Carrie started to shake her head, then winced and lay still. "No," she whispered after a pause. "I can't seem to remember anything."

"That's all right," I said. "You probably have a concussion. I came to the school this afternoon to see you. When I got here, most of the building was dark. Then I heard someone come running out of this office. He disappeared down the far corridor."

"Who?"

"I don't know. I ran after him, but I wasn't fast enough. I never got a good look at him."

"Someone was here in the office with me?" she repeated, frowning. "Someone hit me on the head?"

"Yes."

"I don't understand. Why would anyone want to do that?"

"I don't know," I said.

Carrie put her hands to the floor, palms down, bracing as though she meant to push herself up. Then she felt the stickiness beneath her fingers and hesitated.

"That's blood." She lifted her hands and looked at them, staring as though uncertain whether they belonged to her. "Is it mine?"

"Your forehead's bleeding pretty badly. I called for an ambulance. It should be here any minute."

"My head hurts."

"I'm sure it does," I said, as she maneuvered herself awkwardly into a sitting position. "Just stay there. Don't try to get up. Do you want me to run some cold water on a towel for your head?"

"No." Carrie's eyes shut briefly as she grimaced against the pain. Then they opened again and found mine. "Don't leave me," she said.

"I won't," I promised. I reached out and covered her hands with one of my own. She felt incredibly fragile beneath my touch. "Is anything coming back to you?"

"A little, I guess." She paused, then sighed. "It's still not very clear. I remember staying late to finish up a few things because you were coming to see me about something."

I nodded encouragingly. "Henry Pruitt."

"That's right." Carrie managed a wan smile. "I didn't want to talk about him. But you surprised me when you called and I couldn't think up a good excuse fast enough. . . ."

It seemed rude to press her when her defenses were down, but now she'd piqued my curiosity. "Why didn't you want to talk about him?"

"Why should I? What happened between me and Henry was private, personal. I'm sorry he died. Really very sorry, if you must know. But that's not something I want to share with other people."

"So you were here in the office waiting for me," I said. "Alone?"

Carrie thought back. "I think so. I mean, I must have been, right? It's not like anyone from the school would have done this."

"Do you remember hearing anything? Seeing anyone?"

"No . . ." She shook her head slightly. "I don't know . . . Wait, I do remember something. I was getting a file out of the cabinet in the front of the room."

She and I both turned to look. The top drawer was still rolled open.

"Then the phone on my desk started ringing. That's where the main office number rings and I remember thinking, who would be calling the school *now?* I wasn't going to pick it up. If it was a parent, they could call back tomorrow. But then I wondered if it might be you, calling to cancel, so I walked over to get it."

"Who was it?" I asked.

"Nobody," said Carrie. "Or maybe a wrong number. There was just a dial tone. And then . . ."

"What?" I asked after half a minute had lapsed.

"Nothing," she said slowly. "Nothing at all. That's the last thing I remember until I woke up down here on the floor."

"It sounds like someone distracted you with the phone and then snuck up behind you and hit you on the head." I rose up onto my knees and looked at the telephone on her desk. The receiver was resting in its cradle. "Did you hang up?"

"I don't know."

"Maybe the police can dust the receiver for fingerprints. Or maybe they can trace who made that last call." My gaze went to her purse, resting on the blotter not far from the phone.

"By the way," I said, "last time you saw your purse, where was it?"

"I keep it in my desk." Carrie's hand lifted, finger pointing toward a bottom drawer that was slightly ajar. "It should be there."

"It isn't," I said. "It's on top of your desk."

"Oh crap," Carrie muttered. "So that's what this was about. What kind of world are we living in when you're not even safe in an elementary school? I probably didn't have more than twenty or thirty dollars in there. Who would hit someone over the head for that?"

Carefully, using a tissue I got from my bag, I picked up Carrie's purse and handed it to her. Finally, I could hear the wail of sirens, growing steadily closer. A sweep of lights played across the front windows of the building as the first of the emergency vehicles came flying up into the driveway.

"The front doors are unlocked, right?"

"Right." Carrie was pawing through her purse. She didn't look up. "The cleaning staff arrives around seven. The building's left open until they get here. Then after they're done, they close up everything for the night."

I stood up anyway, intending to meet the EMTs in the lobby and show them where Carrie was.

"My wallet's here," she said, sounding surprised.

Almost to the office door, I paused and looked back. She'd flipped the billfold open. I could see credit cards in the sleeves. "How about cash?" I asked.

Carrie had already opened the wallet to check. I saw her reach in and withdraw something. Even from across the room, I heard the gasp of her indrawn breath. Leaving the office door open, I hurried back to her side.

"What?"

She was holding a small scrap of lined paper. As I watched, her fingers opened and it fluttered to the floor. Carrie's eyes rolled back in her head. I scrambled to catch her as she fell again.

The sheet of paper sailed gracefully to a stop, landing face up. I lowered Carrie down to the floor, then looked to see what had caused her to react like that. The message on the paper was brief; its words printed in black, boldfaced letters that stood out in sharp contrast to the white background.

I read it and felt myself go cold.

*Consider yourself warned,* it said.

"Then what happened?" asked Sam.

He made an excellent audience, though he'd frowned through the entire section of the story where I'd been chasing Carrie's assailant through the dark school building. I couldn't say that I blamed him. What on earth had I been thinking?

"The police and EMTs came charging into the building like they thought they were U.S. soldiers liberating Baghdad." I said, pleased to move on to an easier topic.

I'd arrived home earlier to find Sam cooking dinner in my

kitchen: steak and potatoes, his favorite kind of meal. At some point he'd spoken with Bob and they'd decided between them that Davey was going to spend the night with his father. When, I'd wondered briefly as Sam sat me down and fed me dinner, had my fiancé and my ex-husband managed to become not only friends, but also accomplices?

Sam had brought Tar with him. The big black Poodle, resplendent in his bright blue wraps, had been sacked out on the kitchen floor with Faith and Eve while we ate. All three had been rewarded with several pieces of steak when we cleaned up afterward. When Sam was planning to be away for any length of time, he hired a dog-sitter to come in and take care of his other Poodles. I was beginning to suspect he'd made such an arrangement tonight.

Dinner over, we'd moved into the living room and gotten comfortable. Sam doesn't always enjoy hearing about my exploits, so I'd been judiciously quiet about my day during the meal. Of course, he knows better than to trust my silences either. Little by little, he was dragging the story out of me.

"Carrie was unconscious again," I said. "I told the EMTs what I thought had happened. They got her right on a stretcher and wheeled her out. Then I talked to the police for a while."

Sam leaned back on the couch, stretching his long legs out in front of him. "Anyone you knew?"

"No. They looked like two junior officers who'd drawn the short end of the stick and gotten stuck patrolling the backcountry." As cities go, Stamford, especially the northern, residential area, is generally pretty quiet. "The excitement probably made their day."

"I'll bet. You showed them the note?"

I nodded. "By that time, I'd slipped it into a baggie. And I told them to tell Detective Marley that what happened to Carrie might be connected in some way to Henry Pruitt's murder. I'm not sure they bought it, though. Especially since Carrie's purse was out and her cash had been stolen. I got the impression they thought it was probably just a kid looking to score some easy drug money."

"Someone looking for an easy score wouldn't have hit her over the head," said Sam.

"Nor would they have left a warning behind. Carrie told me she didn't want to talk about Henry. And Jenna Phillips said that the police never questioned either one of them. I hope Detective Marley does follow up and find out what Carrie knows."

Sam looked thoughtful. "You'd have to think that if she knew anything about Henry's murder, Carrie would have gone to the police already. Unless she's involved in a way that she doesn't want anyone to know about."

"Maybe the killer only suspects that she knows something," I said, thinking aloud. "Something Carrie might not even be aware is important. What if she saw something when she was with Henry? Or maybe he spoke to her about something that he'd seen? Henry's job took him all over the neighborhood. And according to everyone who knew him, he was a real busybody . . ."

My voice trailed away. Sam's hand had reached across the small gap between us on the couch. His fingers were skating slowly up and down my arm, and I was finding it harder and harder to concentrate on Carrie's plight and Henry's murder. That was probably just what he had in mind.

"Rebecca Morehouse," I said.

"What about her?" Sam smiled and leaned closer. His hand grazed my throat, fingers dipping inside the collar of my shirt. If he was paying any attention to what I was saying, I would eat my shoe.

"Henry wasn't killed while he was seeing Carrie," I said, not without some effort. Sam's fingers were now working their way down my buttons. "He was killed when he was with Rebecca."

"Fascinating," Sam murmured. My shirt parted beneath his touch and he slipped a hand inside. Warm skin rubbed against warm skin.

I gasped softly. "Carrie can't talk, or she won't . . . maybe Rebecca will."

"Not tonight," Sam chuckled softly. His other arm curled around my shoulders and turned me to him. His thigh pressed against the length of my leg. His lips were only inches from mine.

"No, not tonight," I agreed.

We had better things to do.

# 25

As it happened, I didn't have to go looking for Rebecca Morehouse. She came to me the following afternoon. And not happily either.

Thanks to a frantic phone call from Alice, I got about two minutes notice that the puppy breeder was on her way. That was just enough time to put the Poodles in the backyard and get Davey tucked away in his room before the fireworks started downstairs.

"Look out," Alice had whispered into the phone. "I just spoke with Rebecca and she is mad in a major way. She told me there was no way I could back out on her now, tried to make me think that my kids would be crying on Christmas morning when they woke up and didn't find a puppy under the tree. . . . God, I hope I did the right thing."

"Alice? Where are you?" I probably sounded confused. There was a good reason for that. I was.

"I'm at home. Why else do you think I'm whispering? I don't want Joey and Carly to hear me."

"Are you trying to say that Rebecca was just *at your house*?"

"Yes, and she's going to be at yours in a minute."

"Why would she come here?"

"Try to keep up, Melanie." Alice sounded exasperated. "You don't have a lot of time. I cornered Rebecca this afternoon after play practice and told her that I'd changed my mind about the puppy I'd reserved. I know we were going to talk to her together, but time was passing and I figured I should probably let her know."

"And?"

"It was horrible. She was livid. Really mad, much more so than I would have expected. I mean, she's still got a couple of weeks until Christmas; I'm sure she can find another family."

Was it just me, I wondered, or were there great, gaping holes in this story? "How did Rebecca get to your house?"

"I'm coming to that. See, we couldn't really talk about it right then because all the kids were around. Even if Rebecca wanted to make a scene, she couldn't. I said what I wanted to say and I left. I thought that would be the end of it."

"But it wasn't."

"Hell no. Rebecca must have looked up my address in the arts center records because she followed me home."

"That's bizarre," I said.

"Tell me about it. Sorry to say, kiddo, I kind of panicked when she showed up on my front step. I couldn't let her in, could I? That would have led to all sorts of questions from the kids. So when she demanded to know why I'd changed my mind, I had to think of something quick. I guess I might have mumbled about you convincing me that she wasn't a conscientious breeder."

That was *so* not what I wanted to hear.

"That's when she stopped being mad at me, which was a good thing. Except that then she started being mad at you. She said she was going to march right over to your house and give you a piece of her mind."

It was grasping at straws, I knew, but I had to ask. "Does she know where I live?"

"She does now," Alice muttered unhappily. "She'll probably be there any minute."

Which was what had led to my shooing the dogs out back and sending Davey upstairs. I'd barely gotten both things accomplished when the doorbell rang. Considering that the Volvo was parked in the driveway, I guessed there wasn't much point in trying to pretend that I wasn't home.

"Rebecca," I said, opening the door. "What a pleasant surprise."

Her small eyes narrowed, concentrating the glare she aimed in my direction. Rebecca had armed herself against the December cold in a dark, bushy fur coat that covered her from shoulders to ankles. Standing on my front step, staring at me through beady eyes, she looked like a squat, angry hedgehog.

"Oh, stuff it," she said, brushing past me into the house. "You can't tell me that ninny, Alice, didn't call and warn you I was coming."

The wind caught the door as I was pushing it closed and it slammed hard. A perfectly audible thump followed. The wreath, hung in haste, had probably just landed on the stoop. I debated opening the door and retrieving it, but one look at Rebecca's face stopped me.

"It was hanging crooked anyway," she said with a smirk. "And you'd tied the ribbon on all cockeyed." Her gaze swept around the first floor of the house. "Still, I guess it's better than what you've done in here, which is basically nothing. Davey doesn't mind not having a Christmas tree?"

"Of course he's having a Christmas tree. We just haven't had time to put it up yet."

"Oh, I see." Rebecca slipped out of her fur and tossed it over the newel post at the foot of the stairs. The woman did have style; I had to give her that. "I would think one of the most important things about being a parent is giving your child enough time."

I might have nodded in agreement but Rebecca wasn't looking at me. Instead she was heading, uninvited, toward the living room. She paused in the arched entryway and took a good look around.

Standing behind her, I tried to envision the room through her eyes. Our house was small and cozy. None of the furniture was new, but all of it was comfortable. It was the kind of furniture that dogs could sleep on and kids could play on, the kind where nobody minded if you put your feet up. As luck would have it, I'd dusted and vacuumed only a few days earlier. There were still plenty of legos and dog toys strewn around but our usual debris was at a minimum. Nevertheless, Rebecca didn't look impressed.

"Some people would say that a single woman who couldn't manage to put together a proper Christmas for her child was not a *conscientious* parent," she said.

I guessed that meant the gloves were off in earnest now.

"Did you come here to discuss my parenting skills?" I asked.

"No." She strode into the living room, chose a chair, dusted it carefully with her hand, then looked at me over her shoulder. "Mind if I sit?"

As if it mattered if I did.

"Not at all," I said. "I think I'll stand."

"Your choice." Rebecca smiled thinly. "As I imagine you already know, I came to talk about my puppies, your neighbor, and the possibility of a lawsuit for slander."

That was when I laughed. Right out loud. I couldn't seem to help myself. I think it surprised both of us.

"You think you're going to sue me," I said. "For *telling the truth*?"

"You don't know me. You know nothing about me. What makes you think that these things you're saying about me are the truth?"

Standing over her, I should have felt that I was the one in the position of power. Somehow, I didn't. I tried crossing my arms over my chest. It didn't help.

"You're right," I said. "I didn't know anything about your practices as a dog breeder, which is why I told Alice to ask some very basic questions. I would have given her the same advice no matter who she was planning to get a puppy from."

"I answered her questions," said Rebecca. "And everything was fine. Until she informed me earlier today that she no longer wanted one of my puppies. I was given to understand that you were the one who made that decision."

"No," I said firmly. "Alice makes her own decisions. Though in this case, I support her wholeheartedly. Yes, you answered her questions, but your answers weren't very satisfactory."

"Really?" Rebecca's brow lifted. "In what way?"

It was looking as though we were going to be here a while. I walked over and took a seat on the couch.

"For starters, the fact that you don't do genetic testing on any of your breeding stock. These days all dogs, even mixed breeds, have hereditary problems. Golden Retrievers are hardly immune. There are all sorts of things you should be testing for. At the very minimum, you should be doing hip x-rays, CERF eye exams, and checking for heart disease."

Before I'd even finished, Rebecca was already shaking her head. "Experience has taught me that none of that is necessary. Luckily, I started with very good stock and each succeeding generation has built upon that solid foundation. My line of dogs is not afflicted with those problems."

"Assuming you're right," I said. A big assumption, considering the fact that the woman did no testing. "Does that mean that you never breed to outside dogs? That all your litters are inbred?"

Rebecca stared at me for a long minute before answering. "Aside from the safety factor," she said frostily, "I also have my finances to consider. If I were to breed to other people's dogs, I would have to pay a stud fee. Either that or give up a stud fee puppy. That would cut into my profit and I would be forced to make an adjustment to my prices."

"Your prices aren't low."

"Maybe not, but they are in line with what the market is willing to pay."

"And you don't offer any sort of guarantee with your puppies."

"What a preposterous idea!" Her eyes flashed with annoyance. "Nobody can guarantee the future. I wouldn't dream of trying."

"There are, however, many excellent dog breeders who do exactly that. People with such confidence in their breeding programs and the puppies they produce that they sell them with a warranty of good health and good temperament. Breeders who will take their dogs back if something goes wrong, or if the owner is unable to keep them for some reason."

Now Rebecca was gazing out the window. Her way, I assumed, of letting me know that whatever I had to say wasn't important enough to devote her full attention to. Abruptly, she turned back. Her eyes locked with mine.

"That's what this is all about, isn't it? I don't know why it didn't occur to me sooner. You're mad because I wouldn't take that stupid dog back after Henry died. That's what made you so determined to cause trouble for me."

"Believe it or not," I said, "I'm not trying to cause trouble for you. I'm simply trying to keep a friend from making a big mistake."

Rebecca frowned. *"That's* what you think my little golden bundles of Christmas joy are, a big mistake?"

There was no way to answer that without being downright insulting. I decided to change the subject instead. "It looks as though, once we get a few wrinkles ironed out, Remington will be going to a good home," I said.

"You see? I told you that would work itself out just fine."

It hadn't worked itself out at all, I thought. Aunt Peg's generosity, her connections, and her determination to do the right thing had made all the difference for both Remington and Pepper. Without her involvement—and by association, mine—who knew what might have become of them? It was too bad that Rebecca couldn't be convinced to care.

"I guess you must have known Henry pretty well," I said.

"What makes you think that?" Rebecca's tone was light, but her shoulders tensed. She sat up just a bit straighter.

"As it happens, my aunt took over the care of Henry's two dogs after he died. In the course of trying to figure out what to do with them, she became interested in trying to solve Henry's murder. We know that in the months before he died, Henry was romantically involved with a woman he'd gotten one of his dogs from. I'm guessing that woman was you."

I thought she might deny it, but Rebecca was made of sterner stuff. Instead, her chin lifted defiantly.

"Much as I don't like you, I'm not about to lie to you. Your assumption would be correct. Henry and I were seeing each other. I suppose you think there's something wrong with that, too?"

"No," I said, puzzled. "Why would I?"

"Henry was a bus driver."

The statement came out sounding like an insult. If that was how Rebecca truly felt, I wondered what she'd been doing with him.

"Henry was a very nice man," I said. "And much more than a bus driver."

Several seconds passed in weighty silence. Finally, Rebecca tipped her head to one side and considered me anew. "Imagine that," she said. "We might actually agree on something after all."

Capitalizing on our brief moment of détente, I stood up. "How about a cup of coffee? I've got some in the kitchen. And my dogs are out in the backyard. I'd like to let them in if you don't mind."

Rebecca thought about that, then got up as well. "As long as it's not instant, I think I might drink a cup. Standard Poodles, right?"

"Right." Surprised that she'd remembered, I led the way to the back of the house.

Faith and Eve were waiting on the back steps. Though the yard was fenced, I seldom left them outside for long without supervision. Now when I opened the door, both Poodles came scooting inside. Eve, clipped down to the skin and shivering slightly, glanced at me reproachfully.

"Sorry about that," I said, running my hands over her cold hindquarter, then rubbing vigorously as she danced underneath me. "I didn't forget about you guys, I just got tied up."

"You talk to them as though they're people," Rebecca said.

"Yup." I went to the cabinet, got out two mugs, and poured the coffee.

"Do you think they understand?"

"I know they do. Milk and sugar?"

"Sweetener, please," Rebecca said. "If you have any."

I did. Minutes later we were settled at the table. I'd given each Poodle a big biscuit. Eve was lying in the doorway on the dining room rug, gnawing on her treat. Faith had taken hers and gone trotting upstairs to look for Davey.

"I suppose you want to talk about Henry," Rebecca said. Her voice was flat; she sounded resigned.

"If you don't mind."

"As if that matters. I mind just about everything that's happened. Talking about Henry is the least of my problems. He was a wonderful man. His death was a huge loss to me and to everyone else who knew him."

I nodded in agreement and waited until she was ready to continue.

"Not only that, but it came as such a shock. Of course, I wasn't there but his neighbor—Betty, right?—told me what had happened. Henry wasn't young, but he'd always seemed to be in good health. I just couldn't imagine what had gone wrong. Then to find out after the fact that he'd been murdered. . . ." She shook her head. "It was simply too upsetting."

"How long had you and Henry been seeing one another?" I asked.

"Just three or four months." She stopped and smiled, her expression softening as she thought back. "But it was a nice several months. Henry wasn't at all what I expected him to be. The first time I saw him he was behind the wheel of that big yellow bus. I'm sorry to say that my first impression of him wasn't very positive. But Henry could be quite persistent when he saw something he wanted."

"I'd heard that about him. I also heard that he was the kind of man who liked to be involved in everything around him."

"Pushy, you mean? Controlling? I suppose that's how he behaved with his daughters, at least to hear them tell it. He tried with me, but I wasn't having any of it."

No, I thought, looking at Rebecca. I didn't imagine she would have.

"Do you suppose that attitude might have gotten him into trouble?" I asked.

"In what way?"

"What if Henry saw something he wasn't supposed to see . . . or knew about something he shouldn't have been involved in . . . ?"

"Like what?"

"I don't know," I said truthfully. I was just throwing out ideas, hoping something might come of it. "Did Henry ever talk to you about things that went on in the neighborhood?"

"Sometimes, but not often. He was very well read, not to mention that he loved to travel. We had plenty of other things to talk about besides Stamford."

"So there wasn't anyone he complained about? Someone who annoyed him? Someone he thought was causing trouble?"

"The neighbor's son annoyed him," Rebecca said. "Though I can't imagine it meant anything. It sounded to me like the usual generational conflict between an older man and a teenage boy. I gather the boy played his music too loud, had visitors coming and going at all hours of the day and night. You know the kinds of things that kids do. Henry seemed to think that his behavior didn't reflect well on the neighborhood."

"Did you tell that to the police?"

"You must be joking," said Rebecca. "I've worked with children my whole life. If every time a teenager annoyed the

236 Laurien Berenson

neighbors someone filed a police report, no one would ever get anything done."

"Yes," I persisted, "but this time the neighbor ended up dead."

"Over a bit of loud music?" She looked at me as though I was daft. "I don't think so."

# 26

Guilt is a powerful motivator. Ask any parent; they'll tell you.

Rebecca was barely out the door before I was dragging the Christmas tree into the house. Davey and Faith heard the commotion and came running down the stairs to help. Of course, the reason there was a commotion to hear was because I had the damn tree stuck in the doorway.

Eve, who had followed me outside when I went to retrieve the tree, was still out there, standing in the front yard, barking. Maybe she was trying to help. Possibly she was thinking that the force of her sound waves could propel the bushy tree through the too narrow opening.

Either that or she was calling me an idiot, doggie-style.

"Ooh," said Davey. Eyes wide, he skidded to a stop at the foot of the steps. "That's not good."

"Tell me about it." I glanced at him back over my shoulder. "Who picked this tree anyway? I'm pretty sure it was you. 'Get the big one,' you said. 'We never get to have a really big tree.' "

And then there'd been that guilt thing again. I had felt bad that we were tree shopping late. And by the time we got to the nursery all the nice medium-size trees were gone. The ones that remained looked spindly and anemic. Pine needles, dry and already falling, carpeted the ground beneath them.

So I'd agreed, reluctantly, just to *look* at the bigger trees. And somehow found myself heading home with a seven-foot Douglas fir tied to the roof of my car.

"Sure I said that," Davey replied. "I'm a kid. You didn't tell me it wouldn't fit in the house."

He had a point. If anyone was to blame for this fiasco, it was me. The adult. The parent. The person who hadn't thought about the fact that a tree whose branches spread six feet across wouldn't fit through a four-foot doorway.

"Besides," Davey pointed out, "you're doing it backwards."

"What backwards?" I let the tree drop, straightened my aching back and turned to face him. "I'm holding it by the trunk. That's the strongest part. You can't drag it by the top."

"Yeah, but the branches go in the other direction. The way you're pulling it, they can't fold down so they have to get stuck."

Damn. He was right.

Now that I was standing up, I could see Eve through the doorway. Muzzle pointed toward the sky, front feet bouncing up off the ground to punctuate each loud yip, she was regaling the neighborhood with the story of our adventure.

"Oh, knock it off," I called crossly. "You're not so smart yourself or you wouldn't be stuck out there."

Eve stopped barking and gave me a wounded look.

"I'm calling Dad," said Davey.

I spun around to face him again. "You are not."

"You're doing it all wrong. You didn't even put the stand on yet. That's supposed to happen outside."

"Says who?" I demanded. It's a sad thing when you find your conversational skills deteriorating to the level of an eight-year-old and he still manages to out-argue you.

"Everyone. Don't you know anything?"

Apparently not.

"Okay." I drew in a deep breath and slowly let it out. "Here's the plan. I'm taking the tree back out to the driveway." Before he could ask, I held up a hand. "I'll go out the back door, walk around the house, and pull it out from the other direction. That should unstick it. Then once the tree is outside, I'll put the stand on."

"Then what?" asked Davey.

"Then we'll worry about the next step."

The answer was a cop-out, parent-speak for *I haven't the slightest idea*. Still, the first part of the plan seemed eminently workable. And, in fact, it was. Once I was pulling the right way, the tree slid free without incurring too much damage.

It came through the doorway so easily, in fact, that the big yank I'd given to dislodge it sent me tumbling backward down the front steps. I landed on my butt in the grass with half the Christmas tree in my lap. Luckily, Davey seemed to have disappeared, so the Poodles were the only witnesses.

Faith looked as though she might be rolling her eyes, but I'm sure it was just a trick of the light.

Christmas tree stands are tricky things. Every year I think I'm going to come up with a better solution and every year I never do. By the time I'd negotiated my way around this one and was ready to resume battle with the doorway, I was sweating freely despite the December chill.

When a pair of headlights turned the corner and drove down the road, I stopped to watch the car go by, just as pleased to have a chance to straighten my back again and take a break. Except that the car didn't drive by. Drawing closer, it turned out to be a dark green Explorer that stopped at the end of my driveway and pulled in.

Bob hopped out, took in the situation in a glance, and grinned. "I think the tree is winning."

"I think your son is a traitor," I replied. Still—and I wouldn't have admitted this for money—I wasn't entirely displeased to see him.

"Step aside, woman." Bob said in a deep voice. "This is man's work."

"Oh yeah?" For a second or two I was tempted to ask him who he thought had been performing such chores in the years he'd been missing from Davey's life. Then, thankfully, the impulse passed.

I shut my mouth and stepped aside.

"Go to it," I said, waving a hand magnanimously. "I'll send Davey out to help. And I'll see you boys inside."

"You're welcome," Bob replied, standing over the tree like a conquering hero and surveying the task at hand.

My grin was cheeky. "I know."


Consensus was, it was the best Christmas tree ever. It was definitely the biggest. With the stand affixed to the trunk, the star Davey placed on the top branch just grazed the ceiling. But once we'd dragged all the boxes of ornaments and frills up from the basement, we found there were plenty of decorations to go around. Oh, and I managed to get the wreath re-hung too.

We awoke Saturday morning, on the first official day of Christmas vacation, with a house that was finally looking ready for the holidays. Christmas was still seven days away and Davey was already in a state of high excitement. I could only hope he wouldn't be able to sustain that mood for the next week, or one of us might quietly go crazy. When Bob came to pick him up for their day together, it was one of the rare occasions when I wasn't entirely sorry to see him leave.

Two cups of coffee later, I was having a last look at my Christmas shopping list which, thankfully, was mostly complete when the doorbell rang. I wasn't expecting anyone, but Sam often stops by on weekends. Or, I thought, heading to the front hall, it could be Aunt Peg, in the neighborhood and dying to let me know how her sleuthing was coming.

It was neither, as I saw when I looked through the small pane of glass next to the door. In fact, it was someone entirely unexpected. Annie Gault.

I shushed the Poodles and pushed them behind me before opening the door. Some people are intimidated by big dogs, even friendly looking Poodles. And Annie, her face screwed into a mask of anxiety and a knit cap pulled low over her forehead, already looked uncertain enough.

"Hi," I said. I drew open the door and a blast of cold air immediately entered the house. Which was more than could be said for Annie. She remained standing on the step. "Can I help you?"

"Maybe." She tipped her head to one side and frowned up at me. "Maybe we can help each other. Is it okay if I come in?"

"Sure." I stepped aside. I hadn't been blocking the doorway, but maybe it had looked that way to her. "I just didn't want you to get run over by the dogs."

"Don't worry about that." Annie hopped up the step and extended a hand for Faith to sniff. "I love animals." Then her gaze went to Eve, and she stopped in her tracks. "Whoa, what'd you do to that one?"

The continental, complete with wraps, tends to have that effect on people. "It's a show trim," I said.

Annie still looked blank.

"I show her in dog shows, and for Poodles, it's required that they look that way to compete. Don't worry, she's very friendly."

"She doesn't look unfriendly." Annie was still gawking. "She looks weird. Like, seriously weird." She stooped down to Eve's level and crooned, "Poor thing, did someone dress you up to look like an idiot?"

Eve wagged her tail in reply. The "someone" in question wisely didn't say a thing.

"That's really out there." Annie glanced up at me over her shoulder as Eve licked her fingers happily and Faith crowded in to get some attention. "Seeing you around school and all, I wouldn't have figured you for someone kinky."

"Kinky?" The word seemed to stick in my throat. I wasn't sure I'd have figured myself for someone kinky, either.

"You know . . ." She indicated the Poodles. "A little on the bizarre side. Like this."

At least, I consoled myself, she hadn't made it sound as though she thought that was a *bad* thing.

And still Annie hadn't given me a clue as to why she

was there. Instead she seemed quite content to sit on the floor and play with my Poodles. I nudged Faith's hind-quarter aside and closed the door. I supposed I'd find out in time.

"Would you like some cider?" I asked.

"Nah, I'm good."

Annie braced a hand on the floor and pushed herself reluctantly to her feet. Faith and Eve seemed equally sorry to see her go.

The Poodles are excellent judges of character. They're friendly to strangers, but they're too discriminating to love everybody. And though they tend to hide it well, there are some people they take an immediate dislike to. Interestingly, I've yet to like someone that my dogs didn't. The fact that Annie had passed their inspection made her rise a notch in my estimation.

"I guess you're wondering why I'm here," she said.

Bingo.

"I was hoping maybe we could talk." She looked around: living room, dining room, up the stairs to the second floor, then back at me. "Like, in private."

"This is as private as it gets," I said. "If you're looking for Davey, he isn't here. Let's go sit down."

Annie hesitated briefly. I pretended not to notice and led the way to the living room. She pulled off her parka and cap as she walked and tossed both over the back of the couch. "Nice tree."

"Thanks." She was stalling, but what the heck, I wasn't in any hurry. "We decorated it last night."

"I've been asking around about you," she said after a minute.

"Oh?" That was a surprise.

"Yeah. People say you like to solve mysteries. Like you're a detective or something."

"Actually, the 'or something' part is more accurate."

I tried out a small smile. Annie didn't match it. She looked very serious.

"I'm thinking maybe I could hire you," she said. "We could do a deal."

"Whoa," I said. "Wait a minute. You don't understand. I'm not a real detective—"

"I'll tell you what I need." Annie pressed on as if I hadn't even spoken. "I'm looking for that thing that's called client privilege, or confidentiality, or something like that. You know, like priests have in the confession booth?"

"You want to tell me something and you want to make sure I won't tell anyone else."

"That's right. Can you do that?"

"Maybe. But if I can't tell anyone what you're going to tell me, how does that help?"

Annie shrugged, looked annoyed. Like she didn't want me to be asking questions. As if I could help it. That's what I do.

"Look," she said, "it's not as if I've thought this whole thing through. All I know is, I need some protection here. Some anonymity. Like, nobody ever has to know that this information came from me."

Now that was easier. "You can't hire me. At least not unless you're looking for a teacher. But I can give you my word that nothing you say will get passed along in a way that will hurt you. Is that good enough?"

Annie considered. Her fingers had been gripping the arm of the couch but when Eve wandered over to say hello, her hands transferred themselves to the Poodle's topknot and began to rub. For a dog "in hair" that's a recipe for disaster. Under any other circumstances, I'd have stopped her immediately. Now I bit my lip and hoped Annie didn't do too much damage before she managed to blurt out what she'd come to tell me.

"You won't tell anyone who your source is, right? I need you to promise."

"I promise," I said. I really hoped I wasn't lying.

Annie nodded. Her hands returned to her lap. I tried not to sigh with relief. I did reach down and beckon Eve to my side. Faith's short coat was impervious to careless attention. If Annie wanted a dog to pat, hopefully she'd look to the older bitch.

"I guess you heard about what happened to Ms. Baker," she said.

There'd been a report in the Thursday newspaper; one that thankfully hadn't mentioned my involvement. By the time a reporter had talked to the police at the hospital, I'd been long gone and the officers hadn't given out my name. A follow-up in Friday's paper had said that Carrie was recovering nicely, though she still had no memory of the details of her attack.

Maybe it was time to give Annie a jolt, I thought. Something to get her moving. "Not only did I hear about it," I said, "I was there."

"You were?"

"That's right. I was the one who found Carrie . . . Ms. Baker . . . after she'd been attacked. I chased her attacker through the school but he got away."

"Did you see who it was?"

"No, I never even got close. Why?" I nailed her with a hard stare. "Do you know who it was?"

"Not for sure," Annie whispered. "But I think I might have an idea."

# 27

"If you have information like that," I said, "you don't need to be talking to me. You should be talking to the police."

"Like that's going to happen," Annie scoffed.

She reached out and hauled Faith into her lap. The Poodle is big for lapdog duty but she did her best, managing to get most of her front end draped over Annie's legs. Faith's head reached almost as high as Annie's, blocking my view of the girl's face. Once we had a canine barrier between us, however, Annie seemed to relax a little. Like maybe she thought I couldn't try to force her to do something as long as my dog was in the way.

"Why not?" I asked. It was a reasonable question. As far as I knew, Annie was a law-abiding citizen. If she had information about a police matter, I couldn't see any reason why she should run it through me.

"Look, it's not that easy, okay?"

"Life isn't easy," I said tartly. "This person you're trying to protect hit an innocent woman over the head and put her in the hospital. He's also likely to have been involved in Henry Pruitt's murder."

The police hadn't released information about the note that had been found in Carrie's purse. Even so, the reporter who'd written Friday's follow-up article had uncovered the connection between Carrie and Henry and speculated as to whether the two acts of violence were related. So I probably wasn't telling Annie anything she didn't already know. If she read the newspaper, that is.

"I'm not trying to protect anyone," she said. After a moment, she added in a smaller voice, "Except maybe myself."

I stared at her and sighed. It looked as though we'd reached an impasse. "Why don't you tell me what you know? And when you're done, we'll figure out what to do with it."

"You'll keep my name out of it," Annie said firmly. "You already agreed to that."

"I'll keep your name out of it," I repeated. It looked as though this time I meant it.

She nodded and we sealed the deal. Still it took her a few minutes to get loosened up enough to talk. Her hands rubbed restlessly over Faith's neck and shoulders; her eyes darted around the room. I thought about the two cups of coffee I'd drunk earlier and wondered if I had time to take a bathroom break. Before I could come to a decision about that, Annie finally began to speak.

"At first when Henry died I wasn't going to say anything because, hey, I wasn't really sure, and besides it's not my problem. Also too, well . . . I got my job because Henry was gone, so I didn't particularly want to look a gift horse in the mouth. You know what I mean?"

Close enough, I thought. I nodded, encouraging her to go on.

"But now with Ms. Baker getting hurt, I figured I really ought to tell somebody. Because Ms. Baker is a nice lady and none of this is her fault. She'd never even hurt a fly. So I'm thinking this shit is getting out of hand and it's gotta stop."

"What has to stop?" It took effort not to sound as impatient as I felt.

"Johnny," Annie said softly. Her eyes dropped. She buried her face in Faith's topknot. "Johnny Bowen."

Finally, we were getting somewhere. Maybe.

"What about him?" I asked.

"He's um . . . dealing."

"Drugs." That had to be what she meant, but I said it anyway just to be sure.

"Yeah," she said, then added quickly, "But it's not like he's some big slimeball or anything. And he doesn't sell the hard stuff, mostly just a little weed. He's small time, you know. The neighborhood supplier."

*The neighborhood supplier?* Outrage flooded through me. That neighborhood was only a couple of blocks from my own. An area that was filled with kids. An area that shouldn't have had any need for a *supplier.*

"Now you're mad," said Annie. She looked upset.

"Damn right I'm mad." I shot up out of my chair and began to pace. "Johnny Bowen is selling drugs to kids—"

"No," she interrupted, shaking her head furiously. "No, he isn't. He doesn't do that. He only sells to adults. To people who are old enough to know better."

A drug dealer with a conscience? I didn't *think* so.

Then abruptly I stopped and stared at Annie. I wondered if she thought she was an adult, someone who was old enough to know better. And I wondered how this teenager who was driving my son's school bus had come to be so well versed in Johnny Bowen's dealings.

"I don't do drugs, if that's what you're thinking," she said quietly.

I didn't say a thing. I just looked at her, sitting in my living room with a hole through her eyebrow where the hoop used to be, her full lips outlined with a ghoulish-looking black pencil, her pale, slender hands cradling my dog in her lap.

"Okay. It's not like I'm trying to pass myself off as some innocent or anything. Maybe I used to dabble a little. At one time. But I've put all that behind me now."

"I should hope so," I said.

Annie started to push Faith away. "If we're gonna have a fight about this, I'm leaving."

"Sit," I said, waving her back down. "And stop being so

dramatic. How do you expect me to feel, with you coming in here and talking about taking drugs? You drive my son's school bus, for Pete's sake."

"I expect you to believe me." Annie's voice was taut with dignity. "I'm telling you the truth. All of it. So you'll understand that I know what I'm talking about when I say that Johnny was really pissed at Henry Pruitt. Pissed enough maybe to have done something about it."

"Henry found out that Johnny was dealing."

"Yeah. Johnny thinks maybe he suspected for a while. I don't like to speak ill of the dead or anything, but that Henry, he stuck his nose into everybody's business."

She certainly wasn't the first person to tell me that.

"Now you have to understand that Johnny's kind of paranoid anyway. But he got this idea that Henry was watching him all the time. Following him when he went places. He even thought Henry might have bugged his phone."

"You're kidding."

Annie shrugged. "That's Johnny for you. He's a little out there when it comes to dealing with other people. Anyway, he thought Henry was acting pretty suspiciously. He was really worried about what Henry might do next."

Johnny was the one dealing drugs, I mused. And he'd thought his neighbor was acting suspiciously?

"Why didn't Henry go to the police?" I asked.

"I don't know," said Annie. "I don't know anything at all about his end of it. Mostly what I'm telling you are things I heard Johnny say. Maybe Henry needed proof or something. Maybe that's what he was waiting for."

"What about Carrie Baker? Where does she fit into this?"

"I think Ms. Baker was just in the wrong place at the wrong time. Like Johnny saw the two of them together a bunch of times, added two and two and got five. He knows I work at the school and he kept asking me all sorts of stuff about her. He even had this idea that maybe I should spy on her or something, try to find out what she knew. . . ."

Annie's voice trailed off. She chewed on her lip and looked pretty guilty. I wondered how close she'd come to following Johnny's suggestion. Whether she had more reason to feel bad about the attack on Carrie than she'd initially let on.

"And did you?" I asked.

"No."

I wasn't sure if I believed her, but it probably didn't matter now. What did matter was that Annie realized she'd made a mistake and was trying to rectify it. Now I had to figure out what to do next.

"How about if we go to the police together? There's a man named Detective Marley—"

"No way!" Annie bounded up off the couch so fast that Faith went tumbling to the floor. "You and I made a deal, and that wasn't any part of it. I'm not talking to any police."

"Why not?"

"Do I look stupid to you?" She pursed her lips in exasperation, probably thinking that I was the stupid one. "If I go to the police and tell them that Johnny Bowen is dealing drugs, the first thing they're going to do is ask me how I know. What do you expect me to say to that? That I'm a good guesser?"

All right, so that was a problem. But anything I might report to the police would only be hearsay, especially if I refused to identify my source.

"What if we just tell them that we know Johnny was really mad at Henry, that he'd made threats against him . . ." I paused. "Had he made threats against him?"

Annie shrugged; her features were set in stubborn lines. It looked as though she'd probably given me all the information she was going to.

"You're so hot to talk to the police," she said, "why don't *you* tell them that?"

"Because I'm not the one who heard Johnny talking about how angry he was at Henry Pruitt. It won't carry the same weight coming from me."

"Sorry." Annie picked up her coat and hat, spun around, and headed for the door. "That's all the weight it's going to get. If the police don't believe you, that's their problem."

"Wait!"

Annie didn't even pause. She opened the front door and marched down the steps, pulling on her jacket as she went. The Poodles followed her to the bottom of the stairs, then stopped as Annie went on across the yard, looking back at me to see what I wanted them to do next.

"Annie?" I called.

She didn't turn around, but her stride shortened fractionally.

"You did the right thing."

She waved a hand back over her shoulder, more of a brush off than an acknowledgment. I'd been dismissed.

"Come on guys," I said to the Poodles. I patted my thigh to call them to me. "Let's go inside."

So I called Detective Marley myself. I mean, really, what choice did I have? The information I had was incomplete, but it was better than nothing.

Unfortunately, the detective didn't seem to think so. "Let me get this straight," he said. "You're telling me *now* that Henry Pruitt's neighbor is dealing drugs?"

"That's right. I just found out."

"And how did you happen to come by this information?"

"You know. It's kind of a word-on-the-street thing." Did I sound like a bad episode of *Law & Order* or what?

"My men are on the street," said Marley. "They haven't heard anything about that."

"Look," I tried again. "All I'm saying is that Johnny Bowen had good reason to be upset with Henry Pruitt. He was dealing drugs, he suspected Henry knew it, and he thought Henry was going to turn him in."

"And yet . . ." He paused. I thought I heard the sound of

papers being shuffled in the background. "Mr. Pruitt never contacted us about this alleged problem."

"I can't help that. Maybe he was killed before he got the chance. Johnny Bowen also suspected that Carrie Baker knew what he was up to."

Marley's sigh was audible. "She hasn't mentioned anything about that to us."

"The thing is, Johnny might have been wrong. Maybe she doesn't know anything. I'm told he's kind of paranoid—"

"Who told you that?" Marley inquired, his voice steely.

"A friend."

"Does this friend have a name?"

"Umm . . ." I waffled only briefly before keeping my promise to Annie. "No."

"I see. Well, thank you for the information. We'll be sure and look into it. Perhaps when Ms. Baker regains her memory . . ."

He was blowing me off. Totally. Even without Annie, I'd expected him to accord me at least *some* credibility. Was the idea so far-fetched that a civilian might come up with information the police didn't have? Apparently, Detective Marley seemed to think so.

"Maybe this is why Henry didn't contact you," I said.

"Pardon me?" The detective had been on the verge of ending the call. Now I had his attention again.

Of course, judging by the sharpness of his tone, maybe that wasn't such a good thing. I didn't let that stop me. "Maybe Henry didn't tell you about what Johnny was doing because he was afraid you wouldn't believe him. Maybe he tried to wait until he had proof. Maybe the waiting killed him."

"You may, of course, feel free to believe that," said Detective Marley. "But please rest assured that we are actively investigating every possible avenue of suspicion. . . ."

Yada, yada, yada, I thought. I wondered if the detective actually believed that any more than I did.

"I'm sorry I wasted your time," I said and hung up.

# 28

So I did what I always do in times of trouble. I went to see Aunt Peg. She didn't seem terribly surprised by my arrival.

"It's about time," she said, ushering me inside.

Walking through the throng of Poodles that had accompanied her to the door was like wading through thigh-deep water: slow and a bit cumbersome. Once the dogs realized we were heading for the living room and got turned in the same direction, however, progress became much easier. I'd left my own two Poodles at home. What I wanted to discuss with Aunt Peg was serious; I was trying to keep distractions to a minimum.

"How about a nice piece of cake?" she asked before we could find our seats.

So much for the no distractions theory.

"No, thank you," I said. "No cake. No small talk. Sit. What do you mean it's about time? Were you expecting me?"

Aunt Peg, never one to take orders, remained standing in the middle of the room. She looked bemused. "You realize your manners leave a lot to be desired. Of course I was expecting you. I've been expecting you since yesterday. It's a sad thing when the only knowledge I have of my own niece's exploits is secondhand."

"Sam?" I asked. I supposed he'd told her about my meeting with Carrie.

"Of course, Sam. Who else would be keeping me informed? Certainly not my own relatives. Though if I had *my* way"—Peg's steely gaze fastened on me reproachfully—"Sam would *be* a relative."

"Yes, I know." No use ducking that thorny issue. Better to concede right off the bat or she'd only keep bringing it up. "I meant to call you, it's just that I've been busy."

"Or maybe you forgot all about me when you got bumped on the head?"

I stared at her. "I didn't get bumped on the head. That was Carrie Baker."

"Oh, my mistake." Aunt Peg didn't look chastened. Actually, she looked slightly disappointed that I *hadn't* been the one to get knocked around.

Giving up on cake, Aunt Peg finally took a seat. Then I did as she requested, filling her in on everything that had transpired since we'd last seen each other in Bertie's hospital room.

"Annie Gault," she said when I got to the part about that morning's visit. "I've heard that name before."

"She's Davey's new bus driver. The girl who took over Henry's route."

"That's right. I've heard him talk about her. He's utterly fascinated by the fact that she has something stuck through her eyebrow."

Funny, I thought, Davey had never mentioned that to me. I stared at Peg through narrowed eyes and wondered if she might be the sort of person who would sneak my son off to a tattoo parlor when he got a little older. Probably.

"What are you glaring about now?" Aunt Peg asked.

"Nothing." No sense putting any ideas in her head. "Forget about the pierced eyebrow. Listen to what she had to say."

Peg was uncharacteristically quiet while I related my earlier conversation with the bus driver. For once, I got to go all the way from beginning to end without having to stop and answer a dozen questions.

"We have to take Annie's information to the police," she said at the end.

"Been there." I sighed. "Done that."

"And?"

"Detective Marley asked for proof—"

"Oh pish," said Peg. "Why should you be the one who has to come up with proof? That's his department."

"The problem was that I couldn't give him Annie's name. So everything I told him sounded like rumors or hearsay. He wasn't at all convinced that I knew what I was talking about."

"Damn."

Aunt Peg isn't prone to using swear words, even mild ones. So the fact that the epithet had slipped out had to mean that she was feeling pretty provoked. It wasn't hard to guess who might have been getting on her nerves.

"Henry's daughters?" I said.

She growled under her breath. The Poodles, draped over the furniture around us, lifted their heads and pricked their ears with interest. "I'm about ready to strangle both of them. When it comes to dogs, those two women don't have an ounce of sense."

"What have they done now?"

"For starters, they've informed Cindy Marshall that the wonderful home she found for Pepper and Remington won't be needed after all."

"Do they have an alternate plan?"

"eBay," Aunt Peg muttered.

I wasn't sure I'd heard her right. "Pardon me?"

"eBay," she snapped. "You know, the on-line auction site?"

I hoped she was joking. Judging by her glower, however, that didn't seem to be the case. At least she wasn't growling anymore.

"I don't believe eBay lets people auction off live animals," I said.

"As if those two would let a little thing like that stop them. Robin and Laurel are determined to make some money off those dogs. Apparently, they've found a way to circumvent the rules. They haven't listed Pepper and Remington as animals, they've listed them as clues."

"You're kidding."

"Do I sound like I'm kidding? *Clues!*" Aunt Peg snorted the word. "In an on-going murder investigation. Their listing talks about how Pepper and Remington are the only surviving witnesses to an unsolved mystery."

"What a truly terrible idea." I was appalled. "That's their father they're talking about."

"A father who apparently didn't suit them well enough when he was alive. Now that Henry's gone, they're going to capitalize off his death any way they can. I suppose I should be shocked that people will descend to this level, but having seen the lengths that people are willing to go to in order to have their fifteen minutes of fame, I'm sorry to say that almost nothing surprises me anymore."

"Have you tried notifying eBay about what they're up to?"

"I sent an email, but I haven't heard anything back yet. I just found out about this whole scheme this morning when the two of them dropped by to see how their property was doing."

Knowing Aunt Peg, I was sure that the daughters' property was doing very well indeed. Though now that I was no longer preoccupied with my own news, I wondered where the two Golden Retrievers were. I'd expected them to greet me at the door with Peg's Poodles.

"Don't even get me started," Aunt Peg said. Mind reading is another one of her skills. "I know I told you the boys were such dolls that I'd brought them into the house so they wouldn't be lonely out in the kennel by themselves. Well, Robin and Laurel weren't having any of it. They'd paid for kennel runs, they said, and that was where they expected their dogs to be housed."

"It didn't occur to them that Pepper and Remington would be much happier in here with everyone else?"

"I don't think they give a fig for anyone's happiness but their own. What they do care about is protecting their supposed assets. They didn't like the idea that their Goldens were outnumbered by my Poodles. As though my dogs might rise up in insurrection against Pepper and Remington because they were different."

That was so silly it was almost laughable. I gazed around at Aunt Peg's house dogs. Six big black Poodles, all now blissfully asleep around us. "They look ready to revolt, all right."

"I can't even argue with the two of them anymore." Aunt Peg threw up her hands. "It just makes me too crazy. I took the boys back down to the kennel. In a little while I'll go get them and bring them back up."

Low as my opinion was of Henry's two daughters, I did have to admit one thing. *I'd* never managed to out-argue Aunt Peg, and unfortunately I'd had plenty of practice. I wondered what their secret was and whether or not they'd be willing to share it with me before they left.

"So then we agree," she said.

I looked up, wondering what I'd agreed to while I'd let my thoughts wander.

"If Detective Marley wants proof, you and I are going to have to get it for him."

I might have mounted a feeble protest but what was the point? Deep down inside, I was pretty sure that was exactly why I'd come to see Aunt Peg in the first place.

"What would you suggest?"

"We need to get back into Henry's house," Peg said decisively. "If Annie is correct, Henry was already in the process of gathering evidence. He hadn't taken it to the police, so where is it? Maybe it's still sitting right there, waiting for us to come and find it."

"Maybe it's something like those pictures," I said. "We need to have another look at them."

Aunt Peg nodded. "At them and everything else we can lay our hands on." Abruptly, she rose from her seat. "Let's go."

"Right now?" I was talking to empty space. Aunt Peg was already striding from the room.

"No time like the present," I heard her say from the front hall. "I assume Davey's taken care of?"

"He's with Bob." I got up and went after her.

"Perfect." Standing by the door, Aunt Peg already had the closet open and was pulling out her coat.

"Aren't you forgetting something?"

She paused, turned, looked down at the Poodles that had followed us to the door, then up at me. "What?"

"Johnny Bowen."

"What about him?"

"What if he's home when we get there? I can't imagine he's just going to hand us the key so we can go snooping around again. He must be feeling pretty desperate. The attack on Carrie Baker shows that. I don't know about you, but I'd rather not cross paths with him, especially not until we have something concrete to take to the police."

"Johnny isn't going to bother us," Aunt Peg said calmly.

"How can you be so sure?"

She wound a scarf around her neck and tucked a pair of wool gloves into her pocket. "Because we're not a couple of ninnies, that's why. We're not even going to approach Henry's house until we know he's nowhere around. You and I are going on a stake-out."

Aunt Peg sounded positively delighted by the prospect. I wondered if she'd considered all the ramifications of her impromptu plan. "In my Volvo?" I asked.

"Don't be silly. We'll take my minivan. Neither of the Bowens have seen it and the windows are tinted so they won't be able to look inside. We'll just park a little way down the road and observe for a while. Once we figure out whether or not Johnny is at home, we can make our move."

Aunt Peg with a plan was like a Border Collie with a

flock of sheep: it would be easier to stop a force of nature than it would be to deter her from her chosen path. Twenty minutes later, she and I were sitting parked beneath a tree three houses down from the Bowen residence. From that vantage point, we could see a small detached garage behind the house. The door stood open; a racy looking Mazda was parked inside.

I'd seen Betty's Volkswagen; process of elimination gave the sports car to Johnny. We hunkered down to wait. Ever prepared, Aunt Peg pulled a deck of cards out of her glove compartment, shuffled, and dealt.

She was whipping my butt in our third game of gin when Betty drove up, parked in the driveway, and began unloading groceries from the backseat of her car. After a minute, Johnny came out to help. When the car was empty, both went inside. A few minutes after that, Johnny emerged by himself. Pulling on a battered-looking leather jacket, he turned up the collar against the cold and climbed into the Miata.

The engine raced as he pulled out of the driveway and shot past us. Aunt Peg and I ducked down in our seats, but we needn't have worried. Johnny didn't even glance in our direction.

"Time to go," said Peg. "That was easy, wasn't it?"

Maybe too easy, I thought, but I was already scrambling out of the van and following her across the road. It was too late for second thoughts now.

# 29

It wasn't until Betty Bowen opened her door in response to our knock and she and Aunt Peg came face to face that I remembered belatedly that the last time they'd seen each other, things hadn't ended amicably. In fact, they'd ended with Betty feeling angry and insulted by my aunt's behavior. Then I'd soothed Betty with Oreos. Too bad I hadn't thought to bring a supply of cookies along.

In the brief moment before either woman spoke, I wondered whether Aunt Peg was remembering their last encounter as well. And whether her plan had taken their recent hostilities into account. Aunt Peg makes a habit of rising to the occasion, however; I never should have doubted her.

"I've come to apologize," she announced. "Truly, I behaved like the worst sort of boor. When Melanie pointed out the error of my ways, there was nothing I could do but come straight here and tell you how sorry I am."

It was a performance worthy of Old Vic; I was rather hard pressed to keep a straight face. But if my aunt was laying things on a bit thick, Betty didn't seem to mind. She looked inordinately pleased by Peg's remorseful tone.

"Not at all," she replied. "Once Melanie explained that it was Henry's awful daughters who'd gotten you so wound up, I understood immediately. Even Johnny, poor dear, makes himself scarce when those two are around. Too bad you didn't arrive a few minutes sooner, you've just missed him. Perhaps you'd like to come in?"

Aunt Peg looked like she was about to agree. Next thing you know the two of them would be sitting down, chatting away, while our chance to search Henry's house before Johnny returned disappeared. I grasped the back of Peg's coat and yanked hard; a small reminder to keep her mind on business.

"I have some warm cider on the stove," Betty was saying. "Surely you have time to share a bit of Christmas spirit."

"I wish we could," I said before Peg could reply. "But my aunt and I have a number of stops to make this afternoon. I'm afraid we don't have time."

"And you came all the way over here just to apologize to me." Betty beamed happily. "Wasn't that nice of you?"

"We were also hoping you might be able to let us into Henry's house one last time," said Peg. "As you know, I still have his dogs. Pepper and Remington have settled in reasonably well, but I was hoping to pick up a few things to make them feel more at home. You know—toys, leashes, maybe a dog bed."

It wasn't the best excuse I'd ever heard. Most dog people would have wondered why it had taken Aunt Peg more than two weeks to realize that she needed those things. Fortunately, Betty Bowen wasn't a dog person. Nor, however, was she a pushover.

"I don't know if I should. Robin and Laurel made a point of asking for their father's key back. They were very anxious to make sure that nothing in the house was disturbed." She paused, then added, "However, as Henry's neighbor, I felt it was up to me to look out for his interests, too."

"You copied the key before you gave it back," I guessed.

"It seemed like the wise thing to do. Not that I've used it since, of course."

"Certainly not," Peg agreed amicably. "I'm sure it was only for emergencies."

"That's right. On the other hand, knowing the way Henry

doted on those two dogs, he'd probably be the first to say that something that contributed to their comfort constituted an emergency."

We waited outside while Betty fetched the key. It seemed to take her a long time. I was beginning to wonder whether she'd misplaced it when the door finally opened again.

"Here we are," she said. One hand held out Henry's key; the other gripped a tall insulated thermos. "I know you said you were in a hurry, but it occurred to me that since the thermostat's turned way down in Henry's house, you're going to be cold over there. Here's some hot cider to take with you. This batch has cinnamon in it and a few special herbs. It's my mother's own recipe, perhaps a little on the sweet side, but it will warm you up in a hurry."

"That was very thoughtful," said Aunt Peg. The promise of something sweet always gets her attention. She took the thermos and tucked it into the crook of her arm.

Betty was right; it *was* cold inside Henry's house. Obviously, his daughters had no intention of burning any more oil than it took to keep the pipes from freezing. I shut the door behind us then walked through the kitchen, heading for the stairs at the front of the house. I was almost there before I realized I'd lost Peg. I retraced my steps and found her in the kitchen, opening cabinets.

"Why are you looking in here?" I asked.

"Because that's where we'll find glasses. Ah, here we are." She lifted two glazed mugs down from a shelf beside the sink.

Chilly as it was, I had no intention of wasting what little snooping time we had sipping Betty's cider. As Aunt Peg opened the thermos and poured out the steaming liquid, I left her behind and went to see what I could find. A few minutes later, she joined me upstairs in Henry's office, carrying a mug in each hand. By then I'd opened the desk drawer where we'd found the pictures two weeks earlier. Now the drawer was empty.

"Damn."

"What?" Peg came up behind me and peered over my shoulder.

"They're not here."

"Maybe you're looking in the wrong drawer."

Could be, but I didn't think so. Starting at the top, I methodically opened each desk drawer in turn. Not only did I not see the missing pictures, I didn't see much of anything.

Aunt Peg sipped from one mug and held the other out to me. "Maybe Robin and Laurel cleaned out their father's papers."

"Either that or Johnny has." I took the mug she offered and set it down on the desk top. "I wish we'd taken a closer look at those pictures when we had a chance."

"At the time, we had no idea they were important. Now that we know the pictures aren't here, maybe we should start in a different room."

"Go ahead," I said. "We can split up and cover more ground." I looked around, my gaze coming to rest on the squat file cabinet pushed up against one wall. "I wonder if that's been cleaned out too."

"We looked there last time we were here," Peg pointed out.

"Yes, but then we weren't looking for evidence." I rolled out the top drawer and began thumbing through folders. Nothing looked terribly interesting.

So much for my hopes of being able to prove my suspicions to Detective Marley. I wondered if there was any point in contacting Henry's daughters and asking if they were the ones who'd removed the pictures. And if they still had them. And if they'd let me look at them.

Which all sounded like entirely too much speculation to me.

"What was that?" Peg asked. She hadn't left, after all.

"What?" I glanced up.

"I heard something." She set her mug down next to my

untouched one and crossed the room to the door. "Down-stairs."

Quickly, I rose to my feet. "Something like what?"

"I don't know—" Aunt Peg looked suddenly pale. She leaned heavily against the door jamb.

"Yoohoo! Ladies! Where are you?" Betty's voice came floating up the stairs.

"Up here," I called back. Aunt Peg didn't say a thing. "Looking for dog toys."

I joined my aunt in the doorway as Betty reached the top of the steps. She was carrying the empty thermos and smiling happily. "There you are. I'm so glad you enjoyed my cider. Wonderful recipe, isn't it?"

"Delicious," I lied. I hadn't even tasted it.

Peg, who had, nodded fuzzily. Both her hands were still braced heavily against the door jamb. I shot her a concerned look.

"I knew you'd like it," Betty was saying. "Everyone does. Especially Henry. I told him it was my own secret recipe and he drank it right down. Such a neighborly man, Henry was. He'd never have thought of refusing a nice cup of cider."

And just like that, it all came together. Despite what we knew about Johnny, he wasn't the one we'd needed to be wary of. It was Betty, the helpful neighbor with her sweet, poison-laced cider who'd been the threat all along. Betty who was standing in the hall with her empty thermos gazing contentedly at me and Aunt Peg as though everything was going exactly according to plan.

"Tell me more about Henry," I said. I didn't want Betty moving past me into the office where she'd see that only one of the mugs on the desk had been emptied.

On the other hand, I really wanted to have a look at Peg's mug myself. I needed to know how much cider she'd consumed. Her demeanor was beginning to alarm me; her breathing was rapid and shallow. I slid my arm around her, offering support if she needed it.

Aunt Peg stumbled briefly, leaning into me heavily as if I'd pulled her off balance. Her head bobbled; her lips passed close to my ear. She whispered a single word under her breath, "Act!"

Relief flooded through me, even as I struggled to re-balance my aunt on her feet. I almost smiled but caught myself just in time. Trust Aunt Peg to be on top of things right from the beginning. She must have guessed what Betty was up to, and was now giving the woman the result she'd hoped to achieve. But it was only an act, thank God.

"Henry was a snoop," Betty said. "A busybody. Someone who had to have his finger in every pie. He never should have quit that high-powered job of his. After that he had too much time on his hands. He was always digging into things that didn't concern him."

"You must have hated him." I propped Aunt Peg against the banister, where she listed to one side with a goofy grin on her face. Her acting skills, I decided, were a bit over the top.

"Didn't hate him," Betty said matter-of-factly. "Just needed to shut him up."

"So you gave him some cider from your old family recipe."

With a satisfied look at Aunt Peg, Betty didn't even bother to deny it. "Yup. That did the trick, all right. Ambulance came and took him away, and the doctors decided he'd died of heart failure, just like they were supposed to."

"Not for long," I said. "They ran more tests and found out about the antifreeze."

Betty merely shrugged. "Times are changing, I guess. Used to be, nobody looked into things that closely."

"Used to be . . . ?" I echoed. My voice trailed away as my thoughts whirled. Henry wasn't the first victim. She'd done this before.

"The world's a hard place," said Betty. "A woman's got to look out for herself and her own, because I'm here to tell you, no one else is going to. A man gives his wife a few pops with the back of his hand, there isn't much the law can do about that. A woman who didn't want to keep landing in the hospital might have to figure out a way to end her own troubles."

I remembered the collection of framed photographs Alice and I had seen on Betty's mantel. Pictures of her, pictures of Johnny. But none of her husband, Johnny's father. I imagined his cause of death had been listed as heart failure, too.

"It was one thing when he only hit me," Betty said. "But the day he took off his belt and went after Johnny . . . well, that was when I knew I had to do something. He thought he was the one with all the power. I guessed I showed him differently."

"You certainly did," I agreed. "And when Henry found out that Johnny was dealing drugs, that made him a threat, too."

"Johnny's a good boy, a little wild sometimes maybe. But he's my son, and he's all I have. Henry came to me with what he'd found out, can you believe that? Like he thought I might not know what my son was up to in his own home. He had the nerve to tell me that if I didn't put a stop to what Johnny was doing, he was going to go to the police."

So that was why Henry had never reported what he knew, I realized. He'd been hoping that Betty would solve the problem herself. And she had, just not in the way he'd anticipated.

"Why are you telling me this?" I asked.

"Why not?" said Betty. "Pretty soon it isn't going to make any difference what you know. It's not like I couldn't figure out what the two of you were up to, the way you kept coming back and looking around. That one . . ." Her eyes shifted in Aunt Peg's direction. "She seemed pretty smart. I'd been wondering what I ought to do about that when you two showed up today and gave me a golden opportunity."

Like Betty, I glanced over at Aunt Peg. Her act was getting more convincing with each passing minute.

"It's only a matter of time before the cider begins to work

on you, too," said Betty. "Doesn't matter what I say now, you won't be around long enough to tell to anyone else."

I stepped out of the office and into the hallway. Peg was still on her feet, but she seemed only vaguely aware of her surroundings. Maybe she'd drunk more of Betty's concoction than she'd realized.

"Aunt Peg?" I said. "Are you okay?"

"Of course she isn't okay. You don't listen too good, do you? I guess she must have been the brains of your outfit."

"Oh, shut up!" I snapped as I moved to Aunt Peg's side. Grasping the rail between cold fingers, she gazed at me with blank, unfocused eyes. "I thought you said you were acting," I whispered furiously.

"No." Shaking her head was an effort. As was answering. "I was telling *you* to act. I was hoping Betty might confess."

Gently, I lowered Aunt Peg until she was sitting on the floor, her back propped against the banister. She needed help, and soon. "Betty did confess."

"Did she?" Peg sounded surprised. Abruptly, she turned her head away. "I think I'm going to throw up."

"Good. Best thing for you." I held her until the spasms had passed, then stood up and pulled out my cell phone.

"Hey! What do you think you're doing?" Betty dove toward me, reaching for the phone.

I held it away, blocked her with my other hand, and punched out nine-one-one. "I'm calling for help."

"Too late for that now. By the time anyone gets here, you'll both be gone."

"No, we won't," I said. "I never drank any of your poison. And I'm going to get my aunt to the hospital where they can fix what you've done to her."

"No!" Betty screamed. She lifted the thermos and brought it crashing down on my arm.

Busy with the phone, concerned for Aunt Peg, I didn't see the attack coming. My fault for not taking a woman twenty years older than me seriously as an adversary. Pain shot up my arm; tears sprang to my eyes. My fingers flew open. The cell phone hit the hardwood floor, bounced, and skittered away.

Before I could go after it, the older woman was upon me. One of her hands grasped my neck. The fingers of the other clawed at my eyes. Desperation had lent her surprising strength.

I tried to retreat, but I couldn't; Aunt Peg was on the floor beside me, the banister was at my back. There was nothing to do but grab Betty's hands and try to wrestle her away. Both feet braced, she didn't budge.

Her nails raked down the side of my face. I felt the skin tear. I scrambled for a hold of her wrists. She twisted and swore. An elbow jabbed into my stomach. Then she was pushing me away, my back bending painfully over the railing.

Betty had the leverage I needed. As one foot left the ground, I realized what she meant to do. Aunt Peg had drunk the tainted cider; I would die from a fall down the stairs.

Until that realization hit me, I hadn't actually believed I would have to hurt her. I'd been trying to push her away, not inflict harm. But now I was fighting for my life, and my desperation matched hers.

I grasped Betty's arms and tried to shove her aside. She didn't move much, but it was enough for me to regain my balance. I got both feet back on the floor; my back pushed hard against the banister. When she launched herself at me again, I was ready.

And I was angry. We were wasting precious time. I needed to be getting help for Aunt Peg, not grappling in a hallway with a madwoman. As Betty came at me, I threw myself to the side, twisting in the air to reach back and shove her away.

She flew past me and hit the rail heavily, grunting with the impact. Briefly, her startled eyes met mine. Then momentum carried her further. Arms pinwheeling in the air, Betty overbalanced. For a split second, she teetered on the lip of the railing.

Scrambling back, I tried to reach her. My fingers grasped only air as her legs flipped up and Betty somersaulted over the edge. She landed with a heavy thump on the stairs below, her body rolling like a limp bundle of old clothes until she'd reached the landing at the bottom.

Heart racing, gasping for breath, I gazed downward through the uprights. Betty lay sprawled on the floor below. She wasn't moving.

Aunt Peg was next to me on the floor. Her dark eyes fluttered open. "I don't feel very well," she murmured.

"I know," I said, reaching for the phone. She didn't look very well either. "Help is coming."

"Tell them to hurry," she said.

# 30

To my enormous relief, an ambulance arrived within minutes. It was followed almost immediately by a police cruiser. Betty was lying in the front hall, moaning. I hurried the EMTs past her and up the stairs to Aunt Peg, explaining what had happened as we went. In no time, Peg was on her way to the hospital.

I wanted to go with her but too many things still needed to be sorted out with the police. I got Detective Marley on the phone and told him the story from start to finish. This time he was inclined to listen. The officers on the scene bagged the thermos as evidence. By the time I left Henry's house, Marley was on his way and a search warrant was being obtained for the Bowen residence. Johnny hadn't returned yet; the officers were planning to detain him when he did.

I sped to the hospital behind the second ambulance carrying Betty Bowen. Aunt Peg's stomach had already been pumped when I arrived and she'd been given an antidote to the ethylene glycol. Since she had already thrown up much of the antifreeze she'd ingested, the doctors were confident of her full recovery.

Betty wasn't so lucky. The fall had broken her hip, her collarbone, and one of her legs. Those bones would mend, but her other troubles were only beginning. When she awoke at the hospital, she claimed to have no memory of the events

Detective Marley was anxious to question her about. In the meantime, however, her house had been searched and her fingerprints lifted from the thermos carrying the deadly liquid that had killed Henry Pruitt and nearly done the same to Aunt Peg. The search also turned up a cache of drugs, enough to bring an indictment against Johnny as well.

According to what I read in the newspaper over the next several weeks, the police were considering exhuming Betty's husband's body. With new technology now available, they could check for traces of ethylene glycol to determine his actual cause of death. It was looking as though it would be a long time before either of the Bowens would be causing problems in the neighborhood again.

Aunt Peg was released from the hospital in time to attend Davey's Christmas pageant. Ably directed by Rebecca Morehouse, the play went off without a hitch. Nobody fell from the stage, no one lost any teeth. Davey remembered both his lines and performed them at the top of his lungs. Sam, sitting between me and Aunt Peg in the audience, captured Davey's acting debut on his video camera.

Alice Brickman, with Peg's help, had finally found a Christmas puppy that met everyone's approval. She was planning to wrap up a collar and dog bowl along with a picture of the Golden Retriever she'd reserved from Cindy Marshall and leave them under the tree with the rest of the presents. The new puppy, already named Berkeley, would be delivered a few days later after the holiday excitement had died down.

The year before, there'd been a Christmas gathering at Aunt Peg's. This time it was my turn to play hostess. I'd finally gotten the rest of the decorations up; even Faith was wearing a red bow that Davey had tied around her neck.

Sam and Bob both arrived early. Each slipped several gaily wrapped packages under the Christmas tree. If I hadn't been busy attending to last-minute details, I'd have gone and had a look. Instead I finished basting the turkey and watched as Davey showed off his new train set.

Aunt Peg arrived next, looking robust and inordinately

cheerful. Henry's daughters had struck out on eBay when their auction closed without a single bid. Their father's murder solved, both women had been anxious to return home for the holidays. Before they left, they'd finally agreed that Aunt Peg could dispose of Remington and Pepper as she saw fit. Like the Brickmans' new puppy, Henry's Goldens would be going to their new home in early January. Upon her arrival, Peg checked to make sure that I wasn't serving cider, then helped herself to some eggnog and found a seat on the couch.

Aunt Rose and Uncle Peter called to say they were running late, so the next time the doorbell rang we all knew who to expect. Everyone crowded into the front hall to welcome Bertie and Frank and the new baby to her first Christmas celebration. Scarcely more than a week old, Emma seemed remarkably unimpressed by all the fuss. In fact, she slept through most of it.

"Don't worry," said Frank. "She'll make up for it later tonight."

"I can't imagine why I ever thought of sleep as a waste of time," said Bertie. "Now I fantasize about it. Eight long, uninterrupted hours. Just the thought sounds like heaven."

Davey stood on his toes to peer at Emma, who was cradled in her mother's arms. He'd seen her in the hospital but this was the first time he'd been close enough to touch. His hand reached tentatively, grazing her smooth pink cheek. "Can I hold her?" he asked.

The adults glanced at one another over Davey's head. He'd been wonderful with Faith's puppies, I thought, but a baby was entirely different. Especially one this new. I could understand if Emma's parents felt reluctant.

But Bertie didn't even hesitate. "Certainly," she said. "She's your cousin. The two of you should start getting to know one another."

"Come sit with me on the couch," said Aunt Peg. "Then Bertie can put her into your arms."

"You're afraid I'll drop her." Davey stuck out his lower

lip. "You don't think I'll be careful enough. That's why you're making me sit."

Aunt Peg looped an arm around Davey's shoulder and led him into the living room. "Let me tell you something," she whispered. "They made me sit down the first time, too."

"They did?" Davey was suitably impressed by that information. He knew nobody bossed Aunt Peg around. "I guess it's okay then."

Davey got settled on the cushions, then held his hands out wide. Sam disappeared and came back a moment later with a camera. Gently Bertie lowered the sleeping infant into Davey's arms.

I could tell she was heavier than he'd expected. Bertie adjusted Emma's blanket and showed Davey how to support her head. He tried several positions, maneuvering until he had her just right. Then he exhaled a sigh and held the baby to him as though she was the most wonderful thing he'd ever seen.

"Smile," said Sam. The request was superfluous. Davey was already beaming.

The camera flashed and Emma opened her eyes. For a moment, she screwed up her face as though she was going to cry. Her tiny fist waved in the air. Then her eyes locked with Davey's and her expression relaxed. Her fingers closed around his thumb and held on tight. Her blue eyes blinked; her ruby lips pursed in a smile of her own.

"Perfect," Sam said in a hushed voice. The camera flashed again, the light reflecting in dozens of shiny ornaments on the Christmas tree.

Perfect indeed, I thought.

Please turn the page for an exciting sneak peek of
Laurien Berenson's next Melanie Travis mystery
RAINING CATS AND DOGS
now on sale at bookstores everywhere!

"I'll tell you the secret to happiness," said Aunt Peg. "It's this: Never grow old."

I looked at my aunt, who'd turned sixty-three on her last birthday. From my vantage point three decades younger, that seemed pretty old to me. I resisted the impulse to say what I was thinking, but my discretion didn't help. Aunt Peg was able to read minds, or something close to it.

And not just mine, either. Peg always seemed to know what her big black Standard Poodles were thinking. She had six of them, all retired show champions, all related to my two, Faith and Eve. Now she gazed pointedly in my direction and lifted a brow.

Faith, who was lying under my chair with her long muzzle resting on my foot, cringed slightly and turned her face away, as if maybe she didn't want to witness what was coming next. I think she can read minds, too. When it came to psychic ability, I seemed to be the only one who had gotten left out.

"Age," Aunt Peg said loftily, "is merely a number on a calendar. What matters is how you feel inside. The enthusiasm and curiosity with which you greet each new day. The boundless energy you devote to the things that interest you."

"Boundless energy?" I repeated. I may have sunk lower

in my chair. The mere notion of trying to muster such a thing seemed like entirely too much effort.

We were having this conversation at five o'clock on a Thursday afternoon. I'd already put in a full day of work, attending to my job as a special needs tutor at Howard Academy in Greenwich. My eight-year-old son, Davey, was at spring soccer practice. My new husband, Sam, would be picking him up and bringing him home within the hour. I was supposed to be cooking dinner.

Instead, I was planted at my kitchen table, hands wrapped around an oversize mug of fully caffeinated coffee. Aunt Peg had her usual tea. Sprawled on the floor around us were five Standard Poodles of various ages. My two plus the three Sam had brought with him when he'd moved in three weeks earlier. My house was small and cozy. There wasn't nearly enough room to accommodate five large dogs, not to mention an extra adult. No matter how badly Davey and I both wanted him there.

So far, Sam and my marriage—which had begun with a spur-of-the-moment elopement to Vermont over spring break—had all the elements of a three-ring circus: thrills, chills, laughter, and suspense. Oh, yes, and great sex.

Okay, so maybe it was better than most circuses I'd been to.

Still, it was a challenge to comprehend how this was all going to come together. And combining two households might prove to be the least of our worries. I was thirty-four and had been a single parent for most of the last eight years. Sam was two years older, previously divorced, no children. Both of us were accustomed to living life on our own terms, keeping to our own schedules, and, for the most part, answering to nobody but ourselves. Both of us were willing to compromise; we just hadn't figured out yet how to make everything work.

And the cramped living quarters, which had the eight of us—Poodles included, naturally—constantly tripping over one another, weren't helping.

"All right, maybe not boundless," Aunt Peg said. She peered at me closely. "And here I thought marriage to Sam would be good for you. Are you sure you're getting enough sleep?"

There we were, I thought, back to that great sex thing again.

"I'm fine," I chirped, straightening in my seat. "Quite fine. Positively fine."

"Well, if you don't mind my saying so, you look like hell."

As if my minding would have stopped her. As if my objections to anything Aunt Peg proposed ever slowed her down for even a minute.

"No, I'm just regrouping," I said. "Conserving my energy for later. Faith and I are going to our first obedience class tonight."

"Oh, really? I'd forgotten all about that."

Aunt Peg thinks she's a good liar. At one point in my life, when I knew her less well, I had thought so, too. Now, however, I can spot her ulterior motives a mile away. And this impromptu chat, occasioned by Peg showing up at my door with a box of cinnamon buns in her hands and an innocent expression on her face, had all the earmarks of an inquisition.

"Tell me again," she said casually, "why you decided Faith needed a second career in obedience."

This would be after the Poodle's first career as a show dog. Faith, like Aunt Peg's Standards, was a show ring champion. She had also recently become the dam of a champion when Peg had finished Zeke, a puppy from Faith's first litter. Eve was Zeke's littermate, and she was working toward her championship as well. So far, she had amassed twelve of the fifteen points necessary to earn her title. With luck, I would have her finished by summer.

"Instead of something fun," Aunt Peg continued, "like say . . . agility?"

Agility—dogs and their owners racing pell-mell around a course of obstacles, trying to beat the clock while running through tunnels, in and out of weave poles, and over jumps—did look like fun. It was also currently all the rage. Obedience trials, on the other hand, had been around for decades. That sport was more disciplined and exacting. When done correctly, it did not involve any running, or yelling, or fits of helpless laughter.

Aunt Peg was doing agility with Hope, Faith's sister. And, as always, she expected me to follow in her footsteps.

Except that, for the first time, I was putting my foot down.

"Obedience," I said firmly. "Faith and I are going to have a great time."

"But she's already obedient. For one thing, she's a Standard Poodle, which means that she was born knowing ten times more than your basic retriever or terrier."

You'll have to forgive my aunt. She loves all dogs; she truly does. But in her heart of hearts, she's totally Poodle-centric.

"Plus, the very fact that she was a show dog means that she's already learned to do all sorts of things: she comes, she stands, she stays. She walks beautifully on a leash."

I nodded in agreement. "That's why we're not starting in the beginner class. I spoke with the instructor about it when I signed up. Even though Faith and I don't have any background in obedience, Steve was fairly confident that being in the novice group would bore us silly. Tonight's class is for the more advanced dog and handler teams, those who already know the basics and are working toward a degree. We'll have to play catch-up, obviously, but since Poodles are such quick learners, Steve was sure that after a couple of weeks we'd fit right in."

"You'd fit right into my agility class, too." Like a foxhound on a fresh scent, Aunt Peg hated to give up.

"But that's just it. It would be *your* agility class. And once again you would have excelled at something before I even had a chance to try."

It wasn't that I resented Aunt Peg's success in the dog show world. Quite the contrary, I was in awe of all she'd accomplished. Her Cedar Crest Standard Poodles were known nationwide for their wonderful quality, their superb temperaments, and their excellent health. For three decades, she had produced and managed a line of dogs with which anyone would have been proud to be associated. More recently, Aunt Peg had turned her hand toward judging, and with assignments coming in from all over the country, she was quickly making a name for herself in that arena, too.

In the dog show world, most people knew me first as Margaret Turnbull's niece. Even though I'd worked hard for the things I'd accomplished, I knew there were competitors who felt that I'd never paid my dues, that my success was due to Aunt Peg's influence. And the worst part was, I wasn't sure that the critics were entirely wrong.

Faith, my first Poodle, had come from Aunt Peg, after all. She wasn't the medium-quality dog most beginners have to contend with, but rather, a beautiful Standard Poodle who'd finished her championship easily, despite my inept handling. Aunt Peg had steered me toward the better judges and told me which ones to avoid. She'd taught me how to clip and blow-dry, then set the lines on Faith's trims, and cleaned up my fumbling attempts at scissoring.

I was enormously grateful for everything Aunt Peg had done for me. But where Poodles and dog shows were concerned, I'd been standing in her shadow from the very beginning. It was time for me to try something on my own—an enterprise where Aunt Peg's name wouldn't open any doors or smooth my way along, where Faith and my success or failure would be based solely on our own merits.

"Obedience," I said firmly.

Aunt Peg looked surprised by my conviction. That made two of us. Or three, if you counted Faith. She glanced up at me, then placed her muzzle back into position on my foot. Nothing like a gesture of support from the peanut gallery.

And the decision was made.

\* \* \*

Which didn't prevent me from having to defend it once again over dinner. I'd had a pot roast sitting in the Crock-pot all day while I was at school, so coming up with the rest of the meal was pretty easy. Aunt Peg left just as the men in my life were arriving home. I'd invited her to stay for dinner, but she declined. Having lived alone except for her Poodles since her husband, Max, had died several years earlier, I think she found the chaos inherent in our current living situation to be a little overwhelming.

Unfortunately, she wasn't the only one.

Sam and Peg greeted each other at the door, then he walked her outside to her car. Davey, predictably, raced straight for the kitchen. Since he was still wearing cleats and shin guards, the clatter he made on the wooden floors got Sam's three Poodles—who weren't used to living with a child yet—up and barking. Faith and Eve knew full well there wasn't anything to get excited about, but bowing to peer pressure, they joined in anyway.

A full minute passed before the din quieted and I could even get a word in. "How was soccer practice?" I asked, directing the question to my son's back. His head was stuck in the refrigerator.

"Great." Details weren't Davey's forte. He didn't bother to turn around. "When's dinner? I'm starving."

"Soon. Wash your hands and set the table."

"If I do, can I have a sticky bun?" His eyes lit on the remains of Aunt Peg's bounty, sitting on the counter where she'd left them behind.

"After dinner," I said.

"What's after dinner?" Sam asked. He walked up behind me and slipped his arms around my waist. I leaned back into him and our bodies fit together effortlessly.

It had always been that way between us. Right from the beginning, there'd been that frisson of awareness, that undeniable attraction, whenever we were together. It had taken us three years, one broken engagement, and a host of other complications before we'd managed to get ourselves married.

Looking back, I wondered what had taken us so long.

"Cinnamon buns," I said, prudently neglecting to mention that I'd already eaten two myself. "Aunt Peg left one for each of us."

Sam and Davey quickly set the table while I prepared the plates. The Poodles milled around our legs in a happy state of confusion. All of them, Sam's and my dogs alike, knew better than to beg for food. But that didn't stop them from wanting to be on hand in case something should happen to fall on the floor.

Like the humans in their house, the Poodles hadn't had quite enough time yet to meld into a cohesive pack. Sam's three had to be wondering about their change of abode, which had brought with it cramped living arrangements and the necessity of sharing their person with others. Faith and Eve were accustomed to having Sam around. They just weren't entirely sure about welcoming three canine interlopers into their space. But Poodles are nothing if not adaptable, and so far, the crew was making do with typical élan.

Sam and I had already begun house hunting; finding a more appropriate home for our blended family had been the first thing on our agenda upon our return from Vermont. Sam's house was bigger than mine, but it was also half an hour north in Redding. With Davey happily ensconced in a nearby Stamford elementary school, and my job in Greenwich an easy commute away, it had seemed the best decision was to wedge ourselves into Davey and my small cape for the time being.

It was a decision I was trying not to regret more than once or twice a day.

"Don't forget I have class tonight," I said, when the pot roast had been served and eaten and we were all munching happily on warm, gooey cinnamon buns. Sam and Davey had been discussing whether there'd be time to fit a game of Scrabble in around Davey's homework.

"That's dumb," my son said.

"What is?"

"I'm a kid. I have to go to school. But why would any-body want to go to classes if they didn't have to?"

"They're for Faith," I told him. "It's obedience school. We're going to see if she can earn a Companion Dog degree to go along with her championship."

"Of course she can." Davey licked his fingers, a breach of etiquette both adults at the table decided to ignore. "Faith is the smartest dog ever."

The accolade was pretty much true. Until I'd become a Standard Poodle owner, I'd had no inkling of the scope of the breed's intelligence. Poodles didn't just learn by rote, they thought and reasoned things through. They also possessed a tremendous desire to please, as well as an unexpectedly well-developed sense of humor, all of which combined to make their temperaments nearly irresistible. Living with a Poodle wasn't like owning a dog, it was akin to adding another member to the family.

"Too bad Tar is still in hair," said Sam. "He could proba-bly benefit from a few obedience classes."

As one, our gazes went to Sam's big black male Poodle. Asleep and snoring softly, he was lying flat out on the kitchen floor. His spine was pressed up against the pantry door, probably because he remembered that that was where I kept the biscuits. The profuse hair in his topknot—kept long and thick for the show ring, and confined at home in protective, colored, banded ponytails—had flopped forward over his face. They rose and fell with each breath he took.

The most notable thing about Tar, however, was that some-how he had managed to get comfortable on the floor, and then had fallen asleep with one of his hind feet resting in the water bowl. The fact that his shaved paw and the bracelet above it were wet and cold apparently had made no impres-sion upon him. At least, I noted, he hadn't tipped the bowl over.

Not yet, at any rate.

Tar was an undeniably handsome Standard Poodle. His show career thus far had been stellar. Having recently won his fourth Best in Show, he was currently one of the top Non-Sporting dogs in the Northeast. What Tar wasn't, poor thing, was brilliant.

Oh, tell yourself the truth, I thought. Tar wasn't even terribly smart. In a household where most of the dogs' IQs approached that of the human inhabitants, Tar was an anomaly. A sweet dog, to be sure. A loving dog, even a trustworthy one. One who always tried his best to please, however limited that effort might be. Tar was a Poodle who meant well, but he couldn't think his way out of a dark corner.

When I'd only seen Tar at dog shows and at Sam's house, his limitations hadn't been that obvious. But now that I lived with him full-time and dealt with him on a daily basis, it was hard not to compare him with his more intellectually endowed peers. And to see that he came up short.

"Tar is very sweet," I said slowly. I knew how I'd feel if someone insulted one of my Poodles, so I chose my words carefully. "But I'm not sure that obedience would necessarily be the right option for him."

"I'm not saying he would be a star," Sam said. "But taking a few lessons might teach him how to deal with new things. You know, he could learn how to learn."

"Or how to think," said Davey, shaking his head. "Because that is one dumb dog."

So much for not insulting the new family members.

To my relief, Sam chuckled. "I wondered how long it would take you two to notice. I don't know when was the last time I had a Poodle that was so lacking in brain power." His hand waved in the direction of Raven and Casey, his older females. "Those two know everything. If you told them to cook you breakfast in the morning, they'd ask how you wanted your eggs. But Tar . . . well, what can I say? Everyday he wakes up to a whole new adventure, because nothing he learned the day before ever seems to stick."

Hearing his name, Tar lifted his head. His weight shifted, and his leg moved. His sodden foot slipped off the rim of the water bowl and landed on the floor with a soggy thump. Cold water splashed up onto his close-clipped hindquarter. Expression quizzical, clearly confused, Tar turned to see what had caused the spray.

"I don't think obedience would help," I said.

"Maybe agility," Sam mused.

The thought made me laugh. "I've seen Tar get lost coming down the stairs. And twice so far, I've had to untangle him from Davey's swing set. Something as fast-paced as agility would probably send him into shock."

"You're probably right," Sam admitted. "I bet Faith would be good at it, though."

"Don't even start," I said. "I just had this conversation with Aunt Peg—"

Abruptly, Tar leapt to his feet. He crossed the kitchen in a single, athletic bound, barking ferociously as his front paws slammed against the back door hard enough to make the glass rattle. Immediately, the other Poodles were up and on alert. Their outraged voices joined his. I spun in my seat and looked to see what had caught their attention.

The Poodles had all been out in the fenced backyard earlier; the outside lights were still on. Silhouetted in their glow, a large orange cat was clearly visible through the window above the sink. He must have been standing balanced on the windowsill; his yellow eyes calmly scanned the room.

Tar was a mere few feet away, barking so hard now that the effort bounced him up and down on his hind feet. The cat cocked his head in Tar's direction but didn't retreat. The Poodles' raucous ire at his invasion of their space didn't seem to faze him one bit. His fluffy tail lifted high in the air and swung slowly from side to side. A gesture of disdain if ever I'd seen one.

"I didn't know you had a cat," said Sam.

"I don't. He must belong to one of the neighbors, though I've never seen him around here before."

"You'd think a cat would have more sense than to come here," said Davey. "This place is like Dog Central."

"Maybe he's lost," Sam said.

I looked again and the cat was gone. Now that he'd removed himself from their sight, the Poodles quieted. They were beginning to look rather sheepish about their outburst. I stood up, walked over, and peered out the window. The cat had disappeared.

"Wherever he came from, he's gone now," I said. "And speaking of which, Faith and I have to go, too."

"Go ahead," said Sam. "Davey and I will clean up. Then after that, we'll hit the books."

He made it all seem so simple, I thought as I dug out Faith's choke chain and leather leash. No need to arrange for a babysitter. Or worry that if I took Davey to class with me, his homework wouldn't get done. Marriage might not be the easiest thing I'd ever done, but it definitely had its perks.

*Melanie Travis has her hands full with her two young sons, a part-time job, and a half dozen Poodles to her name. But even with the busy holiday season approaching, she still has time to sniff out a Christmastime killer . . .*

There's nothing lovelier than Christmas in Connecticut, but Melanie can scarcely find a moment to enjoy the festivities. With her youngest son approaching toddlerhood, she's decided to return to her old job at Howard Academy, a posh private school attended by the children of Greenwich's well-heeled gentry. Balancing work, motherhood, and the hectic dog show circuit takes some fancy footwork, especially when the headmaster taps her to be the chairman of the school's Christmas Bazaar.

The Christmas Bazaar is Howard Academy's biggest and most important fundraiser, so Melanie feels the pressure to make it a huge success. She even enlists her long-suffering sister-in-law Bertie to help with the Santa Claus and Pets Photo Booth. But everything goes awry when a prize show dog goes missing and Santa turns up dead. The dog's owner is one of the school's most perfectly pedigreed alums, and she enlists Melanie to help find the purloined pooch. But just as Melanie starts pawing at the truth, she digs up a sleighful of sinister secrets that leaves everyone feeling less than merry . . .

**Please turn the page for an exciting peek of Laurien Berenson's newest Melanie Travis mystery THE BARK BEFORE CHRISTMAS coming in October 2015!**

# CHAPTER 1

"Here," said Bertie, handing me a slicker brush. "Don't just stand there. Make yourself useful."

The directive involved a Poodle. Nothing new about that in my life.

This Poodle was a cream-colored Miniature puppy, sitting on a nearby grooming table. The puppy looked as though she'd recently been bathed and blown dry. Now she needed the dense hair on her legs raked with a slicker so that Bertie could scissor her trim. When I glanced her way, the Mini gazed at me with trusting brown eyes.

I can talk and brush a Poodle at the same time. I've been doing it for years. Sad to say, I could probably do it with my eyes closed. And since I'd shown up at my sister-in-law's house unannounced, interrupting her preparations for the upcoming weekend's dog shows, I suppose I deserved to be put to work.

*Make yourself useful.* It's my family's rallying cry. We have my Aunt Peg to blame for that.

Dog show aficionados know Peg as Margaret Turnbull, breeder and exhibitor of some of the best Standard Poodles in the country over the past four decades. In recent years Aunt Peg has shifted her focus; now she's a much-in-demand Toy and Non-Sporting Group judge. But one thing hasn't changed a bit. Aunt Peg still has impossibly high stan-

dards and she blithely expects everyone in the vicinity—
especially her relatives—to live up to them.

I've long since accepted the fact that Aunt Peg is always
going to find my efforts wanting. But Bertie, bless her heart,
she keeps trying. Maybe that's because she's a relative new-
comer to the family. Married to my younger brother, Frank,
Bertie is also a successful professional handler. She has a
thriving business and a competitive string of dogs, several of
which were currently in the process of being prepped for the
weekend shows.

It was Friday, so I'd known that Bertie would be busy.
Still, that hadn't stopped me from dropping by without
warning. I needed someone to talk to. Someone with an im-
partial opinion who would either take my side and commis-
erate or else do exactly the opposite—tell me to grow up,
stop complaining, and get to work.

Either way, I knew I could count on Bertie to talk me
down off the ledge. She always had before.

So there I was, standing in Bertie's finished basement—
which doubled as her kennel and grooming room—on that
cold December morning. A French Bulldog was air drying
in a crate with a towel draped over its back. Two Schipperkes,
a Briard, and a pair of Toy Poodles were observing the activity from inside the long runs that lined the room's walls.
Bertie had a silver Bearded Collie out on a second grooming
table. It looked as though she'd been getting ready to grind
the dog's nails when I arrived.

It was no wonder that I'd barely gotten my coat off before
Bertie was already putting me to work. Tit for tat, Aunt Peg
would have said.

I took the red slicker brush from Bertie's outstretched
hand and raised the Mini puppy into a standing position on
her tabletop. Lifting a hind foot, I began to brush upward
through the plush leg hair with a sharp, practiced flick of my
wrist. Bertie turned on the Dremel tool and quickly shortened
and shaped the eight nails on the Beardie's front feet.

Then she put down the grinder and said, "Well? You drove

all the way over here, you might as well spit it out. What's the matter now?"

I didn't stop brushing, but I did angle my body in Bertie's direction. "Do you want the long version or the short version?"

She let her gaze drift around the room of half-groomed dogs. "It's not like I don't have time to listen. Tell me everything."

"You know I went back to work part-time, right?"

"Sure. You got your old job back at Howard Academy. Special needs tutor just like before."

By *before,* Bertie meant prebaby. My younger son, Kevin, had been born two and a half years earlier, and the single semester I'd taken for maternity leave had stretched to several by mutual consent. The school had been happy with the teacher they'd hired as my replacement and I'd been delighted to be a stay-at-home mom. It was a luxury I hadn't been able to afford when my older son, Davey, was born.

But over the summer my replacement had left and at the start of the current school year, I'd found myself teaching once more. I loved my job; I always had. The kids I worked with were wonderful and it was enormously satisfying to know that I could make a difference in their lives.

For three happy months, I'd been juggling part-time work at Howard Academy with my family life at home. In fact, the transition had gone so smoothly that I'd agreed to step up to a full-time position when the new semester began in January.

Bertie reached around for a back paw. The Beardie lifted its leg obligingly. "So what's the problem?"

"The Howard Academy Christmas Bazaar." I snorted with annoyance. "That's what."

"If you want me to bitch and moan convincingly on your behalf," Bertie said, "I'm going to need more information than that."

"How much do you know about Howard Academy?"

"Pretty much just the basics." She paused, then added,

"Considering that *my* child goes to public school." Bertie and Frank's four-year-old daughter, Maggie, was in her first year of preschool and enjoying every minute of it. "Exclusive private school in Greenwich, Connecticut. The kids that go there are all like Richie Rich, trust-fund babies getting started on the educational path that will take them straight to the Ivy League. Am I close?"

"Yes, and no," I told her. "That may be the school's history and its reputation but it's no longer entirely correct. Actually, Mr. Hanover would be very disappointed to hear his beloved institution characterized in that way."

"He's the Big Cheese, right?"

"He is indeed. Not that anyone would ever dare call him that. Our headmaster is quite dignified, and very much aware of the significance of his position."

"In other words," said Bertie, "a prig."

I wished I could tell her she was wrong, but Russell Hanover II didn't just govern Howard Academy, he also shared the school's conservative ideology and its firm belief in its own importance. Fortunately, however, that was only one side of my boss. He was also a man who worked hard, played fair, and stood up for his teachers when they needed his support. All of which made me feel compelled to defend him.

"He may be a bit of a prig," I said. "But it's not on purpose."

Bertie shot me a look. "Is there any other way?"

I thought about my answer as I moved around the grooming table to work on the puppy's off-side legs. "Mr. Hanover honestly wants what's best for his school and for his students," I said after a minute. "He's aware that both he and Howard Academy are in a position to influence the next generation of this country's political and financial leaders. And he doesn't take that responsibility lightly."

"*Oh my God.*" Bertie swept the Beardie off his table and led him across the room to an empty run. "I can't believe you just said that. This Hanover guy must be turning you into a prig, too."

"Hardly."

Bertie cocked a brow. "Are you *sure?*"

"Be quiet," I said with a laugh. "And listen to what I'm trying to tell you. At one time, what you said about HA's student body would have been true. But things have changed dramatically in the last couple of decades. Now the byword in education is diversity, and that includes extending a helping hand to those less fortunate. In the current school year, nearly one third of Howard Academy's students receive either full scholarships or financial aid."

"So what? That place has the money."

"That's just it," I told her. "It doesn't. The endowment funded by the Howard family a hundred years ago when they donated their property and founded the school is pretty much gone. So every dollar that's given away in scholarships has to be raised, primarily through alumni donations and school benefits."

Bertie fastened the latch on the Beardie's pen, then straightened and stared at me across the room. "I thought we were going to be talking about you. Why is any of this *your* problem?"

"Normally it wouldn't be."

I sighed. Loudly. And mostly for effect. The Mini puppy who, like all Poodles, was attuned to the people around her, tipped her head to one side and cocked an ear in my direction.

"Let me guess," said Bertie. "We've finally worked our way back around to the Christmas bazaar."

"Bingo. It's one of the biggest fund-raisers of the whole year. Mr. Hanover called me into his office earlier today. Apparently you're looking at its new chairman. As of a few hours ago, I'm in charge of the whole shebang."

"That sounds like a big job."

"It is!" I wailed. "It's *huge.*"

"And when does this happy event take place?"

"Next weekend. Saturday."

Her eyes widened. "*Eight* days from now? You must be kidding. How are you ever going to pull the whole thing together by then?"

"Well, there's good news and bad news about that."

"Shoot," said Bertie.

"The good part is, most of the advance planning has already been done. The committees were formed six weeks ago and everyone is already working on their assignments. The whole school has been buzzing about the event for the last month."

"Okay." She nodded. "So what's the bad news?"

"The woman in the middle of all that activity, a parent volunteer who was the former chairman, eloped to Cabo San Lucas yesterday morning. Apparently she tendered her resignation as chairman of the bazaar by e-mail. Mr. Hanover was *not amused*."

Bertie and I grinned together.

"Maybe you should follow suit," she said. "E-mail Hanover and decline the position."

"That's not an option," I told her. "The parent was a volunteer. I'm an employee. Mr. Hanover thought that giving me the position was a great idea. He said it would ease me back into full-time work before the next semester starts."

"Right," said Bertie. "Because that's what every mother wants before Christmas. More stuff to do."

I lifted my hands helplessly. "I didn't have a choice. Mr. Hanover steamrolled over all my objections. He said the event was already primed and all I had to do was step in and make sure that nothing went seriously awry."

"*Awry?* That's the word he used?"

"You betcha."

"Prig," Bertie said again. "With a capital P."

The Mini's puppy's legs were finished. I moved on to the rounded pompon at the end of her tail. "He's actually a pretty good guy," I told her. "You'd probably like him if you met him."

"Well, that's not going to happen," Bertie replied. She reached into a pen and scooped out a Toy Poodle. Then she turned and looked at me, her eyes narrowing suspiciously. "Is it?"

"I don't know," I said innocently. "Could be."

Bertie crossed the room and plunked the Toy Poodle down on the other tabletop. "Melanie Travis, what are you up to now? And what makes you think there's even the slightest possibility that I might want to be involved?"

I gestured toward the Mini, now brushed, and fluffed, and ready to scissor. "This one's good to go. Don't you want to work on her next?"

"If you think I would even dream of letting you change the subject, you must be delusional." Bertie retrieved a cloth case from a nearby shelf, unzipped it, and set a pair of Japanese scissors down on the edge of my grooming table. "Here you go. Your trims are every bit as good as mine. Have at it."

Aunt Peg would have disagreed with that assessment. Not me. I accepted the compliment with pleasure, and went to work.

The Mini Poodle was young, but she already knew what was expected of her. When I slid my fingers beneath her chest, lifted slightly, then dropped her front legs into a square stance, she raised her head and held the position. I picked up the scissors, ran the long blades lightly up the puppy's leg to lift the hair, and began to trim.

"I agreed to go back to work at Howard Academy as a teacher," I said. "Not a circus ringmaster."

"We're talking about a few booths in a school auditorium, right? How bad can it be?"

"Have you ever *been* to the Howard Academy Christmas Bazaar?"

"Heck, no. Why would I want to do that?"

"It's mayhem. Out-of-control chaos. A veritable zoo."

Bertie, busy popping the rubber bands that had held the Toy Poodle's long topknot hair up and out of the way, thought for a minute then said, "Luckily you're very good with animals."

"That's not funny," I grumbled. "But it does segue nicely into my next point."

"Which is?"

"One of the attractions is a Santa Claus and Pets Photo Booth. The school has hired a photographer and students have been encouraged to bring their dogs and cats to the bazaar to get their pictures taken with Santa. Mr. Hanover's secretary is already working on the arrangements but he wants me to help out, too. He thought it would be right up my alley."

"I can see that," said Bertie. She turned on the water in the big, utility sink and checked the temperature with her fingers. The Toy Poodle was about to have a bath.

"The pictures will be uploaded on the spot and parents will have the option of having them turned into Christmas cards," I said, raising my voice to be heard above the running water. "It's a great idea and I'm hoping that the booth will be a big moneymaker. I thought I'd walk around the shows this weekend and try to drum up business among the exhibitors."

Bertie wasn't the only one who'd be spending the next several days driving back and forth to the "Big E" Exposition Center in Massachusetts. My son, Davey, had his Standard Poodle, Augie, entered in the dog shows as well. The big black dog had spent the previous five months away from the show ring, growing hair—enough to balance out his new continental trim. Davey was delighted that his pet was finally ready to make his adult debut.

"You'll be swamped," said Bertie. "Especially if you have to oversee that booth *and* everything else."

"That's what I'm thinking."

"You ought to tell Hanover that you need some help."

"I already did."

Bertie was bent over the sink. She had one hand covering the Toy Poodle's eyes. The other held the nozzle and directed the spray toward the loose topknot hair. She looked back over her shoulder at me and frowned.

"No," she said firmly. "No way."

"It will be fun," I told her brightly.

"No, it won't. It will be chaos. You just told me as much. Besides, I'm busy next Saturday."

"No, you're not. I looked at the calendar. It's December. There isn't a decent dog show within two hundred miles."

"I'm sure I must be doing something."

"You're not," I said. "I even checked with Frank. He told me you were free."

"Frank's a traitor," Bertie muttered. "I wouldn't believe a word he says."

Funny thing about that. I'd felt the same way about my feckless younger brother for years. But meeting Bertie was the best thing that ever could have happened to him. Not only had she become a steadying influence in his life, but it also turned out that Frank's desire to live up to his wife's expectations was the impetus he'd needed to finally outgrow his irresponsible ways.

"Come on," I said. "Give me a hand. It's for a good cause."

Bertie sighed. She was wavering, I could tell.

"Between the kids, and Santa, and the pets, there's going to be a lot going on. You know I'll need someone there who's really good with dogs. And the best person I could think of was you."

"Not Aunt Peg?"

I lifted a brow. "Can you picture Aunt Peg in an elf costume?"

"Wait a minute." Bertie spun around. "You didn't say anything about an *elf costume*."

"Umm . . ."

"Before you answer," she warned, "bear in mind that it's a deal breaker."

"Then no," I said quickly. "The costume isn't mandatory. Though I bet you'd look cute in a pair of striped tights."

That was an understatement. Bertie was gorgeous. She had thick auburn hair, killer cheekbones, and the kind of body that instantly rendered every other woman practically invisible. If anyone could pull off a forest-green tunic and pointy shoes, it would be my sister-in-law.

"Don't even think about it," she said.

"All right, you don't have to dress up. But will you come and help out? If I'm going to tackle a project this size—especially with Mr. Hanover watching—I'm going to need back-up I can count on. It's just for a few hours. And I'll owe you one."

"You're not going to let me say no, are you?"

Not if I could help it. I'd beg if I had to.

Bertie went back to bathing the Toy Poodle. Even though her back was turned, I heard her mutter, "Someone should have warned me before I married into this family."

"I tried to," I told her. "You didn't listen." *And thank God for that,* I thought.

"All right," said Bertie. "I'm in."

# Grab These Cozy Mysteries
## from
# Kensington Books